Quiet
WEALTH

J.L. DRAKE

QUIET WEALTH

QUIET MAFIA SERIES

Cover Design by Spellbinding Design
Editing by Lori Whitwam
Formatting by RedDoor Author Services

Letter to my readers

In 2016, I wrote my Devil's Reach Trilogy and took a stab at writing in the motorcycle genre, and with little research made it my own. I purposely don't read in the genres I'm writing, so there are times I will do something that isn't normally found in those kinds of worlds.

Well, flash forward to 2021, and I'm back at it again, so please remember this is my interpretation of the mafia world. It's a modern mafia with a refined darkness.

Family, Strength, Loyalty, and Protection

-Jx

Dedication

To first loves, who held our fragile hearts and helped strengthen us along our journey.

Pronunciation of Main Cast

Elio – Ell-e-o
Capri – Ca-pre

Sienna – See-enna
Giovanna – Gio-vanna

Francesco – Fran-cesco

Piero – P-ero

Mariano – Mari-ano

Niccola – Nee-cola

Chapter ONE

In order for you to understand where I'm coming from, you must understand what really happened from the very start.

Sienna

Sicily, Italy

I covered my ears and hid in the space between the wall and the bed. The smell of dirty clothes and old shoes made my stomach turn. The sound of staggered footsteps came closer, and I tucked my legs up closer to my chest. Tears stung and ran down my cheeks as I lay there, terrified.

"Who did this?" Andrew, the father with a temper like a light switch, held up a half-eaten bag of potato chips. "Tell me now or you'll all be punished."

Their oldest son, Renzo, who always seemed to have it out for me, screamed, "She did it!"

Before I knew what was happening, a hand wrapped around my ankle and jerked hard, tearing me out of my hiding place.

I taught myself how to mentally check out whenever I was alone with Andrew and Julie, the mother. I didn't understand why they hit me or why they made me watch their kids eat and have fun while I had to sit in the corner of the kitchen all alone, sometimes even overnight.

I came to this house when I was five. All I was ever told was that I had to stay here until my mother came back for me. It had been four years since I arrived, and I had heard people snicker and say *she's his obligation* enough times to wonder what that meant, and I didn't even know who *he* was. All I knew was that these people didn't like me, and I didn't like them.

"I hope you're full," Andrew hauled me to my feet and pushed me out the bedroom door, "because it will be the last meal you'll get for a while." I followed blindly, not at all listening. I didn't have to. I knew what was coming.

I wiggled as little as possible as the leather strap tore at my skin. Blood dripped from the wounds, as some spots were barely healed from the last time. I tried hard not to allow myself to let the pain win. There was a part of me that knew this wasn't right, that if the cops came, they could go to jail for what they did to me, but I had my own reason for staying right now. Besides, the last time I left and was returned, they put Renzo in charge of watching over me, and that was something I never wanted to have happen again. I hated the way he looked at me.

"You hungry?" Renzo came into the kitchen around five in the morning. I jerked awake from my uncomfortable sleep and groaned silently at how sore I was. I knew he had been watching me through the night as he often did whenever he got me into trouble for something I didn't do. I knew the rules and tried hard to follow them blindly, knowing never to question.

I looked away, but he grabbed my chin and forced my head upward to look at him.

"That sucks," he eyed my bruised cheek, "but better you than me."

I hate you.

Renzo was seven years older than I was and the oldest of all their kids. If he didn't like you, you were his pawn. My only friend here, Cara, said her brother Renzo was like a boy she had seen on a TV show. He was tall with lots of muscles. Once, when we were watching a movie, she pointed out a boy to me and said that he reminded her of Renzo, and he was a jock. I guessed he was okay looking if you were into boys at all. I was young and had my own version of what good looking was, but I certainly didn't care. I was quite sure even if I were older that Renzo would not interest me.

I knew that boys shouldn't hit girls, especially when no one was looking and especially just to get the attention off themselves. It was creepy the way he stared. I noticed that Andrew looked at Julie like that whenever she wore her green dress.

Someday I will leave this place. It's not forever, I reminded myself as his fingers ran up and down my arm. I pulled it away from him, pretending to scratch.

"Sienna," he rubbed his nose and spoke very slowly as he studied me, "I need you to do something for me."

I listened, terrified of what he was going to ask.

"It's time for you to tell Andrew that you want to start working at the dockyard."

"What?" That threw me. "Why?"

"Because," he twisted a piece of my hair through his fingers, "I asked you to, that's why. Don't you dare question me." He pulled my hair hard, bringing tears to my eyes.

"I don't like it there. You know that," I stammered. The last time I found myself alone there, while trying to hide from Andrew, one of the workers grabbed me and wouldn't let me go. It took Julie screaming at him to set me free. The fact that I still got hit for not coming to her soon enough was worth it. The dockyard was where they put us to work at ten. The thought of going there was why I started taking money wherever I could find it, just small coins here and there so it wouldn't be noticed. I sometimes even went through pockets, desperate to try to hide away enough for a bus ticket for when I got the chance to follow my plan. I knew I didn't have a lot of time left, and I dreamed of getting a ticket to somewhere safe, far away from here. I planned to get myself a hoodie to hide my face, especially from older people who might have questions about where my parents were or why I was on my own. I would lie in bed and think about where I would go or where my Mama was. That thought always twisted my insides. Andrew didn't like it when I asked questions and would yell about how she'd left me, and he ended up stuck with me to feed and care for. I hated that I knew nothing about who I was or where I came from.

"You will or…" He went to the cabinet, fiddled with the lock, and tugged the half-eaten bag of chips down. He crushed a handful of them to dust and held his hand like he was going to sprinkle them around me.

"Want to rethink your offer?"

"A beating or the dockyard?" I hissed with my heart in my throat. "I'll take the beating."

"Stupid girl." He sprinkled the chips around my feet and over my lap and then freed one of my hands. "Need to make it look real." He chuckled like a crazy person.

I cringed, knowing a beating and another empty belly would be coming very soon.

A door upstairs creaked, and Renzo jumped, causing the bag of chips to fall on the floor, and the rest of them scattered everywhere. The panic on his face made me realize he could be scared too.

"Shit," he hissed as he raced through the kitchen door and out into the living room.

Chicken.

Sweat quickly formed on my forehead, and my legs started to shake. Once again, the fear that lived deep within my belly shot through me, and I knew I was really in for it this time.

Normally, I'd sit there and wait for my punishment, but when I covered my mouth to keep from screaming, something came over me, I moved without thinking. I undid my other hand and bolted for the outside door. Renzo must have spotted me through the window, and I could hear his laughter as I ran.

I raced down the path through the thick woods. The deeper I went, the more I could breathe. We were never allowed past the property line. They had made that clear the very first day I arrived, but I didn't care. I wanted to be free and ran as fast as my legs could go.

Renzo's laugh echoed in my head as my legs pumped and my lungs felt like they would burst. I tried to outrun the sound of it, and it helped for a while.

I didn't remember tripping on anything, but I landed hard with a mouthful of dirt. I lay still for a moment, trying to hear past my own gasping breaths until I dared to stand and look around. I stood beside the edge of a small pond. I had no idea there was such a place anywhere in the area. A rope hung from a tree, proof that this was used in summer as a swimming pond. I could only imagine what it would be like to swing from it and land in the water with a splash. Big, beautiful flowers—I knew they were plumeria—grew all around the edges. It was so pretty. The beauty of it all only lasted for a moment before the entire weight of what happened hit me hard.

Unable to bear the thought of it all, especially in this beautiful place, I buried myself in the branches of a tree and pressed my cheek against the rough bark as I hugged the trunk and sobbed. Life seemed so unfair to me. Why was I not wanted? How could my Mama leave me with the Di Vaio family? How did she not know how horrible they were?

"Are you okay?" A boy's voice made my eyes snap open wide as I instantly swallowed my sobs, frozen in fear. "Sorry," he said, and as I slowly turned to face him, he lifted his hands to show no harm, his wet t-shirt dangling from his fingers. "You just sound really sad."

"I'm—" I tried to catch my breath. "I'm okay."

He nodded but made no move toward me. He just took a seat on a rock in front of me. I took two small steps to the side, away from the tree branches. He looked to be a few years older than I was. He had dark hair that matched his dark eyes. They were so intense it nearly made my tongue suck back into my throat when I tried to swallow.

"How did you hurt your face?" He spoke quietly, the way you would to a puppy.

I quickly covered my bruises with my hands and blushed in embarrassment. He came up on me so quickly I didn't have time to react.

"I fell," I lied lamely, looking into those dark eyes.

"Must have hurt." His voice stayed soft.

"I fall a lot," I admitted for some reason. "I'm used to it."

His head tilted to the side as he studied me.

"It's not a big deal." I tried to recover, not wanting pity from a stranger, let alone a boy.

"Is that why you're crying?"

"No." I sniffed and dried my cheeks. "I wish." My voice ran away from me.

He turned his back to me as he reached for a new shirt in his bag.

"Are you scared of something?" I watched as he tugged the t-shirt over his head. He didn't seem old enough, but I saw he had a tattoo on his shoulder blade. It was a gold crown with a black bird below it. I could see it against his tanned skin, but then in a flash it was gone under his shirt.

I blinked when he turned back to face me and tried to remember what he had just asked. He took pity and asked again.

"I think I was born scared."

He studied my face again then nodded, almost like he understood my comment.

"You want to swim?"

I shook my head. I took another small step to test my shaky legs. "I should get back." I tried hard for a smile, but my lips just made a funny twitch.

"Where do you live?"

"For now, I live at the Di Vaio house." I saw that he flinched at where I lived.

He stepped forward and offered me a hand. He was very formal. "I'm Elio."

"Sienna." I hesitated but slipped my hand into his. "Thanks for talking to me."

"I'm always here." His eyes shifted over my shoulder, and I turned to see what had caught his attention. Someone was coming toward us. My world dipped, and I fought to stay standing.

"I gotta go," I quickly muttered and raced away from him, taking a curved path I hoped would get me back to the house. I knew my beating would come and that it would be the worst one I'd ever gotten, but I sure didn't want him to see me get it.

I stayed away from the swimming pond for three months, but I thought about it every day. Most of us at the house were homeschooled by Julie, which made it even harder to find time to disappear. When the opportunity came one day, I slipped away and found my way back. Elio wasn't there, but I enjoyed just sitting and looking at the water. I went as often as I could after that, always being sure I wouldn't get caught.

I leaned against the tree and pulled out the little notebook Cara gave me the other day. One of the movies the older kids were watching said it was good to have a journal to help control your thoughts. I liked that idea. I took pride in how well I could spell. I believed it was from all the late-night reading I did, desperately longing for an escape. My favorites were *The Lord of The Rings* and *Harry Potter*. Both were about surviving and making it through to the other side.

I scribbled the date in the top left corner and started to pour the earliest memories I had on the small white pages, not wanting to forget them. Faint images broke through the surface of my brain, and I remembered the smell of something old. My mother wore a green jacket, and I also remembered being held in her arms, and the comfort of that fleeting memory sent a tear down my cheek. More words came, and five pages later I closed the book and looked back in the direction of the house. I held the notebook to my chest, suddenly nervous of what could happen if they ever found my private thoughts. I used the Ziplock bag that I'd brought my lunch in and slid the notebook inside and hid it well under a rock. I felt a lot better about leaving it there. I raced back home, feeling lighter than I had in a very long time.

A few times, Elio came. He never stayed very long, but he would always talk for a few minutes before he left. Other times, I might find a bit of food waiting for me in our spot with a note. The first one said *Thought you might like to try my mama's tortellini. -E*

Even cold, it was the best thing I'd ever tasted. I only could handle a few bites, but *oh* how I loved it. I tucked his note inside my notebook and wrote about his kindness toward me. Carefully removing a small piece of a page from the back of the notebook, I responded with *It was great. Tell your mama thank you. -S*

I smiled when I wrote the "S," mimicking his signoff. I tucked it next to the paper bowl the pasta was in and leaned back, enjoying the comfort of a full tummy and the knowledge that I had a friend.

Even though I barely knew the boy, something drew me here, and I knew he was a major part of it. It was a welcome, safe place for me. Elio never made me uncomfortable or said hurtful things. He just occasionally left me bits of things to eat, and sometimes left notes. He always checked to make sure I was okay. That was the way it went for two years, just little moments together, but treasured ones. It allowed me little glimpses of what a real friend was like. Cara was wonderful to me, but Elio was different.

"Right there." Elio pointed as he flipped his shaggy hair out of his face to show me where the frog had just laid her eggs.

"Where?" I leaned in and lost my balance, and the first thing that raced through me was that my good outfit was going to get wet, and how was I going to explain it.

"Whoa!" Elio grabbed my hand and pulled me back to steady me. "You good?"

"Yes, thanks." I smiled slightly, beyond thankful he saved me from a lashing, but what really surprised me was I didn't flinch when he grabbed me. I felt no fear with him.

"Right there, there it is." He went back to our quest.

Weeks later, I returned to the pond with a fresh new journal in hand, proud that I had managed to save up for it without anyone noticing. As I always did, I checked our secret spot and saw a note sitting next to a plastic-wrapped chocolate chip cookie.

Something sweet? I have to go away for a few days, but I will be back Sunday. Meet me here at 1 p.m.? -E

I tucked his note away safely with the others and wrote a reply.

The cookie was very good. Thanks. I will try! -S

I took my place under the tree and let the summer

sun warm my face as I thought about what I wanted to write today. Elio's face worked its way inside my head, and I found myself growing warm on the inside. Before I knew it, I was scribbling my thoughts out on the page.

To me, boys were nothing but annoying, mean, and cruel, but when I met Elio he showed me that isn't always true. Maybe kindness could be found in others, but they need to be good, like Elio. Like when he saved me from falling in the pond or when he brings me treats and leaves me notes just so I know he is thinking of me. I like that in a person. I want that in a person.

Questions for Mom: Is it strange that when he's near me, I feel warm and my head gets foggy? Is it normal for me to study parts of his face that I like? His lips and dark eyes. But more than anything, is it normal that I want to spend all my time with him?

I dropped my pencil into the center of the book with a sigh. I would give anything to have my mother answer these questions. Slipping it into a new bag, I tucked it away with the rest of my journals and walked back while I enjoyed the lovely taste of chocolate that still lingered on my tongue.

It wasn't easy for me to get away, and as I got older it became even more difficult. I was working at the dockyard, and my life had become even harder, especially now with the unwanted attention my developing figure drew from the workers and the boys at the house. I didn't like their attention. I wished they would look at me the way Elio did. He made me feel pretty and smart. He often liked me to read out loud to him, and I loved nothing more than sharing with him that way.

When I turned sixteen, my life went from bad to worse. I was embarrassed to see Elio now, as I didn't want him to see the bruises were getting worse. Though Renzo was old enough to leave the house, he stuck around. I was sure it was just to torture me. He would pinch my arms or twist my wrist, which left red marks, then bruises. Then one day he found the money I had stashed in my mattress, and in that one night I went from someone with one small hope to just plain hopeless. Finding money had never been easy, but now that everyone's pay went through Andrew, he only gave us enough to buy a few clothes, and we even had to hand over the change and receipt to prove we hadn't kept any.

My only blessing was their youngest sister Cara, my only girlfriend. She didn't use me to do her chores or to take punishments for her. She hated it here just as much as I did, and she was their own child. We would talk and dream about what we would do if we ever got away from here. We sometimes talked about boys, and I told her my secret about the swimming hole. After that, once a week she would cover for me so I could race down to the swimming pond. I would stay very close to the shore and use a small piece of stolen soap and wash. It was wonderful to be able to bathe without fear. Renzo was never far away at the house, and the small washroom we were allowed to use had no lock on the door. He had made enough comments to let everyone know he claimed me as his. The very thought made me fold inward. So far, he hadn't made any attempt to touch me, but I knew that day wasn't far off.

One sunny day when I arrived at the pond, I checked our spot and found at least eleven notes that he had left me. I loved that he had started to number them so I could read them in order.

I waited on Friday – meet me here Wednesday? -E

The frogs had more eggs. -E

I miss my pond friend. -E

I hope you're coming by soon. -E

Are you okay? It's been a really long time since I've seen you. -E

I'm going to keep these notes here so you can see them. -E

I hope you like the flower I picked. It made me think of the ribbon you sometimes wear in your hair. -E

I closed my eyes and wished I were able to be here with him more. It had become harder and harder to get away, but it wasn't the only reason I didn't come. As I tucked the notes away, I noticed how dirty my hands were.

Stripping down to just my bra and underwear, I slipped into the water and allowed myself to float, proud that I had finally learned to swim. I splashed in the water, happy for a brief moment. Puffy clouds made their way across the blue sky, and I let myself drift away with them, enjoying the freedom. The smell of the plumeria filled the air, and I pretended it was Mother Nature gracing me with a gift of her perfume.

"I was beginning to think you were avoiding me." His voice traveled across the water and vibrated through me. I ducked down, careful to keep my body underneath the water, so just my nose was above the surface. "It's been quite a while since I've seen you here." He peered into the hidey hole where we hid our notes and grinned. "I see you got my notes."

He was right. I had been avoiding him, but it had come with a cost. His kindnesses and our chats had been so important to me. I realized how much I had missed him. I was lost and felt angry and sad all the time.

He tugged off his t-shirt with one hand and stood in his jeans. I saw the way they hung low on his hips. Elio was two years older than I was, and his body was that of a fighter. Strong, lean, and had that V that Cara always drooled over. Yes, Elio looked spectacular.

"And you're swimming." He placed a hand over his heart playfully. "That hurts."

I couldn't help but smile at that, even as I swam a little bit farther away from the shore. It was true that I didn't like people looking at my body, especially because of all the bruises. I was also self-conscious about being so thin, although I had put a little meat on my bones lately. Most of all, I didn't like the attention I got from the men at the dockyard and the house. It made me feel uncomfortable. I had developed quickly over the past few months, and it was difficult to hide my shape under my clothes.

I treaded water and tried to think of something to

say as he dropped his jeans and waded into the water in just his boxers. He dipped under the surface and came up right in front of me.

His dark eyes seemed to be even more intense today, and I felt a jolt when I took a leap and stared into them. It was like someone poured a bucket of warm water over me.

"Sorry," I whispered, and his eyes softened like he was happy I spoke. "Things have been hard, and I got a little…" I trailed off, unsure how to explain myself.

"Lost?"

"I think to be lost you need to have been found at some point," I fought back an urge to cry. "I didn't have a starting point. So…" I shrugged.

"I missed our notes."

"Me too," I confessed.

"But I missed you more." He smiled sweetly. Elio would often be bold with his kindness. I admired that he could say what he wanted without a care.

His eyes flickered as something raced through his mind. I could feel his body language change.

"Do you trust me, Sienna?" I licked my lips and thought about his question. "You know me well enough to know I wouldn't hurt you, right?"

I nodded because it was true. Elio had never said or done anything to hurt me in any way. In fact, he had cared for me over the years and never asked for anything in return. I felt like he knew me better than anyone else.

"May I take you to show you something?"

Nerves tried to take control, but I fought them back.

If I was gone for much longer, I would get a beating. However, the idea of seeing something besides the ugly walls at the house or the dockyard intrigued me.

"All right." I nodded, and a genuine smile spread across his face.

"Good." He motioned for me to follow him back to shore.

Of course, my eyes wandered as he pulled on his jeans, and again when he moved to lift his shirt over his head. Only once did I catch him watching me as I buttoned my shirt part way up and wrung out my long dark hair.

He waited until I had my shoes on and crooked a finger for me to follow him.

"Where are we going?"

"I want to show you my home."

What?

Chapter TWO

Elio

As much as it hurt when Sienna pulled away, it was for the best. I had to deal with a few things myself. But I couldn't help but be more pleased that she was here now and willing to go somewhere with me. It only took a childhood to get here, but I knew this needed baby steps.

From the first day we met, there was something about her that I found interesting. I believed it was that she wasn't frightened of me. Most people were, and it was hard to grow up like that. Now, as an adult, it was an asset rather than something I hid from.

I glanced over my shoulder and saw she was hesitant. Poor girl was always on edge and jumpy. I wished I could have taken her from that house, but I had bigger things to deal with, and it wasn't safe at my house either. My only saving grace was that the swimming pond was on our property, so she would be safe any time she hung out there.

"Not too much farther," I reassured her and watched as she wrapped her arms around her midsection.

I had watched Sienna become even more beautiful as the years went by, not that I would tell her that. I believed she had enough men in her life looking to get a piece of her. Her long, dark, damp hair fell to her mid-back. Her frame was small, but she looked healthy for once, not to mention she had a few curves that I couldn't help but admire. She was the classic sexy Italian woman, and she nearly brought me to my knees when she stepped out of the water earlier.

"This," I forced myself back to where we were and held up a branch to let her see my home, "is where I live."

She stepped out and came to a stop. She shook her head and looked back into the forest and back to the villa again.

"What?" She almost sounded upset. "This? This is where you live?"

"I do."

I saw the panic that swept over her, and I felt her pull away.

"Is something wrong?"

"I feel like a bird let out of the cage for the first time." She rubbed her eyes. "I can't believe I didn't know this was here. It's beautiful."

I didn't want to let her talk herself out of coming with me, so I took her hand and started to walk forward.

"Come on, let me show you around."

She came, but I could tell it took a lot of effort.

When we rounded the back yard, she gasped at the sprawling, rectangular stone pool. A few cabana huts were nestled between the white lounge chairs that lined one side of the pool. Archways outlined the five double doors leading inside, and the view took your eyes over the cliff and down to the crisp blue ocean below.

Francesco, the head of the house staff—at least that was what we led others to believe—appeared in his usual suit and tie as we stepped onto the patio.

"Good afternoon, Mr. Capri. Will you and your guest be joining us for lunch?"

I squeezed Sienna's hand to let her know it was all right. "Yes, we will be."

"Elio," she whispered, but I shook my head with a smile. I wanted this to happen.

"Very well." He nodded politely and led the way to the long table under one of the cabanas. He pulled out a chair for Sienna while I took the other. I reluctantly broke my hold on her hand, one that I had very much enjoyed.

"Elio," she repeated, "what am I doing here?"

"We're having lunch." I poured her a glass of ice water. "And my family wanted to meet you." Her eyes nearly bugged out of her head, and her face went pink.

"Now?" She looked around in a panic. "With me looking like this?"

"I think you look nice."

"Nice," she hissed. "I'm still wet. I must look like a half-drowned rat."

"You could never look anything like a rat, Sienna, so I totally disagree. You look beautiful."

"I swear, Elio, I will cut you from your navel to your hairline if you're serious right now."

"Ha!" I laughed out loud. I had never seen that fire in her before, and I really liked it.

"You forget the kind of men I have to live with…" She trailed off when my mother arrived with her arms stretched open for a hug.

"Elio, my dear son, you finally brought her to us."

I leaned forward and moved the steak knife from Sienna's reach.

"Mama." I quickly jumped up and kissed her cheeks. "This is Sienna."

Sienna stood and hesitantly offered a hand, but my mother leaned in for a hug, and I noticed Sienna's face softened for just a moment.

"It's lovely to meet you, dear. You can call me Andrea, and this is my husband Piero." My father, an older version of myself, offered a hand, then he laughed and pulled her into a hug. We were a true Italian family. No one was unwelcome, until they gave us a reason to change our minds.

"We've heard about you for years." My father took a seat at the table and reached over to pour my mother a glass of sparkling wine. "I won't lie, we may have believed you were imaginary, but when Elio started collecting your notes, we had to believe you just might be real."

Sienna glanced up at me like she was trying to read my thoughts.

Good luck with that.

"I apologize for how I must look. We just had a swim." She blushed as her hand went to her hair while looking down at her damp clothes. "If I had known I was meeting you today, I would have dressed appropriately." She threw me a look, and I smirked, entertained by her glare.

"Nonsense." My mother waved her off. "I think this is the first time I haven't been in the pool before lunch." She leaned back while Francesco placed a plate of fresh fruit in front of her. "Why don't you share a little about yourself, since my son seems to have kept you all to himself."

"Well, um." She fought to think as a plate was placed in front of her. She took a deep breath and looked at me, then her chin lifted as she turned to face them. "I'd really love to sit here and give you a beautiful story about my loving parents and the opportunities that I was given, but I can't." I could feel the sadness in her voice. "All I know is what I've been told, that my father left after he got my mother pregnant, she moved here from somewhere, and we stayed with a friend of hers. Until one day she left, and I was told I had to live with one of his friends. I've never seen her since." She gave a shy shrug. "As you can see, I don't know much about where I came from. My life began rocky, and my memories are vague."

"Oh." My mother's face fell.

"Like I said, not exactly a beautiful tale," she whispered and cleared her throat.

"I understand you're living with the Di Vaio family?" My mother leaned in closer.

"I am."

"So, it's true?" My father eyed me and shook his head. I gave him a nod to let him know I would be looking into who exactly was living at that house.

"Yes, sir, and I'm looking forward to the day I can leave. If they let me."

"Let you?" I asked and caught Francesco holding a finger up to me that he would be right back. I gave a nod and went back to watching her.

She bit her lower lip and looked up at our faces. "I've been working at the dockyard for a few years now. I'm not afraid of hard work. I just don't get my pay, as it all goes through Andrew Di Vaio. He only allows me money to buy clothes. Without money, it would be nearly impossible to go. I represent income for them, so it might not be easy to do."

"You're always welcome here, dear." Mama put her hand over Sienna's and gave her a warm smile.

"That's very kind, thank you."

It wasn't lost on me that Sienna only ate the fruit and not the actual meal. The Italian in Mama wanted to insist that she eat, but I gave her a warning not to push. I knew Sienna was never fed much. I knew she always ate what I left for her, and I was happy to be able to do that, but a meal like the one we were having would overpower her stomach.

As the afternoon went on, I could feel her anxiety level rise. I knew it was her fear of being away from the house too long. My parents enjoyed talking to her. Despite what she had been through, she was quite smart and had a fire to her personality that I found very intriguing. However, I knew she needed to get back and stood to give her the out she needed.

"Thank you for such a lovely afternoon." She hugged my mother. "Forgive me for not staying longer, but I must get going."

"Wait, wait." My mama held up a camera, and as she snapped a few photos, it surprised me that Sienna leaned into me and smiled warmly. Even my mother seemed pleased and snapped a few more as we were hustling around the table.

"I will walk with you." I waited for her to say goodbye to my parents then led her back toward the path, her hand in mine.

She remained quiet for most of the way. I knew I had dropped her into a world she wasn't ready for, but if I didn't do it then, when? I started to get nervous and decided to be honest with her the way she had been with us.

"Sienna," I reached out to stop her, "I'm sorry if that was a lot. I just wanted my parents to meet you."

"Why?"

"Because I really like you." What was she not getting?

"You can have any girl out there. I have nothing to

offer you."

"You're different from any girl I have ever met."

She closed her eyes, and a tear leaked out. I reached up and gently dragged my thumb down the damp path, catching the tear at the corner of her lips.

"You're right. We are very different."

"I didn't say that."

"I know, but it's true." She smiled and slid her hand from mine. "Thank you for an afternoon I will never forget." She leaned up and gently kissed my cheek then disappeared through the brush back to what I knew must be hell for her.

Chapter

THREE

"You look happy lately, my friend." Francesco set a cold beer in front of me. "Would this have something to do with a certain young *bella donna*?"

"Perhaps." I grinned and pushed out a chair with my foot, so he would join me. Francesco was actually our *consigliere*, but he was so much more than that. He was like a big brother to me, easy to talk to, and always had the best advice. He often stepped up when my father had a lot to deal with. Like right now, I knew something big was brewing by the way the staff in the house were practically tiptoeing around and my mother was constantly watching the phone. So far, I had purposely not asked about it. I had other things on my mind.

"Perhaps?" he repeated then pulled out a few photos. "Then perhaps you would not mind if I threw away these photos?" He held up a picture of Sienna that my mother had taken and wiggled his eyebrows. I snatched the photo from his hands and stared down at her. She was looking directly into the camera. Her hair had dried wavy after our swim, and the ends had caught the breeze and brushed across her cheek. I couldn't tell if her eyes were a dark hazel or a deep navy blue. Either way, I found myself lost in them. I was careful about how much I stared at her in person, not wanting to make her uncomfortable, so this was the perfect opportunity to study her face.

"I know that look, Elio." He pulled my gaze to his with his tone.

"Is it possible, Francesco? To be in love so soon? Before one has had time to test the waters and know what else could be out there?"

"There is no starting point for when to love, Elio. That's not how it works. Someone much higher than us presents the opportunity. You can either embrace it when it comes and see where it takes your heart, or let the moment pass and hope another will come that will be more worthy of it. Only you can make that choice."

"What if I don't want anyone else?"

"Then you hold on to her." He paused, and I saw that familiar smile appear that smoothed the stress lines around his mouth, and I knew his wife was on his mind.

"Are you thinking of your Mariella?"

"Mm." His smile grew. "Listen to your heart and

hold her tight."

"There seem to be so many obstacles to being with her." I sighed deeply to make the point.

"Obstacles will always be part of love, Elio. If love was easy, where would be the challenge in that? It takes work to be in love. When it isn't, well, that's when you must tread carefully."

"How can I show her that I am worthy of her, make her see that I'm worth loving back?"

"By being you. You have a steady hand, a head on straight, and you lead with your heart."

"And what about the family business?" I challenged.

"If she loves you, she'll love all of you. Just go slowly."

"I hate that house." I flicked my head in the direction of the De Vaio house. "Renzo should be tied to the back of a pickup and dragged over shards of glass."

"I don't disagree." He huffed with a smile at my choice of words.

"I saw it in his eyes that he wants her. It took everything in me not to drag him outside and beat his face in."

"You said your part for now. The time will come for that, but there's no reason to scare her until she knows the truth. Who knows what story Renzo might plant in her? You must be patient."

"There you are." Mama raced toward us, fluttering her hands nervously. "We have guests, so please get dressed. Your father needs you to befriend the son."

"Mama." I hated that part of the business.

"Elio." Her face told me not to push, and a strangeness settled into the air. "Please."

"Very well." I headed back inside and noticed Francesco darted toward the staff corridors, no doubt to warn them to get ready.

Despite the tension in the house, I took a moment to remove a photo from a frame and replaced it with the one of Sienna and me. Our fingers were laced together, and my lips were pressed to her fingers. Such a simple moment, but yet so special. I held on to it for an extra beat then sat it next to my bed. I was looking forward to showing it to Sienna the next time I saw her. With one more glance at her smiling face, I hurried to my closet to get ready. My father had stopped in to quickly brief me on who was coming, and I knew I had very little time.

I rolled my eyes at the blacked-out Mercedes E-Class that led the four cars up our long driveaway. You might as well have spray painted *mafia* on the side of it. I rested my forearms on the railing of the balcony and watched as a fat man waddled over to help his over-the-top dressed wife and son, who looked to be my age. The DeSimone family were the head of their syndicate, which was much smaller than ours and was wedged southeast of our northern territory and just northeast of the Coppolas'. For years, they had tried to hold their own, but, as my father explained, they just didn't have the power we had to rule. We hoped they would want us to absorb their territory, which would allow us to expand our reach.

"Elio." My father stood in the doorway of my bedroom. "It's time to come down, son."

I pushed off the rail and fell into step behind him to go meet a family from an old syndicate south of Florence. I'd never met them before, mainly because they kept a low profile and had never been that active. Now, for some reason, they wanted to meet with my family to discuss boundaries. I felt uneasy when I noted how my father's shoulders stiffened as Francesco opened the door for the fat man and his family to come in.

"Dom Capri," he held his hands in the air, "what an honor to meet you."

"You as well, Roberto."

My father immediately waved him to follow, and he turned toward the hallway that led to his office. Apparently, he wasn't wasting any time.

There was an awkward moment of silence while the rest of us stood there, then Mama cleared her throat and stepped forward.

"Please, do come in." She forced a smile on her face and pointed to me. "This is my son, Elio."

"Bria and Mariano."

"Elio, show Mariano around, please." Mama fluttered her hand at us. "Come along. We'll go to the living room where we can chat."

Then it was just the two of us. Normally, when I had to entertain, I did the same thing. I showed them around and then got us something to eat so we wouldn't have to talk much, but to my surprise, Mariano started to laugh.

"Funny," he followed me outside, "we're nearly adults, and yet they treat us like children. Rather than being in there learning the family business, we are brushed off and sent to play."

"I'm sure there's a reason." Relieved that he seemed easy to talk to, I handed him a beer from the ice chest near the grill, then waved for him to sit with me by the pool.

"I guess." He shrugged, letting it go, but I saw his gaze dart to the family ring that I wore. "Lucky. How bad was the initiation?"

I admired the ring in the light as I remembered what I had to do to earn my position as an underboss.

"Not bad."

"Did you look him in the eye as you pulled the trigger?"

"There wasn't a trigger." I eyed him and let his imagination run wild with how I might have done it. "He deserved it, and it's one less bastard to worry about."

"Were there any witnesses?"

I could tell he was more than ready to do the same as I had done to prove himself. He was as eager for details as I had been at that point in my life. Later, the faces became blurred, and you lost count of how many souls you had collected.

"Not anymore."

"Nice." He tapped his beer to mine.

For the next three hours, we chatted about everything from our childhoods to friends to girlfriends.

"Stella," Mariano held on to his chest dramatically, "her body is shaped like an hourglass, and her lips are as full as the moon." He smiled and touched his lips. "Not to mention the way she kisses me." He rolled onto his side on the oversized lounge chair and finished off his third brew. "And what about you? You seem to understand what I'm saying."

"Not really," I lied not liking the idea of sharing anything about Sienna with a stranger, and I knew she wouldn't like it either. I tucked an arm under my head and stared up at the late afternoon sky where the clouds worked to build mountains over our heads. "But I know she's out there just waiting for our paths to cross."

"She's out there," he agreed then moved to sit up. "Three brews and my bladder's full."

"Three doors down on your left." I pointed to the house and bent to clean up the bottles. "I'll meet you in there after," I called to him, and he waved.

I was curious about what was happening with the meeting inside, so I made my way toward the living room where my mother seemed much more relaxed with the company than she had earlier. Then I heard my father laughing from his office, and my defenses lifted.

"There you are, Elio." Mama beamed up at me as she poured a glass of white wine. "I was just sharing about how you found love by a pond in the middle of the woods." She cooed like it was romantic, and I shifted uncomfortably.

"Sounds like Sienna is a very lucky young lady to find such a handsome young man." Bria, who looked to be at least twenty years younger than her husband, crossed her legs and made a show of it.

"Thank you." I shot Mama a glance, which she quickly picked up on and changed the subject. "Bria, have a little more of the cheese and pears. They are at their peak of ripeness just now, and we must enjoy them while we can."

"I'd be happy to. They are delicious." She leaned forward and gave me another show. I turned on my heel and hastily left, nearly bumping into Francesco, who stood by the entrance of the kitchen looking uneasy.

"Is everything going well, Elio?" he asked as I walked by.

"Please make sure I'm on the opposite side of the table from the wife." I groaned and rolled my eyes.

"Only if you promise not to leave her alone with me either." He chuckled darkly as he clearly had not enjoyed his own encounter with her.

"Deal." I laughed and raced up the stairs, surprised to be met at the top by Mariano.

"Hey, sorry. My papa was using the restroom downstairs, and your mother said to use the one up here."

"Oh, okay. I'll be right down."

"Sounds good."

The rest of night went smoothly, and Francesco, true to his promise, kept Bria well away from me. Mariano and I decided on a plan to meet in the city for drinks later in the week. I found I liked talking to him, and he seemed to enjoy it as well.

After they left, I heard my parents quietly talking outside, but when I joined them, they quickly changed the topic.

"Everything all right?" I took a seat next to my mother and eyed them both.

"Yes, son, and thank you both for your help in entertaining tonight." My father gave me a squeeze on the shoulder. "I think they will be a good asset to the family business, plus their syndicate is fading fast and the wolves are circling."

"What do they bring to the table, Papa?" I was curious why these people had surfaced all of a sudden.

"They have a connection with Naples." He gave me a dark look, one I knew all too well. The Naples syndicate had been after us for a long time. The news of my father's recent illness spread quickly, and the sharks were out for blood. Little did they know my father was an ox, and it would take more than a mild heart attack to bring him down. Nevertheless, we had a bright, bold target on our backs.

"Roberto wants to join us and help keep Sicily under our rule."

"Do you trust him?"

My father thought for a moment, then he looked at Mama. "I don't think we have a choice right now. Not with your two uncles over on the mainland working in the north. Until they return, we need all the help we can get."

"A watchful eye and an open ear are more important than you know," Mama said quietly. "It's a powerful tool to have, despite," she paused, "an inappropriate trophy wife. She was interested to hear of your love interest." She gave me a knowing nod as if to say *Now you know why I brought up Sienna.* We could never be too careful with what we shared with people.

"Understood." I read her loud and clear.

"Elio." My father drew my attention to him. "What are your feelings toward their son?"

I leaned back and nursed the water Francesco had given me. I felt better now that I knew what was going on and that my father felt good with his decision.

"I like him. We're meeting up in the city later on in the week."

"Did he pry?"

"Only about my initiation." I held up my ring. "I didn't say much, and he never once asked about the business."

"Did he share anything with you?"

"No, we kept it light."

"Good." He lit his cigar and puffed the smoke away from us. "I think this is good."

Chapter FOUR

"What are you doing?" Cara hissed at me. "Hurry up!"

I felt around between the seats of the truck, desperately trying to find my necklace. Renzo had ripped it off my neck the night before in another of his attempts to touch me. The fabric stank of cheap beer and cigarettes, and I almost lost my stomach contents when my fingers touched something wet. Just as I was about to give up hope, I felt the chain with the tips of my fingers.

"I feel it!"

"Come on, come on!"

It was the end of our shift, and I knew we had about another minute before he would come out to the dockyard office and spot us. I hooked the chain and pulled it free.

"I got it!" I quickly tied it in a knot and was about to shut the door when we heard his voice.

"What the fuck!"

"Run, Cara." I pushed her hard, so she'd go. She hesitated then ran, knowing this was my fight. If she got hurt again because of me, I would never forgive myself.

"What the hell are you doing here? Are you stealing from my truck?" He came up and grabbed me by the hair and tossed me against the truck. My shoulder hit the door hard, and my temple smacked the mirror. I slid to the ground in a heap and lifted an arm in an attempt to protect my face. His fist rose, and I squeezed my eyes shut and waited for the impact, but none came. I opened an eye and found him staring down at me.

"You just make me so mad sometimes."

What?

"Here." He reached for my hand and hauled me roughly to my feet. "What's that?" He fingered my necklace with his filthy hand. "Nah, you don't need that. I like my girls without the bling." He ripped it off and tossed it on the ground, sending the teddy bear pendant hard against the knot in the chain. "Now, I want you to go get yourself cleaned up. I'm going to take you out. Go get pretty now."

"I would rather you hit me again." I spat on the ground next to him.

His eyes bulged, and he whipped around, grabbed my neck, and pushed me up against the truck. My windpipe struggled for air while he stared into my eyes, begging me to challenge him again.

"I said go get ready."

I held my ground when he let go, and he muttered and walked away. I caught sight of Andrew in the window watching us, and just like always, he glared and moved out of view. Dismissing the pain that wrapped around my head, I wiped the dirt from my face.

With a sniff, I picked up my broken necklace and hurried down the road. I had been hit more times than not, but this time something was different, and it scared the shit out of me. I knew it was only a matter of time before Renzo would force himself on me, and that would be the day I knew I would snap and check out for good.

Working at the dockyard, I quickly learned to keep my mouth shut and listen. Lunch times were particularly interesting, as the stories about the mafia encroaching on the dockyard were becoming story time. Many times, I dreamed of leaving a note asking one of them to crush Renzo's kneecaps.

I made it to the general store and let my tears fall, and the shakes overcame me. I wanted to be scrappy. I tried to hold my own, but the reality of it was I wasn't good at it. I wore my heart on my sleeve, and I cared too much. I had never really gained the *kid left behind* thick skin.

Easing onto the step with my back against the wall, I tried to find a peaceful place in my mind, anything that would give me some strength.

"Sienna?" A familiar voice found me, and I opened my eyes to see Elio's mother with an arm full of bags.

"Sweet girl, are you all right?" She put her bags on the ground.

I started to cry again. Her caring voice struck a chord inside me, the mother figure I had never really had.

"Oh, come here." I buried myself in her arms and let a stranger give me comfort, forcing away my problems, if only for a moment. "You're shaking." She pulled back my face, and her thumbs brushed across my forehead. "Is that blood?"

I nodded, and she walked me to over her fancy, expensive car, and I tried to pull away, as the thought of getting some blood or dirt on those beautiful seats worried me.

"Please just tell me who did this. Was it someone at your house or someone else?" She began to look around like they might return.

"House," I whispered to reassure her she wasn't in any danger.

"All right," she nodded, "no arguing. I'm taking you to my house to get cleaned up."

I didn't have it in me to protest further, and the idea of having a safe place to go even for a while did seem appealing. She opened the door for me and fiddled with her phone before getting back behind the wheel.

The leather seats of the car were soft, but the cool air she directed toward my face felt even better. We rode in silence for a bit. She glanced over a few times and once thumbed around with the temperature.

"I will not ask too many questions," she said quietly after we turned onto the road, "but have you eaten today?”

"I had a little, yes," I whispered.

"I imagine the Di Vaios don't cook for you often?"

I lowered my gaze and twisted the ring on my finger.

"You don't have to answer me."

"I get by." I shifted uncomfortably, more embarrassed than anything else.

"I see." She kept her voice low as she parked outside the front door in the middle of the horseshoe shaped driveway. I had never seen the house from this angle before, and it was utterly stunning. It looked like a painting, everything so perfect.

Francesco appeared out of nowhere to open her door. He stood and waited for her to get out.

"Sienna, one last thing."

I turned to look at her as she spoke.

"Can you tell me exactly who hit you?"

"Which time?" I shrugged. "I am used to it. Please don't worry about it."

Her frown turned up into a sad smile, and she let it go.

I felt uncomfortable once again returning to the Capri home in my less-than-clean work clothes, shorts, a tank top, and flats. I wore many hats at my job, and this week I was filing paperwork in the back, only now I wished I had worked in the front office today, as I would have at least been in a dress. I was short and loved nice clothes and high heels, but all that would have done was bring on more attention from the men. I tried only to wear clothing that didn't draw attention. My head hurt from where I bumped it on the mirror, but the cool air and fresh smelling house helped calm my nerves.

"What can I get for you, dear?"

"A drink of water would be nice, thank you."

"Will you eat something?"

"Yes, just something small, though, thank you. Would you mind if I used your washroom to clean up?"

"Of course. Here, take this to clean that cut, and then I'll start on something for us to eat."

"Thank you." I turned to follow Francesco up the massive stairs. The place was like a dream, winding staircases, massive flowerpots with every flower you could imagine, floor to ceiling windows, open walkways, and an incredible view of the ocean. I was awed that people lived in such places.

"How long have you worked with the Capri family?" I asked Francesco as we walked down a long hall. I felt a little uncomfortable not speaking to him.

"Since Mr. Capri was twenty-two, and we've been very close since."

"That's a long time. Do you have any family? Children?"

"I have kids, but my wife and I divorced when they were very young." He shrugged as though he was fine with it. "But I was blessed with two handsome sons." He beamed and stopped to open his wallet. He held it out, indicating a family photo. "I don't get to see them as often as I'd like, but we are close, and that's what matters."

"I bet." I forced a smile. The warmth of a real family

was not something I could relate to. I knew enough to understand it existed; it just never had for me.

Francesco opened a door to a guest room and stood to the side to let me enter.

Wow.

Canopy bed, open glass door to a massive balcony, and the bathroom was bigger than the De Vaio house. The walk-in shower could fit at least five people.

On instinct, I crossed my arms and felt unworthy to be there.

"Anything you need should be in here. Please feel free to take your time." He hesitated for a moment and seemed about to say something then changed his mind.

"I'm sure I will only need a few minutes. Thank you so much, Francesco." I placed a hand on his arm, then on sudden impulse reached up and kissed his cheek.

Francesco, who was taller than I was, with a hint of salt and pepper along his sideburns, sputtered a little then tugged at his tie. "Miss Sienna, if you ever need help, you need to understand that I can help you."

"What do you mean?"

"No one should hit a child or a young woman. Such scum." His face softened as he sidestepped my question. Then he placed a kind hand on my shoulder and smiled warmly. "You're safe when you are here."

"Thank you, Francesco." I let out a shaky breath and knew in my gut he meant it.

I used the cloth Andrea had given me to dab the wound on my temple then pinched it together and used a bit of tape to close the cut. Satisfied it would hold, I covered it all with a small bandage. I knew it probably needed a stitch or two, but this would have to do. It wasn't the first time I'd had to do a makeshift job. I washed my face and finger brushed my hair as best I could then swallowed a couple of Advil from a bottle in the cabinet. A wave of self-pity overcame me as I studied myself in the beautiful mirror.

I closed my eyes and put my hands on the sink and let out a silent scream, wishing things were different, that my mother hadn't left me with an empty promise to return, and that I'd had a better life than the one that was forced on me.

The idea of leaving the Di Vaio house terrified me as much as living there did. I'd never been on my own. I had no idea how to handle money, or even how to get a job other than the one I'd been given at the dockyard, and then there was the one thing that rested in the center of my heart. What if my mother came looking for me? What if all this time she had to wait for some reason and finally came to find me and I wasn't there? Then what? If I ran away there would be no way for her to ever find me. I pushed back the thought that I wasn't sure I could ever forgive her for abandoning me, anyway. The worst part was I knew nothing about who I was or where I came from. Cara told me to make up a new past, one that I wanted. I tried, but I always circled back to the start.

I shook myself free of the thoughts that threatened to overpower me with more self-pity and forced myself to stand up straight and smile into the mirror. I had to move on.

"Sienna?" Andrea knocked lightly on the door. She came into the room to check on me. "I just wanted to see if you needed anything."

"I'm fine, thanks. I was just heading down."

She smiled and came toward me, wrapping her motherly arms around my shoulders.

"Oh, sweetheart, I'm so sorry for what you are going through."

"I'm okay, really." More pesky tears leaked out. "I just," I stumbled to find the right words, "I'm just thankful you're so kind to me."

"Of course, Sienna. You mean so much to my son, therefore you mean so much to us." She kissed the top of my head and gently dried my tears with a tissue from her pocket. "Now, come. We will eat together."

"That would be wonderful." I sniffed and fought the raw emotion back down.

I followed her downstairs and heard a commotion as we neared the front of the house.

"Where is she?" I heard Elio speaking to someone in the entryway.

"She is all right, *figlio*, but did you speak to…?" His father lowered his voice, and I couldn't hear the rest.

"Of course, Papa, I did. Why do you question me on that?"

"Then I need to make some calls."

I rounded the corner to see Elio in a pair of jeans and a damp dress shirt.

"Calm down, dear," Andrea spoke up, as she was a few feet ahead of me. "She just needed a moment to clean up."

When he spotted me, I saw relief rush over him.

"Hi," I whispered, uncomfortable with the attention on me.

"Mama texted me and said she brought you here." He came over and wrapped me in an unexpected hug. I hesitated but returned his embrace and found myself leaning my head against his shoulder. His strong arms and the smell of his skin had all kinds of feelings racing through me. "Are you hurt?"

"Just a bump, nothing that won't heal."

As he pulled me back to inspect my head, I noticed Andrea and Piero exchange a glance.

"She needs to eat." His mother nodded for us to go outside. "Papa and I will join you shortly."

Elio took my hand and led me out to the patio area. He pulled out a chair and nodded at Francesco to go ahead and serve us.

He watched me take a bite as he rubbed his stressed face. His mother appeared at the doorway and waved him over.

"Excuse me." He politely left the table, returning a few moments later with something in his hand.

"Sienna." My name rolled off his tongue and smacked me right in the center of my stomach. "I'm not someone who dances around a topic, so I'm going to be blunt."

"Okay." I placed my fork down on the table, but he handed it back to me and urged me to continue to eat.

"You wouldn't know this, but you helped me

through a very difficult time in my childhood, and I feel that I may have helped you as well?" He waited for me to answer.

"You did, and you still are." I looked directly into his eyes to let him see I was being truthful.

"Are you attracted to me?"

I felt the heat of the blood as it rushed up into my neck. I forced myself to ignore it even as I felt the warmth stain my cheeks. Elio's earnest expression made me want to be as completely open with him as he was being with me.

"Yes I am."

"And I think you are beautiful, and kind, and you make me feel good inside."

"Oh." I wasn't ready for that.

"I've hesitated to share my feelings for you. From the first moment we met, I knew, but you were just a child. I want to be clear, it is not simple lust, Sienna, it is real love, and it has grown deeply with every year we have been friends. I don't want you to think I'm like the other boys you live with in that house or that place you work. I have respect for you and want to treat you the way a woman should be treated."

I put the fork back down on the table. Every word he spoke filled me with emotion. Elio was saying what I knew he truly felt. I found myself unable to speak, so I just continued to look at him.

"Now." He took my hand and kissed the back of it. "I am not going to ask you to be my girlfriend just yet. I want to earn it and prove to you we are meant to be together. However, I would like to give you this." He pulled out a small box and opened it to show me a chain with a small pendant on it. I studied it and recognized the bird was the same as the tattoo he had on his back.

"I know you already wear one, and I'm assuming it's something special?"

Tears once again fought their way to the surface as I pulled my own broken necklace from my pocket.

"It was my mother's. She gave it to me a long time ago."

He took the broken chain from me and removed the small teddy bear and put it on the chain along with his. He stood and turned me around then brushed my hair off one shoulder and fastened it around my neck. I held the two pendants between my fingers. The little teddy bear that my mother had given me was now accompanied with a black bird.

"It's part of our family crest. The bird is a crow, and it represents family." He stumbled for a moment and went on. "I want you to feel you are part of the family now."

"Thank you, Elio. It's beautiful." It was all I could manage to say. I was overwhelmed with emotion and felt something shift inside me. For the first time in my life, I felt love.

"Now, please, Sienna." He smiled, and the mood instantly lightened. "Eat, or Mama will be after both of us." I laughed along with him as I picked up the fork.

And that was how the next two years went. I would finish my job at the dockyard then race off to my secret life beyond the swimming pond. I was always welcomed with open arms by Elio's parents, who seemed to love me almost as much as they did their own son. Things changed for the better since that day, and life had new meaning. I began to take more care with my wardrobe and my body. It was like parts of me were finally becoming found. Cara was happy for me, too. She even talked about someone she met at the dockyard. I never questioned why Renzo or Andrew stopped hitting me or why Renzo backed off trying to touch me. I was just glad they did.

Elio never forced himself on me, never pressured me. The only thing he would do was gently kiss me on the cheek and wish me goodnight before we would part.

One day, I bolted from one of the bedrooms, hoping I could outrun him, but instead I ran into one of the flowerpots, catching it before it tumbled to the marble floor. I saw a flash of white and knew I needed to run.

"No!" I raced out of the hallway in a fit of laughter with Elio close behind trying to tackle me, his body all sweaty from his workout.

"You can't outrun me, beautiful!" He grabbed me around the stomach, but I was able to slip away and run out to the patio. When I whirled around, he was gone.

"Elio?" I laughed quietly. "Where did you go?"

Francesco chuckled as he stepped out through the

patio doors holding a tray of fresh lemonade.

"Hey." I smiled warmly at one of my new best friends. "Have you seen Elio?"

"I have not." He started to place the glasses on the table.

"I think I outran him." I heaved forward to catch my breath.

"Oh, sweet Sienna." He shook his head knowingly as though what I said was so far from the truth. "No one outruns Elio."

"That so?" I lifted an eyebrow and held out my arms to show him that I just had.

One moment I was standing there, and the next I had a six-foot-three Elio wrapped around my body as we both flew into the pool.

When I kicked to the surface, he had a huge, smug smile on like he was five and had just won a game of tag.

"I thought I lost you." I grinned. As he swam toward me, his expression changed to a more serious one. He slowly backed me up to the side of the pool and used his arms to trap me in place.

"You'll never lose me, Sienna, not if I can help it."

My heart filled, and I found my eyes traveling down to his lips. He often said such sweet things to me, and I never knew how to respond. Love had never been a part of my life until I had let him in, and now…now I knew I did love him. I was young, but not too young to know I wanted more from him. Suddenly, whatever version of love we had, I relished it and would follow him freely.

I moved my hands to his shoulders then slid them

over so my arms wrapped around his neck.

"I don't want to lose you either."

My body responded to his closeness, and I knew he felt it too by the way his pupils dilated and his breathing quickened.

"May I," he stood and steadied himself while his warm hand cupped the side of my face, "kiss you?"

Elio wasn't one to ask for permission from others. He was a natural leader, but he treated me differently, and I loved it. I nodded and waited for him to respond. He pressed his lips to mine and slowly started to move with the kiss I followed his lead and felt a tiny spark of lust brew in my belly. I moved my hands up his arms and back down his back, feeling the heat spread through me like heavy, thick molasses. Once I gave him a little moan of enjoyment, he reached down and urged my legs to wrap around his waist. I felt his interest, and I found myself wanting more, wanting the kiss to go deeper.

"Francesco?" I somehow muttered through the kiss, and that seemed to make him realize that we were on display for all.

"Come on." He helped me out of the pool, and we ran together across the lawn to the pool house.

He shut the door and pulled a couple of long lounge cushions off a pile in the corner and threw a blanket over them. I removed my shirt, and when he turned to me, I threw myself against him, wildly demanding.

"Damn." He threw himself back into our kiss as he walked me backward then pulled away only long enough to lay me on top of the cushions. His thumb hooked into the waistband of my skirt and pulled it down over my wet legs. He stepped back and removed his clothing while admiring me in my bra and panties. I saw him pull his wallet from his pocket, and he removed something then tossed the wallet back onto the wet pile.

He held up the small pouch and smiled at me.

"This is for your protection as well as mine, *cuore dolce*."

I smiled back and nodded my agreement and silently thanked the gods he was such a gentleman. The thought hadn't even entered my head in the heat of the moment.

"Good." He moved in front of me and started to kiss me again. "I only want you, Sienna, only you."

I pulled back from the kiss and inched my way up on the makeshift bed. I unclipped my bra and watched as his face became transfixed. My breasts sprang free as I tossed the bra aside, and then I pulled my bottoms down all the way, kicking them off impatiently as they stuck to my wet toes.

"You can have all of me, Elio."

He slowly knelt between my legs and ran his hands down my thighs then between my legs, brushing over my slick, wet opening. He moved tentatively, as though worried I would change my mind. I wiggled, mad with the need for him to touch me.

"Please take me."

"Oh," he moaned, closing his eyes, "it's just as I dreamed it would be. You are so beautiful." He placed his hand on my stomach for a moment then let his fingers slide down to circle my bud, and I nearly went wild.

He pulled his hand away and began to kiss me all over my stomach, neck, and chest. I shook and pressed against him in desperation.

He moved away for a moment, and I nearly cried out at the loss of contact, but he soon returned and hovered over me. His dark, intense eyes looked into mine.

"Open your eyes, *bella*. Are you ready?" he asked like the gentleman he was, and I nodded, unable to form real words. "If it becomes too much, you must tell me." I leaned up and kissed his lips to tell him I heard him.

Slowly, he nudged my opening, and ever so carefully, he slid inside. I had heard it would be painful, and it was for one sharp moment, and when my eyes flew open to find his, he stopped briefly. Then he began to move very slowly and gently, and the combination of that with how wet and ready I was made me lose all power of thought. It was like nothing I had ever experienced. I felt full and stretched, but when he pulled out and slid back in, every nerve in my body was heightened and I felt pure, hot pleasure.

"Ohh," I moaned.

"*Paradiso*." He squeezed his eyes shut and cursed. "Just like a dream."

In and out he went, and with each little thrust, I wound tighter and tighter until I didn't think I could handle another moment of it.

He suddenly reached down and rubbed my bud, changing the sensation, and I found release in a billion bright lights mixed with his sweet cries of joy from his own climax.

He flopped down next to me and pulled me onto his chest.

"That was incredible," he whispered and brushed my wet hair off my face. "How do you feel? Are you okay?"

I smiled at him. "It was wonderful, Elio."

We lay there holding each other. Neither of us wanted to break apart.

"What's this?" I held up his hand to study the ring on his wedding finger.

"Family ring," he answered as he drew my hand to his mouth to kiss my fingers, then he turned it over and kissed the palm.

"When did you get it?"

"A little while ago." His kisses traveled down my arm as he rolled me over onto my back.

"It's pretty." I smiled up into his dark eyes and felt a rush of heat pool in my belly. "Did your parents have it made?"

"Mmhm." His lips were on my neck, and I fought to think, then realization suddenly dawned and I sat up as real life swept into my thoughts in an instant. I pushed him back, jumped up, and began to pull on my wet clothes.

"I'm so sorry, Elio. Cara said she couldn't cover for me this afternoon. I completely lost track of time."

"Here." He quickly handed me my flip flops.

We both raced through the woods and stopped where we always said our goodbyes.

"I wish so much we could have spent the day

together. I didn't want to end things like that." He was frazzled with the sudden rush.

"Me too."

"I hate that you are going back there, too."

"I know."

"See you tomorrow?" He tugged me in for a kiss then pulled away as my lips under his stretched with a big grin. He grinned back.

"Bye, Elio."

"Goodbye, my Sienna."

We spent the next six months exploring all the many ways two people could make love to one another, and how many times. I would return to the house each night. I would go to the dockyard and work every day. I was treated with disdain and rudeness, but no one hit me, and although Renzo glared at me and made every effort to make my days as horrible as he could, I could handle it because I knew Elio was a just a breath away.

That was, until one day when everything changed, and my life would forever be taken down a different path.

"Where are you going?" Renzo, who clearly had had multiple beers, staggered into the bathroom one evening while I was doing my hair. He leaned his bulk across the doorway, blocking my exit.

"I'm going out. Now, move, Renzo." I put down the hairbrush and glared at him.

"Out where?"

"None of your business." I tried to move past him, but he wouldn't budge.

"Are you going to see your pretty boy? Don't think I don't know about your fancy man in the big, fancy house."

I wasn't ready for that. I thought I had kept my visits a secret. I hesitated to answer, and I knew he saw the truth.

"Does he look at you the way I do?"

"What?" I had to resist the urge to gag.

"Has he seen you naked?"

"Seriously, Renzo? You really need to grow up already."

He shifted his weight off the wall and stood square on both feet as he tossed his empty beer bottle into the sink. The noise was so loud it made me jump, and he took that opportunity to push me backward against the sink and shut the door behind him. His hands were on me, and I fought and scratched at him to make him stop. He put a hand to his now bloody cheek and stood straight.

"You've been tempting me for years, flaunting yourself around, teasing me, and I'll be dammed if he takes the one thing that is mine."

"Enough," I hissed when he came at me again. "I said enough!" I screamed at the top of my lungs then flew at him and with all my force and drove the palm of my hand into his nose. He shot backward and hit the wall and fell into the tub with a howl.

"What the hell, Sienna!" Cara looked terrified as she rushed into the room. "Andrew is going to kill you."

She was right. No matter what I did, I was in the wrong, but assaulting his beloved firstborn just sealed my fate.

I raced past her, grabbed my book bag, and filled it with as much as I could that was mine. This was it. I knew if I didn't leave now, I would never be able to.

"Here." Cara handed me her jar of cash. "Please take it."

"No." I hugged my friend, the only person who always had my back in this awful place. "Come with me."

"I can't, you know I can't." She was just as panicked as I was. It had been beaten into us at every turn that we could never leave. They constantly undermined us and chipped away at our self-esteem. We were kept off balance, never knowing when we would be beaten, never knowing when or if we would eat. I had hit my wall, and if my mother had not come looking for me yet, well, chances were she never would. "Where will you go? Elio's?"

"Yes. I know they will keep me safe."

"Goodbye my friend." She hugged me so tightly I could feel my heart and hers as they said their goodbyes too.

"Bye."

With all my life's belongings in one bag, I raced through the forest, never once tripping in the pitch black, even with tears of hurt and freedom streaming down my face. This was it; I had finally broken free.

The pool lights were on, and one of the doors was

open on the patio. I called out as I stepped inside.

"Elio?" I raced toward the kitchen. "Andrea? Piero?"

As I entered the living room, my world stopped, and it suddenly registered. The house was a mess.

"What?" I whirled around and saw the place looked to be ransacked. Everything had been gone through. As I ran in a panic through the rooms, I saw closet doors and dresser drawers had been left open, and items of clothing were strewn about the floor. The furniture was left behind, but most of their personal items were gone. I found no notes to indicate where they had gone. There was very little evidence left at all to show that the Capri family had once lived there.

Pain burst through my chest as I picked up a picture frame from the floor and brushed my finger over the broken glass. It was taken a few weeks ago, of his family and me at lunch by the pool. Elio's arm was wrapped around the back of my chair, and he was smiling at me while the rest of us smiled at the camera. I couldn't help but wonder why the photo had been left behind.

With a sick feeling that had taken over my stomach, the sad reality slowly seeped into the cracks of my soul. For the second time in my life, I had been abandoned by someone I loved. I tucked the photo in my bag and bolted for the woods.

FIVE

Sienna

Present Day Florence, Italy

"You can do this." Wyatt's big gray eyes pushed through my nerves as I stepped into the studio and took in the staged bedroom ready for the boudoir shot.

"I don't know if I can."

"Listen, pretty lady, we didn't work our asses off at the bar, college, and now as journalists only to have you chicken out now. Being offered a cover shot for *Fab Magazine* doesn't come to most people. If you don't do this, I will, so make your decision fast."

"Offered?" I lifted a skeptical eyebrow his way. "You know Georgio is only using my story to help his own newspaper ratings."

"Even if he is, who cares? It's a chance to step out of the shadows and finally get out a story worth telling."

"I guess." I shrugged and wrapped the robe a little tighter around myself. I let out a heavy breath while the photographer walked toward us. I was offered this huge opportunity after someone somehow got hold of the personal story of my life's struggle and climb to success. The moment Georgio, my boss, heard about it, he saw money and rating charts, and he spent the next six months wearing me down. I was a sucker for a good story, and now I supposed it was time to tell mine. *Maybe, if she's out there, she'll finally be able to find me.*

"Breathe, girl." Wyatt was positively glowing at all the fuss that came with a photoshoot.

As exciting as it was, the interview scared me more than a little. I hoped it didn't dredge up old demons or, even worse, encourage people from my past to come find me.

"Thanks." I closed my eyes for a moment to steady myself.

"Thank me when you're finished." He gave me a hug. "I saw a set of gorgeous twins downstairs, so hustle along."

"What about Rosa?"

"We're off this week, so…"

"Mm." I rolled my eyes at my best friend, who had an on and off again girlfriend for years. Personally, I thought they had been dating for so long they didn't know any other way.

Wyatt and I had been close ever since he helped me get off the streets and find a job at a local pub where he was bartending, even though it was a dive. He pretty much saved my life without ever asking for anything in return. From there, we were inseparable. We got a place together, went to college, and later both got a job at a local newspaper as journalists. We worked so well together that we often worked on the same stories. We were each other's rock, and I would do anything for him.

"Drop the blanket, darlin'." Sean, the photographer, rubbed his lips as he looked me over when I finally let my protective covering drop. It didn't help that I knew he had just finished a photoshoot with Jennifer Lopez.

My attire for the next two-plus hours was a tight, off-white corset dress that wrapped around my body in thin ribbon strips. Chandelier earrings peeked out from my long dark hair that presently had so much volume I was sure they must have been going for an eighties feel.

"Michelle," he snapped at his makeup artist, who was by his side in a flash, "no gloss on the lips. Let's use more subtle tones. I want her eyes to tell the story. Let her natural beauty come from there."

"Yes, of course. I see that."

Before I knew that was happening, my face was wiped clean, and I had makeup reapplied, then I was told to wrap myself in a simple piece of deep red silk and lie down on my side and stare directly into the camera.

"Sienna." He held the camera in front of me and spoke from behind the lens. "Bend your top leg and touch your elbow to your knee. Point your toes and let your hair fall all around you. Like you just laid down. Nothing about this shot should look staged."

Happy with his comment about being real, I immediately shifted my body to match his direction. When I reached to pull the fabric up to fully cover my breasts, he stopped me.

"No, Sienna, let the fabric do its job. I promise this will be beautiful."

"Okay." I took a deep breath and repeated the movements again and let everything just happen naturally.

Wyatt pulled out the article the magazine had given us early to review and started to read a section out loud.

"I was afraid to show my body because of all the bruises, and how my skin exposed the thin bones along my rib cage. I looked weak and unhealthy. My skin and hair were dull from lack of proper nutrition, and my clothes were old and never fit right. I carried my scars on the outside, but the ones on the inside were worse. Embarrassment rested in my reflection and tried to control me. It took years and a lot of work, but now I know I am a strong, confident woman, beautiful on the inside as well as on the outside. I love who I am now and am proud of who looks back at me in the mirror." Wyatt caught my gaze and gave me a smile. "That's why you're doing this kind of photo, Si, to show the world that you know you are beautiful. Do it for you."

I fought tears and gave a slight nod. My best friend knew I needed this, and he had just given me the reassurance I needed. I let out a long breath and focused.

"You hold so much of your story in your eyes. Think about all of it and let me capture it in this photo," Sean demanded.

I closed my eyes and took a moment to dig deep and let all that I held back for years flood my memory and burn the tips of my brain.

Okay.

When I opened them again, I let the pain show.

The shutter clicked away, and the memories attacked my soul like a tiny army with painful spears. I had fought for years to hold back the levy, but if I was going to do this, I was going to do it right. I never half-assed anything, no matter what the toll was.

"She does do that well," Wyatt said from somewhere in the room. "I think I have goosebumps."

"Mm," Sean caught my attention, "that right there," he pointed his camera at me, "is why every man in Italy will be beating down her door."

I pushed the men out of my head, closed my eyes, and let my mind wander to the forbidden corner of my mind where *his f*ace lived. His intense dark eyes stared back at me, and I let all the pain open up and wash over me. It had been ten years since I'd seen the only man I ever loved. I had dated, I even once had a three-year relationship, but my heart was never fully in it. Nothing compared to *him*. My heart raced, sweat threatened to break out, and my stomach churned like an angry sea as my lids opened again.

"Shit," Sean whispered as the shutter clicked, "this is the shot."

I barely heard him as I blinked back the hot rage that boiled just under the surface of my skin. It hurt so damn much.

Click, click, click. The camera moved around while I lay there unafraid to show the world what I was capable of. That I was much more than just a reporter for a newspaper.

"Sienna, Sienna," Wyatt's voice pushed through and brought my attention back to the room, "are you okay?"

I pushed myself to my feet, realizing everyone in the room was staring at me. I was careful that the fabric covered all the right spots.

"Yes, I'm fine." I held up my hand and smiled. "Are we finished?"

"Yes, and if you ever want to work with me again," Sean handed me his card, "I will always find the time for you."

"Thank you." I rushed to get changed and felt almost lightheaded. Perhaps I should get something to eat.

"Come on, lady, it's time for us to go home." Wyatt wrapped his big American arms around me, and we walked out together. "I know that was hard, but I'm so proud of you."

"Thanks." I rested my head on his shoulder as we headed for the train.

It had been eight days since the shoot, and I felt even more nervous than when I did the actual session. I had always been comfortable with nudity, but it was different when someone wanted to share you with the world. It was hard for me to close the gates that I had opened that day, and I feared that seeing the magazine would make it even worse.

"Honey, I'm home," Wyatt said in English as he burst into the living room like a caveman. "Get dressed because, darlin', I have something to show you."

"No way. Me and my sweats are fine right here."

"Okay, but remember you were the one who always asked for a heads up on things because you hate surprises." He made a face like he couldn't understand why I would hate them.

"Dammit." I dragged my tired body from the couch in my room and put on something clean.

"That's my girl." He grinned, knowing I would fold.

"How far is it?"

"Not that far." He led me outside and down a few streets then stopped on a corner and put his hands on my shoulders. "Ready?"

"Ready for what?"

He whirled me around, and my stomach sank as I took in my image on a digital billboard right above the shopping center. It was the red silk shot, and my eyes shouted everything that I had been running from for years.

"Georgio is going to freak when he sees this!" I could hear the pay raise in Wyatt's voice.

"I think I might be sick."

"Sick?" He moved to stand in front of me. "You're

everywhere!" He pulled out *Fab Magazine* from his bag, and there I was again, on the front cover. I snatched it from his hand and flipped to the article where I'd poured out my heartbreak to a stranger for the world to read and judge.

"Yup, this is my hell," I whispered.

"Sienna, what did you think you were doing?"

"I don't know." I hid my face from a woman who looked to be making the connection on who I might be. "Maybe I thought I'd be on page twenty-seven wedged in between two celebrities and their baby drama. Not on the front cover or on a vineyard-sized billboard for everyone to see. Dammit, Wyatt, they might as well have popped my boobs out completely!"

"Yes, that is some magnificent cleavage," he pointed to the magazine, "but it's not slutty, Sienna." His voice became softer. "It's beauty and pain meets raw and exposed." He held out his arm toward the billboard. "It's showing young women everywhere that a true Cinderella story does exist."

"Cinderella got the guy, remember?" I muttered darkly.

"The problem with fairytales is that they don't show you all the heartbreak that they've overcome."

"That would be a long movie." I sighed, trying to see his point.

"Screw Cinderella, be the one that uses this article," he held up the magazine, "to get what you want."

"So, play the villain?"

"*He* did, so why can't you?"

I turned to look at him, shocked that he'd referenced Elio so boldly. Wyatt was the only person who knew my true back story, and never once had he painted Elio as a villain.

He raised his hands palms toward me when he saw my expression.

"I'm sorry. It just hurts me that you hurt so much for someone who left you."

"Everyone I ever cared about has left me."

"Not everyone." He lowered his head.

"No." I felt bad. "I guess not everyone." I threaded my arm through his. "Come on, let's go home. I have a quart of chocolate gelato with our name on it."

The weekend came and went, then Monday came much too quickly, and as Wyatt and I walked toward work, I found myself staring at the billboard wondering if my mother had seen me yet. If she had, would she come looking for me? Was I not worth looking for?

"Stop," I whispered to myself. That was the old me. The new me had a backbone and a new life I really loved.

"Here we go." He held open the door for me, and we quickly zipped past the chatty secretary. She was nice but would talk your ear off about her pet bird. Did anyone really like birds? And who named their bird Chester? I thought that was a cat's name. That just caused confusion for all.

Of course, on cue, my boss appeared at the door to the office with a file in his hand. I shook my head at Wyatt. He hated Georgio just as much as I did.

"First, nice photo." He held up the magazine.

"Second, just as I expected, we got a lot of press from your story." He waved us in and closed the door, which was odd, and motioned for me to take a seat. "I received a call early this morning requesting to have you, Sienna, interview one of the owners of Ricco Oil."

"Ricco Oil? They never let anyone interview them." I glanced at Wyatt, beyond confused.

"Precisely why you will do this interview with Mr. DeSimone."

"Why me?"

"Because of this." He held up the magazine.

"I won't sleep with him."

"They made it very clear it was your article that made him want to meet you, Sienna. Apparently, they want you to write it because you struck a chord with him or something. They say, like you, he started from nothing, and so on and so on."

"Wyatt has to come with me to meet him." I wouldn't do this alone.

"I wouldn't send you to the wolves alone. I already got you cleared, Wyatt, but you will stay in the background unless you feel Sienna can't handle something."

"Okay." My best friend nodded, and I felt mildly better.

"Instead of seeing the negative here, Sienna," Georgio stood and buttoned his jacket, "see it as you're touching people with your story."

"I'm trying," I muttered.

"Well, try faster. He arrives in two hours."

"What?" I jumped to my feet.

"Yes, so get your stuff together and make your way over to the airport."

Georgio was a shark, good at the job, but a shark who could smell a story miles away. Maybe this was an opportunity to show just how good I was at being a journalist. Hell, maybe this story would land me a better job than working for Georgio.

Once I was alone with Wyatt, I flipped open the file. "What does it say about him?"

I scanned the bio report. "Hm." I struggled to get my heels on while I read. "Not much here."

"Well, who doesn't love a little mystery?" Wyatt peered over my shoulder, reading the details. "We'd best hurry. I'll call a cab."

"Thanks." I rushed to the washroom to change into one of the emergency outfits I kept on hand for situations like this.

I downed some coffee and tried not to second-guess my outfit as we continued to dig on our phones. I did what my boss suggested and wore one of my favorite dresses, the one that got me through security lines before. If I was going to get something for my next article that might make the front page, I needed to land the moment.

I got this.

Chapter

SIX

I swirled the rum around and took a moment to appreciate its rich color through the crystal, then placed it carefully on the ledge of the stone balcony. The orange peel twirled through the liquor as it floated up to the top to rest gently on the surface. It was our tradition to use a thin piece of orange peel whenever we used the coin. We considered it good luck.

It wouldn't be a long visit, but it needed to happen to make a point. Sometimes the art of dramatics could be a defining one. Church bells rang off in the distance, and I knew it was time.

It was above-average temperature for May. The sun beat down on my shoulders, warming the fabric of the crisp black suit I had chosen for this meeting. I watched as the Alfa Romeo rolled up to the front stairs below my office at the dockyard.

My cousins, my *capos*, Niccola and Vinni, opened their doors, buttoned their coats, and at the same time leaned to open the back doors of the car then reached in to grab the two men I had requested to see.

I slowly moved closer to the railing, alerting the two men that I was there. Fear flitted across their faces and twisted their expressions into an acceptance of their grim fate. The large coin I was holding traveled between my fingers, and I saw their eyes drawn to it as I marked each of the men with either a head or tail. Once my decision was made, I flipped the coin high above me and caught it as I conceded to fate's choice. Resting a single finger on my lips I gave the signal. *Heads*.

One moment there were two men standing, and then the next there was one.

"Holy shit!" The winner tossed his hands in the air as he looked down at the blood spray from his friend that now stained his coat and ran down onto his shoes. "We had a deal!"

I waited a beat, staring down at the man who couldn't fulfill his job, then I spoke confidently so there was no confusion as to who was in charge.

"And that deal was over when you didn't deliver."

I turned on my heel and let my cousins deal with the situation at hand. I had no interest in what happened next. I had much bigger family shit to deal with.

Pulling my keys from my pocket, I hurried home,

not interested in making small talk with anyone.

"There you are." Mama had her back to me as she kneaded the dough for tonight's meal. Whenever she was stressed, she would give the staff the night off and work her frustrations out in the kitchen, and then feed them as a thank you for taking over their space. It was rather fun to watch, and I knew it was one of the many reasons people loved to work for us. We treated them all as family, but like all families, we had our fair share of secrets and did whatever it took to keep them under wraps.

I kissed her cheek and smiled down, but her expression zoned in on some blood on my cuff. Blood from an earlier unfortunate situation.

"You look stressed, *figlio*. Did everything go smoothly at the dockyard?"

"Yes," I reassured her, but I could tell she wanted to say more. "I'm good, Mama, really. Everything is fine." She went back to kneading the dough.

"I assume they'll clean that up."

"Well," I chuckled and took a seat at the island, careful not to brush against the counter now covered in flour, "twenty-three men have died in that very spot, Mama, and you have walked over the area countless times. Have you ever once seen any red stains?"

"What are your plans for this evening?" She changed the subject, knowing I was right. Sloppy wasn't how I operated. I learned from the best, and I would continue to be the best at what I did.

"Not sure yet. Mariano should be calling this evening, and we have many things to discuss."

"Did he take care of—" She paused when Anna strolled into the kitchen and plucked an apple from a bowl.

"Anna, are you staying for dinner?" My mama was always a polite hostess. We had a rule in our house that everyone had to attend at least three dinners a week, and Sundays were mandatory. Any time we held a dinner for guests, they were hosted at my parents' place. This kept their home as the central place within the family to gather socially. Anyone who was close to our family or lived on our property came and went without a thought. The bar was always open, and you could always count on someone enjoying a drink if you ever wanted company. The doors were hardly ever locked, but if they were, it would warn them something big was up. Everyone knew the rules, and they were there for a reason, so no one would ever question them.

Anna looked over at me, waiting for an invitation. I didn't blink as I kept my expression neutral. Anna was the daughter of one of my father's closest friends since we arrived here. There was a history there, and one we couldn't ignore. She was pretty and smart but not my type. She never said what was on her mind and didn't get my sense of humor. Perhaps I did know I was a little too dark and sarcastic for her comfort, but having to stop and explain everything I had said was utterly maddening.

She flipped her thin, pin-straight hair over her shoulder and sighed at my lack of comment.

"I'd love to. Thank you, Andrea."

Wonderful. I could hear the dinner conversation now.

It would consist of one-word answers and uncomfortably long periods of silence while she tried to anticipate what I wanted to hear.

"Another rum?" Francesco read my face like an open book. "Or perhaps a double?"

"Please." I handed him my glass with an exasperated smile, and he returned the expression in kind as he patted my shoulder in sympathy.

"Elio?" Anna shifted her weight from foot to foot as she always did whenever she spoke to me. "Will you be joining us?"

How could someone who looked like she should have it all together have such an unsure, almost blank expression? It was as if no one was home inside. I wanted to like Anna. She had a pretty decent body, and had a nice laugh, but when you got down to the bones of her, that was it. There was no fire, no passion, no sense of self.

I groaned internally while she waited for my answer. I glared at Mama, who tried to hide her amusement.

My phone alerted me to a text, and I quickly pulled it free, hoping that someone had come to my aid.

Mariano: I need to make a house call. I'll call you later with the details.

Damn, the stars were not in my favor tonight.

Elio: Understood.

"Oh, yeah." Niccola came up behind me and leaned in to read my text. "He's wide open for dinner." He walked behind Anna and gave me a shit-eating grin.

"Really?" She beamed, and when she looked away,

I whipped a lime at his head.

"Looks that way." I ducked as he sent it back, and she didn't even react to the fact that a lime was being tossed around the kitchen.

Dinner was in full swing with all of the kitchen staff and Francesco laughing and enjoying Mama's food. *Arrivederci Roma* by Jack Jezzro played in the background as dessert was handed down the line, and the wine never stopped flowing.

Thanks to my papa chatting with Anna, I was able to slip out, but not before I gave Mama a kiss thanking her for a lovely meal.

"Are you sure you want to go? The night's still young."

"That's my fear." I shifted my gaze over to Anna. She would no doubt be expecting something from me at some point through the evening.

"She's really quite lovely, dear." As she said the words, I noted her shoulders slumped slightly.

"She is, Mama, but lovely doesn't mean she's for me."

"Thank you for staying." She kissed my cheek, and I gave her a hug then threw my father a wave as I left.

I twirled my car keys in relief as I headed outside. I thanked the doorman for opening the door to my matte black Maserati Ghibli. The cool leather hugged me as I ran my hand over the wheel. I tried hard to push back the memory that instantly swept through my mind. I must have been more tired than I thought because I closed my eyes and gave in to the pain that flooded my senses for a moment. It was all I had left.

"You good, sir?" The doorman tapped on my window.

I gave a curt nod, shook my head clear, then started the engine. The smooth sound of it calmed me as it moved down the long driveway and traveled the short distance to my villa. It was only minutes away and on the same land as my parents'. When we moved here, we made sure to all stay close. Until we had total control of our product and people, we were still at risk.

The lights turned on automatically when I opened the door. I made my way inside and headed down the hallway to the kitchen, shrugging off my jacket as I went. I draped it over the back of the chair then removed my watch and placed it on the island. The warm glow from beneath the cabinets gave me just enough light to move about to fix a stronger than normal nightcap.

I sent a quick text off to Mariano.

Elio: How was your visit?

The doorbell rang, and I glanced at the time, wondering who it could be. Skipping the usual camera check, I rubbed my tired neck and opened the door to find Anna looking nervous and unsure.

"I didn't get to say goodbye earlier, and I wanted to." She fiddled with her hands. "Well, good night."

"Night." I smiled to be polite and went to close the door when she spoke again.

"Elio?"

"Yeah."

"Is there any chance I could come in?"

I pressed my lips together as I chose my words carefully.

"Anna, you're a sweet woman who I know will find someone great someday. But I'm not the one."

"I'm not always sweet." She tried again.

Ugh, desperate women were never my thing. I knew her father was important to mine, so I tried my hardest to be kind.

"Don't change who you are to be someone you're not." I leaned against the door, feeling drained on the topic but wanting to be fair. "Truth is, I'm not looking for anyone right now. As you know, my family has been through a lot the past ten years, and I need to focus on that. I'll date, but right now that's as far as I go."

"All I'm asking for is a date."

"It's not a good idea."

She stepped down a stair. "Well, when you're ready."

"I'll know where to find you." I nodded, thankful she wasn't going to push any more. I didn't want to hurt her and was hopeful she'd find someone else.

Once she left, I skipped my drink and headed back inside, changed into my workout gear, and hit the treadmill for a solid hour.

It was important in the life I led to be fast, fit, and lean, as well as to be able to kill someone with my bare hands.

The bottom part of my house was dedicated to all of that. I had the best of the best equipment and some of the top trainers in Italy.

I grabbed a towel and wiped the sweat from my face

and neck as I pushed the button on the wall, knowing I needed a harder workout to be able to turn my head off for the night.

Aldo, the nearly three-hundred-pound trainer who was, despite his size, unbelievably quick, stepped into the room and cracked his thick neck.

"Ready?" he grunted as we both stepped into the ring on the opposite side of the room.

I raised my hands and spent the next two hours fighting to keep my jaw intact.

SEVEN

Sienna

My deep yellow sundress flowed around my legs in the light breeze as Wyatt and I hurried to find the terminal gate. I caught a glimpse of myself in the window and was pleased with my outfit choice. A thin, tan tie wrapped around my waist, and matching heels all paired nicely with my rose-colored sunglasses and gold jewelry. Now that I could enjoy the clothing I wanted to wear, I had a bit of an obsession with fashion.

"There really need to be moving sidewalks out here." Wyatt huffed beside me like he was about to die from the short walk since we had stepped off the train.

"Cardio." I held up a hand to warn a driver to slow down. He seemed intent on making us his new bumper sticker. "You might want to look into it."

"I do cardio."

"Flirting with woman at the coffee stand outside work isn't cardio." I smiled over my shoulder at his deep gray eyes that looked amazing with his tight black t-shirt. "Hold on." I googled Ricco Oil and the last name that Georgio had given us and quickly wrote it on the sign we were to hold up. "I think that's how you spell it." I handed it to Wyatt as we started our dash down the walkway.

"Oh, over there." He pointed to terminal eight, and we picked up the pace. Just as the passengers were coming out, we slipped toward the front, both of us searching for someone who looked like they had a ton of money.

"So, we are going off a name and a photo?" Wyatt pulled out a silk handkerchief and dabbed this forehead.

I chuckled under my breath. "Isn't that what he has to go off of, too?"

"True. It's like a blind date interview."

"No date," I shot back in my normal debate with that topic and held up the white sign that read DeSimone. "Work. This is simply a work date."

"You still called it a date."

"Do you want me to leave? Because you know I will."

"No," he gave a little nod toward the sea of people coming toward us, "because I believe you've just been spotted."

"Oh, God," I whispered at the tall, rather attractive

man walking toward me with quite the swagger. His jaw was defined, clean shaven, and his black hair was styled in the latest clean short look.

"Miss Giovanna?" He stopped in front of me and offered his hand.

"I am."

His face broke into a cocky smile. "I'm Mariano DeSimone."

"Pleasure to meet you. This is my associate, Wyatt Burn."

"Nice to meet you as well."

Wyatt looked to be starstruck, just standing there with a gaping mouth. I gave him a little nudge as I took a step forward.

"We thought you might like to get together after you were settled, but my boss told me you asked to meet right away at the airport."

He picked up his bag and ushered us toward the doors. "I don't have a lot of time, and I wanted to fit this in."

"The interview?"

"I think we would both benefit from it."

"I'm intrigued." I glanced back at my best friend, who seemed to be still stuck in some kind of trance.

We stopped in front of a town car that looked like a modern-day carriage. A man who could only be described as spiffy-looking started to load Mariano's luggage, and another fellow opened the door for him.

"This isn't going to be your regular sit at a table, drinking coffee while I share my story kind of interview,

Miss Giovanna. If you choose to tell a true tale about the oil business and all its struggles, and all the work and effort I have had to put in to get where I am, then you must experience it personally from the inside. This will require you to travel with me." He stopped speaking and stared directly into my eyes. "Are you willing to do that? Go the extra mile? All for a story that will launch your career like no other?"

"Why me?" fell from my lips.

He handed his last bag to the driver then unbuttoned his jacket and tossed it inside the car.

"Because from what I've read, you understand that sometimes the lines between right and wrong may be blurred in order to survive."

I licked my dry mouth and glanced at Wyatt for some kind of answer.

He finally spoke up. "Lines between right and wrong? Wait, will she be in any danger?"

"Ha!" He chuckled lightly. "No, of course not, and I live here in Florence. We will not be going far, and you can call and meet up with her at any time. You have my word she'll never be in any kind of danger." He addressed Wyatt with such confidence that I believed him.

"Look," he rested his arm on the car roof, "I've run my intentions by your boss already. Sometimes you will be required to spend the night, and other times you'll be driven home. Georgio has been emailed the locations that I will be showing you, and you have been cleared from work for the next month if you choose to accept my offer. Though it could be longer if you wish to dive in deeper."

"A month?" I nearly choked on my words.

"I'm due back in the States for my sister's wedding," Wyatt reminded me. "I won't be here to help you over the next while." He looked more than a little unsure.

I took a deep breath, and when Mariano sensed my nerves, he checked his watch.

"I figured your boss ran the details by you already. Here, take my number. Think it over, but I'd like an answer by tonight as I'm very busy."

"Wait." I stopped him when he was about to get into the car. "I'm still not sure why you want your story to be told. And why by me?"

"I read your article a few times. I'm intrigued by you, Miss Giovanna. So, for the same reason you wanted to tell your story, it's why I want to as well." The driver closed the door, and we were separated by a mirrored window. I stared down at the matte black card he handed me. It had gold lettering, and when you tilted it in the light, a strange logo appeared.

"Well, that certainly was not what I was expecting." Wyatt ran a hand through his hair. "This probably will skyrocket your career, and honestly, I would love for you to get the hell out from under Georgio's hold."

"Mm," I thought out loud, "I can't believe he didn't fill me in on those rather important details. He was probably worried I'd say no."

"He's a jerk, but I think you should do it."

"I think so, too. Hey," I turned to him, "us, Wyatt, we need to get out of this together. I might be doing the interview, but I expect you to help me with this so both of our names are in print."

"You really are a good person, Sienna."

"So are you." I waved a hand to stop the cab that was heading our way. "We should get back."

Later that evening, I paced the living room floor, most likely driving the tenants below crazy. His card was in one hand and my phone with the written text to Mariano in the other. A bottle of my favorite wine sat ready to be opened for a celebratory evening, but I was scared to hit send. I couldn't help but wonder who I'd meet and what places I'd see. Not to mention the story that would come out of this. I would be the first person ever to get to do an exclusive on Ricco Oil. It was no secret that every reporter and journalist would give their left arm to get the true story on this company. One day, they just appeared, sank their roots into Florence, and were now a multi-billion-euro company. The company had propped up the economy big time, and word was that anyone who worked there seemed happy. I knew this was going to be the experience of a lifetime, and Wyatt was right about me going for it. The article would open doors that I probably didn't even know were there.

"Send the damn text already." Wyatt tossed himself on the couch then started to pour the wine. The sunflower on the label had a shiny gold outline that caught the light as he poured it. It was the reason I'd picked up the bottle in the first place a few years ago.

"Sienna," he waved the glass around, "stop stalling."

"Okay." I closed my eyes, took a breath, and hit

send. "Oh, sweet Lord, please tell me I made the right call."

A moment later, my phone rang, and I saw it was him.

"Hi."

"Hi, Sienna. I'm happy to hear that you've decided to write my story. I think you'll really enjoy yourself, and at any point you're not, I will have my driver take you home. I want this to be fun as well as work."

My nerves settled, and I felt my shoulders sag with relief. "I'm looking forward to it."

"Good. Do me a favor and please pack a bag and bring something fancy. We never know when we might need to stay in hotels, so please always be prepared."

"I can do that."

"Wonderful. Text me your address, and I'll be at your place early, about eight."

"Will do. See you then." I tossed my phone aside and swung around to look at Wyatt. "And so, it begins." I took the glass from him and tapped mine to his.

At ten to eight, I stepped out on the curb with my bag packed to the brim. I only hoped I was ready for any situation that might be thrown at me. One of the many things I had learned while trying to survive on my own was to always be prepared for the unexpected. And of course, a bottle of Mace for good measure.

"He dresses well *and* is punctual." Wyatt pulled

down his sunglasses as the sexy car from last night pulled up in front of us. The front passenger hopped out and opened the door for me while he slipped the bag from my hand.

"Good morning, Miss Giovanna," he greeted me kindly. "Please take a seat."

"Thank you." I turned to Wyatt, who looked at me with a worried face.

He leaned in and whispered, "I sure wish I were going with you, but I need to prepare for my trip. Your phone location is on. Mace is in the side pocket. Try and have a good time but be alert."

"Thanks." I kissed his cheek and squeezed his hand. "No goodbye." I chanted our special parting words.

"Just a later." He smiled.

I slipped down onto to the leather seat, careful to keep my dress down.

"Good morning," Mariano greeted me briefly then immediately turned his attention back to his phone and started typing.

"Morning," I whispered.

"Would you care for some coffee?" He handed me a to-go cup of coffee that he must have picked up along the way.

"Thank you." I sipped the heavenly coffee and tried not to moan at the rich flavor that smothered my taste buds. "Where are we off to today?" I tried to fill in the gap of silence.

"We," he paused and tapped his phone one more time, "are off to tour the beach."

"Beach?" That was the last place I thought he would say.

"Yes, if you are going to interview me about Ricco Oil, we need to start from the beginning."

"All right, the beach it is." I smiled, but it fell as he went right back to his phone. I guessed his busy life consumed a lot of his time.

The drive was long, and I found myself staring out the window, lost in my thoughts. I remembered why I had moved here in the first place. Cara, my old friend at the house, once showed me a post card she had received from a relative who had visited here. It showed an entire field of sunflowers on the front. It was so beautiful, I often dreamed of lying in the middle of that field watching the clouds drift over those golden heads that looked up without a care in the world. Sadly, when I arrived here, finding that field of dreams hadn't come true yet. I had jumped into my job and lost my way to it. I guessed some dreams were just meant to be just that—dreams. Thankfully, I found a someone along the way who had become a true friend. Wyatt saved me from myself and had proven to me that he could be depended upon.

"What's that?" Mariano pointed to my hand that was now entwined with my necklace.

"Oh." I fiddled with the two pendants. "Just something my mother gave me."

"What is it?"

I shifted uncomfortably and felt my heart suddenly speed up its rhythm, something that came along with any thought of both of my heartbreaks.

"A teddy bear and a crow."

"What do they mean?"

I forced a smile and dodged the question.

"I thought we were here for you."

His phone rang, and he held up a finger for me to hold on. I took a deep breath and turned thankfully back to the window and tuned him out.

Chapter
EIGHT

Elio

"Mariano, how far away are you?" I rubbed my head and glared at the piece of shit who was tied to a chair in front of me. The wind whipped at my jacket, and the birds dipped and soared around us as if curious as to who our guest was today. I could feel the heat of the sun on my shoulders, and I took a moment to look down and watch as it sent sparkles through the salty spray on the ocean below. Waves crashed into the rocks and sent a jolt of cold water up into the sky, perfectly matching my present mood.

"Fifteen minutes. I just need to get my present company set up." He spoke quietly, as though someone was close to him. I rolled my eyes at my best friend. He always seemed to have some woman on the go, and once he got tired of them, he moved on to the next. Money, power, and an easy woman were all Mariano cared about, and I was getting annoyed with him lately. The day he ever settled down would be the day I owed him a hundred grand, and I knew that money was as good as mine.

I knew I didn't really need to wait for him. I held the power here through all the oil that was shipped in and out of our ports, but this was his find, and I wanted him to get his own hands dirty on this one.

"You have ten, or he's gone. Drop the legs off and meet me here."

He chuckled as though my comment entertained him, and friend or not, I felt the need to remind him who he was dealing with.

"I'm not asking."

He cleared his throat. It wasn't often that I needed to pull rank, but lately, he seemed to be preoccupied with his personal life while I handled everything.

"I'll be there," he growled quietly.

I hung up and took note of the time. Reaching into my bag, I pulled out a pair of brass knuckles, slipped them over my fingers, made a fist, and moved closer to the man who sniveled in front of me.

My reputation was known across Italy, and my family was everything, but I wouldn't hesitate to kill during our dinner prayer if it was warranted. Life had led me to this.

"One minute." I flexed my fingers growing more

and more annoyed with Mariano.

I ripped the tape off the man's mouth and pressed my weight down onto the arms of the chair to stare into his terrified eyes.

"Mariano said you were at the docks after hours."

"It must have been someone else, sir." His eyes lied, and I realized my brass knuckles weren't going to be intimating enough, so I tossed them aside.

I pulled out a tin and made a show of emptying the long construction nails into my free hand. Reaching into the bag at my feet I pulled out a hammer and waited for him to talk.

"What, exactly, were you doing at the docks after the shipment left?"

"Nothing." He shook violently.

"The boat left, and yet you hung around and took a call." I reached into my back pocket and showed him a photo on my phone. "Doesn't look like nothing to me."

"I-I was calling my ride." His eyes widened and bounced around.

"I see." I gently pressed one of the long nails into the top of his hand then suddenly slammed the hammer onto the nail head. It shot down through his veins between the finger bones and into the wood of the chair, holding the hand in place.

"Ah!" His scream was muffled by the waves of the sea. "Son of a bitch!" He tried to catch his breath while his brain processed the level of pain he experienced.

I ripped his pocket and removed his phone then pressed his free thumb against the button to open it. I quickly changed the setting so it wouldn't lock again then pulled up his call log. Three times, that same person called him that night, so I clicked the number and held it to my head.

"Don't," he heaved, "please don't." His voice quivered, his tears flowed harder, and the terror on his face made me aware of just how deeply rooted his fear really was.

"Tell me." I held a nail to his other hand and raised the hammer.

"I can't!" he wailed.

"Why not?" I held up the phone to show him it was still connected. "Ring three."

"Because!" His bloodshot eyes rolled back in his head from the pain. "He wants you all dead!"

"Who?" I yelled into the wild wind.

"I don't know," he screamed and cried as I slammed the hammer down.

"Ahh!" He bucked and turned bright red.

"Tell me!" I screamed inches from his face.

"The man in white! *S* something…" His eyes popped open when he realized what he had just said.

"*S* who?" I used my weight to press and rotate the second nail that oozed blood, a dark pool of it now puddled on the ground at the edge of the cliff and caught the reflection of the nosy seagull above. He bucked around, and I released the pressure as I stepped back to think. I thought about all my enemies that started with an S, and many names came to mind.

I dropped down on one knee and forced his head

around to look at me. Marco had been with us since the move to Florence, so whoever this *S* was, he must have just surfaced recently. What did he have on my men to make them turn against me?

"Tell me more, Marco."

"I-I," he slipped in and out from the pain, "I don't know any more than that, sir, honestly." He begged as saliva dribbled down his chin. "I was told to wait around for someone." His red eyes blinked a few times. "Then Niccola spotted me."

"You think it's okay what you're doing?" I asked calmly.

"No, sir." He shook beneath my hands. "He did," he paused to catch his breath, "mention a debt."

"What debt?" I had no debts. I never owed anyone anything. I knew better.

"I don't know. He just said there were debts."

I whirled around and tried to control my temper. "Let me get this straight, you had instructions to wait at my dockyard, and you didn't think to call me? Does that sound like something you should have done?"

"No," he whispered.

"What else do you have to tell me?"

"Nothing more."

I knew there was more; there always was. "So, instead of coming to me with this, you dishonored me and went behind my back to meet someone who was out to get me and our family?"

"I know." His sob broke, and I felt nothing.

"You risked my business, our family, for what?"

"I know, I know," he sobbed. "It was wrong, I buckled and, and…"

I stood, straightened my jacket, and turned to find Mariano racing toward me.

"For God's sake, forgive me."

"No."

I used my foot to tilt back his chair while he screamed and tried to move his nailed hands. I gave him a shove backward, and he and the chair spun slowly in the air then hit the jagged rocks below and disappeared into the churning whitecaps of the angry sea.

Mariano was breathing hard as he stopped short next to me. I watched as a wave hit a rock and shot spray into the air.

"I'm sorry. I had to deal with some—"

"Whatever woman of the week you're sleeping with shouldn't interfere with family business!" I hissed inches from his face. He knew better than to push me. "What do you know about the debts?"

"What debts?" His face shot back as he tugged at the elastic around his wrist. He snapped it a few times as he often did and waited for me to go on.

"If you had anything to do with that, Mariano," I looked down into the sea where the body still tied to what was left of the chair now bobbed around the jagged rocks, "we'll have a big problem."

"Let's not forget that I was the one who told Niccola he was there and to go get him."

I waved him off, not wanting to hear it. He needed to get his shit together. I grabbed my bag and tossed the hammer inside and turned away from him.

"Where are you going?" he grated.

"To hunt down a letter!" I thought I knew all the players on the families' chess boards. None have ever dared step onto my territory before without me knowing about it.

I didn't realize how fast I was driving until the officer pulled up behind me. I pulled to the side and slipped off my sunglasses. He had one hand on his gun, but I knew he would have already run my plate as he approached the window. He knocked twice on the glass, and I lowered it to look up at him.

"Sorry, Mr. Capri." He took a step back, and his hand dropped away from his gun. I could see by the way his eyes shifted around he was nervous to speak to me. He was clearly new, as the law enforcement in the area knew if they stayed out of my business, I would stay out of theirs. "I just wanted to check and make sure everything was all right."

"Everything is fine."

"Very well." He cleared his throat. "You have a good day, now, sir."

I gave a tight nod then shifted into first and pulled away. I drove only slightly above the speed limit until I passed through our iron gates. Within the protection of the trees that lined the long winding drive, I tried to let the stress of my afternoon drift away. It wasn't easy, and it didn't last long, as once I parked and stepped out of my car at my parents' home and spotted the young woman, dressed to kill, waiting for me.

"You must be Elio."

"And you are?" I tried not to sound rude.

"My father is here on business with yours. I thought maybe we could take that sexy car of yours out for the evening."

News traveled quickly when we first arrived here that I was a bachelor and the son of the great mafia boss, Piero Capri, but that role got old quickly. I knew my father often wanted me to occupy the women who insisted on coming along to get a good look at me. I certainly wasn't in the mood for this today—or any day, for that matter.

"As flattered as I am that you would let a complete stranger take you out for the evening—"

"You're not a stranger, Elio." She stepped closer so I could get a better look at her. She had the usual pencil-thin figure, puffy lips, and thick fake lashes that women seemed to think men liked. "We've met before."

"Again, I'm flattered, but—"

"Really?" She interrupted me again. "Why don't we finish what we almost started last time?"

Then it clicked for me. Aurora. Her father was the one we were trying to buy more ships from. Dammit! Her father was a big deal.

"How about this?" I gritted through my teeth. "Tonight's not good, but," I hid my annoyance, "there's a party here in a couple weeks. Why don't you join me?"

"As your date?" A wickedly excited smile spread across her red lips.

"Yes."

"Sounds like a date, then."

"I will send you the details once they're confirmed." I found a smile.

She stepped forward and kissed the side of my cheek. "Can't wait."

I watched as her hips dramatically rolled as she made her way toward the pool. Once I knew the coast was clear, I headed inside to find my father. He needed to know what happened, and we needed to set some new ground rules for me.

Chapter
NINE

Sienna

"So, you walked along the beach and saw some old crap," Wyatt snickered, slipping into his natural New York accent, "while I busted my ass for toothless Joe." Joe was a researcher who Wyatt often had to work with when I was off working elsewhere. He was something else, to say the least. "Who, by the way, spelled 'party' wrong. Party! Girl, my first language is English, and even I can spell party in Italian."

"Don't make me laugh." I had to pull the phone away while I got myself under control. He always had a way of cracking me up, and I loved him for it. "I'll mess up my eyeliner."

"Whatever. You can't screw that face up even if you

tried."

"Right." I rolled my eyes at his lame flirting.

"Well, what's he like?"

"I don't know." I pushed the wand into the mascara tube. "He's nice enough."

"We had a deal, Sienna."

"Ah, fine!" I checked myself in the mirror one last time and gave a silent nod of approval on my dress of choice. It was a white cotton sundress with a soft, brown jacket paired with brown ankle boots.

"You look good. Stop stalling."

I flipped off the light and sat on the edge of the bed, knowing I had ten minutes to spare. "He's nice, easy to talk to, works a lot, always glued to the phone. Oh, he did ditch me at one point and was gone for, like, twenty minutes."

"Ditched you?"

"Yes, something about his business partner. It wasn't a big deal, but it allowed me to do a little window shopping, and the time alone was nice. He has some strange ticks, though, like he has this cream-colored elastic, and every so often he'll snap it."

"Okay, okay." He waited, and when I didn't bite, he let out a frustrated sigh.

"Yes, he's handsome," I laughed, "but there's something about him I just can't figure out."

"Bad or good?"

"Neither, really, it's just something off. I guess how you feel sometimes with Rosa."

"Yeah," he agreed, understanding the feeling.

"When I figure it out, I'll let you know, but," I glanced at the time, "I really need to go."

"All right, no goodbye."

"Just a later." I smiled as I hung up. I threaded my clutch strap over my wrist, took one last glance in the full-length mirror by the door, and left.

The lobby was empty as my eyes searched around, wondering where Mariano might be. I checked my watch and knew I was on time. I stood on the side of the entrance for over fifteen minutes, feeling conspicuous waiting for a man I barely knew.

"Sienna." He came around the corner with his phone held up. He was probably answering another email. "Are you ready to go?"

"I have been," I whispered at his lack of apology for keeping me waiting. He pushed open the door and crawled into the town car that had been waiting for us. I followed him as he slid over and patted the seat beside him, his eyes once again on his ever-present phone.

The restaurant was dark, with low ceilings, and the smell of steak hung thick in the air. I pulled out a tissue and dabbed at my eyes. It took me a moment to get my lungs under control.

"You'll get used to it," he assured me as he prattled off our order to the waiter. After he ordered for the both of us without my input, he seemed to settle.

"All right, Sienna, I'll give you one question that I will answer without hesitation. Use it wisely."

I nodded and thought about where I wanted to start, but instead of diving right in, I thought I would change directions. "Are you close with your parents?"

His studied me as he absorbed the question. "You could have asked me anything in the world, and you choose that."

"True." I leaned back as the waiter refilled my wine glass and our *Tagliatelle funghi e tartufo* was served.

"Why?"

"I believe you have a question to answer first."

"All right." He took almost all the dressing before he offered some to me. "We are close, yes. I love them, of course, but as far as getting along, it depends on the day. My mother can be a lot."

I nodded, not overly pleased with his answer, but who was I to judge.

"You're different, Sienna." He pointed his fork at me as he chewed loudly. "I think this month will be a lot more fun than I thought."

"Good." I couldn't help but chuckle at his bluntness.

Somehow, the three weeks flew by, and despite the fact that he lived on his phone and would disappear every once in a while, I found myself enjoying my time with him. So much, in fact, that I agreed to stay on longer.

He loved to educate me on his family and where they came from, but I found myself getting frustrated with how little information I was really getting regarding the family's oil business. Every time he would occasionally touch on what he did in the business, he would skirt over it and never gave me any details that I could use for my article. Sure, I could piece together a story, but certainly not one that had any real meat to it, and that was what I was expected to produce. I needed to know more about the oil business and how and why they started here. That was, after all, the story I was here to tell.

"You seem extra quiet this morning." He poured himself a cup of espresso and waved at me to take some too.

"Just thinking, that's all."

"About?" He tapped away on his phone while I sipped the heavenly brew.

I thought about Wyatt and how he had left for his sister's wedding in the United States by now and wasn't due to return home for another few weeks. I missed him.

"Sienna?"

"I was under the impression I was going to get an inside look into your world. Please don't get me wrong. This has been a lot of fun and very educational in some ways, but I'm expected to produce an in-depth article on your family's oil business, and so far I only have enough detail to fill about two pages. Where's the action and adventure that you hinted at when we met at the airport?"

He studied me for a moment then rested his cup on the table and stared directly into my eyes. "I haven't been with a woman like you before. I have enjoyed your company very much. I guess I got a little swept away."

Oh...

"This evening, I will share something worthy with you. You have my word." His smile made me match his, and I was excited to see what he had in store for me.

The rest of the day he worked while I tried to type some more on the article in case tonight's promised excitement wasn't what I hoped for. I needed to get something a lot more interesting or I might as well toss the whole thing.

As we drove that evening, my excitement at something happening faded as he talked away to someone on his phone. I finally opened my laptop and clicked on the article, glad to have it with me to occupy my thoughts. I looked up from the screen when the car stopped and immediately felt sick to my stomach as sweat broke out across my shoulders at where we were.

"Are you all right?" he asked as I stood on shaky legs next to the car. I wasn't even sure my legs were capable of moving at this point.

"I am."

"Oh." He made a sound and nodded as though he made the connection. "I'm sorry, I seem to remember something from your article in *Fab Magazine* about your time at a dockyard? Will this be too painful for you?"

I had never gone into a lot of detail regarding my days at the dockyard or of the nightmare it had been for me in that article, but I had touched on it.

"I'm sorry, Sienna. I wasn't thinking, but I just need to grab some files."

"No, no, it's fine." I didn't want my past to keep me from moving forward in this life, and I pushed it down. "Please lead the way."

He waved for me to follow him through an open

gate. The smell of the containers and the sound of the buoys rubbing against the dock made me hyperaware I was out of my comfort zone.

"Tell me, Sienna…" He was most likely trying to distract me. "Why did you agree to write this article?"

I looked up at him and went for it.

"Ricco Oil came out of nowhere and absorbed Vivo Oil in a matter of months. Over the past thirty years, many oil companies have tried to stake their claim here, but they never stuck. You either had one hell of a sales pitch, or you put up a hell of a fight. Either way, your company is booming, and you have many wolves circling waiting to find their way in."

"You've done your research." He smiled.

"I wouldn't be here if I hadn't."

"Well, you wanted to understand what I do," his expression changed to a more serious one, "so you must do one thing for me."

"Okay." I was hungry for it. I needed that big break to get any chance to write for a bigger paper. I wanted more creative control and to be taken more seriously.

"Wait here, and I'll be right back."

"Pardon?" I glanced around, unsure.

"There are cameras everywhere. I promise you're safe." He laughed. "Let me grab the keys and the files, and I will show you something that will interest you in the back of the property." He raced up the stairs and disappeared inside.

"And why couldn't I come up?" I muttered and tried to push back the fact that he often put himself first.

I folded my arms, feeling exposed and nervous. I closed my eyes and tried to settle my nerves. I knew he had read my story, and I was a little hurt he left me there alone, but I knew there were probably things that were not for my eyes.

"Please!" I thought I heard a young voice yell from behind a huge container. "Help me."

I whirled around while goosebumps raced up my arms and around my neck.

"Help!" I heard again.

I glanced up to where Mariano had gone, but the place was pitch black.

In a full-out sprint, I raced across the dockyard, my street instincts kicking in, and tried to follow those cries. The containers were like a maze, and every way I turned I found myself getting more and more lost. My sense of direction was off as I strained to hear that voice again. I found myself at the stairs that led up to the office again and whirled around in a panic. A dockyard was no place for a young person.

"Mariano!" I called up toward the window, but he must not have been able to hear me. A strange noise like a power surge being turned off made it through my wild heartbeat. What was that?

"Where are you?" I called, straining to hear over the wind.

I heard a sound again and ran to look once again behind a container. I froze. A young man was on his knees, elbows out, his hands clasped behind his neck.

"Please," he sobbed, shaking his head as he looked

up at someone holding a gun at his head, "you don't have to do this."

I took a step forward, terrified but unsure what to do as the man with the gun looked directly at me then turned back and pulled the trigger.

Bang!

The sound vibrated through my chest, and time stood still as I slowly absorbed what I had just witnessed.

I tried to comprehend that a man now lay dead a short distance away from me. My numb hands grabbed for the container to hold myself up as the killer continued to stare directly at me. Then, like a shadow in the night, he slowly faded away between the containers.

"Sienna?" Mariano suddenly was there. He grabbed me by the wrist and pulled me back. I nearly lost my footing as he swung me around the corner of the container. He gave me a shake as though it would help me jolt back to life. "What did you see?"

"That man, someone shot him." I started to panic and as he pulled me in tight to his body.

"I should never have left you alone."

"We need to call the police." My brain started to work again. "The killer was tall, taller than me, but-but…his face was slim, and he wasn't wearing a mask. I got a good look."

"Sienna," he stopped me, "no police."

"Why?" What did he mean?

"Because," he awkwardly dried my tears with the palms of his hands, "you don't call the police on these guys!"

"Why?"

"Because," he looked over his shoulder, "they're the mafia."

Chapter
TEN

Sienna

"Are you okay?" Mariano sat across from me in the town car that had just pulled up in front of the hotel.

"Yes," I whispered. I only wished I could back up time and unsee what I had witnessed.

"Because you haven't moved in the past ten minutes."

I thought I nodded, and Mariano pushed a button and muttered something to the driver. I couldn't make out what he said because of the dense fog that had set up camp in my head.

"What was it you were going to show me at the dockyard, anyway?"

"Just a spectacular view of the property…" He

brushed me off and went back to his phone as I went back to my foggy state.

It wasn't until the car stopped and the driver opened the door and got out that I allowed my senses to take in what was happening. Mariano got out of the car, and soon a hand reached inside for mine. I gratefully took it and stepped out, only to find that instead of Mariano's hand, it was the driver who assisted me. Mariano was already walking up the steps to a house.

"Where are we?" I whispered to the driver, who seemed confused.

"This is Mr. DeSimone's house, miss. He thought you might be more comfortable here."

"What?" I shook my head, trying to keep up. "Why here? I don't even have my things."

"A second car is on its way now with your belongings. It shouldn't be long, miss." He smiled warmly and nodded for me to follow Mariano inside.

I walked up the steps and hesitated at the door then turned to scan the area around me. I spotted the lights of a house up a huge hill to the left. I could imagine the view they must have from up there, a good three-hundred-and-sixty-degrees that would take in this house and the surrounding area. It was an impressive looking place. It was too dark to see much more, so with a heavy chest, I stepped inside.

"Mariano?" I called into the dark entryway.

"Come in." His voiced carried from somewhere. The uncomfortable feeling that swept over me earlier this evening returned, and I fought the need to leave.

"I was beginning to think you walked home." He was still in his jacket and shoes as he sat on a stool rather than the comfy looking couch.

"Why am I here?" I blurted.

"You are upset. I didn't want you to be alone in a hotel. I thought maybe you'd like to come here."

I wanted to point out that he could have asked or at least he could act a little more inviting, because standing in his living room right now felt more uncomfortable than my hotel room. I was cold and uncertain about the whole evening.

"Here." He set a clear drink down on the table. "Drink that."

I slowly perched on the edge of the couch and took a sip of the drink. My throat burned, and my eyes teared a little as the vodka slipped past my tongue, but I went with it because I seriously needed a little help with my head right now.

"See," he smiled, "better already."

"Mmm." I shook myself. This wasn't exactly better.

"The guys should be back with your belongings soon. Would you like to stay up for a bit, or would you just like to go get some rest?"

My hand gave away my nervousness by tipping the glass over as I set it down. "Why don't you show me around first?" I tried to recover.

"All right." He jumped to his feet and motioned for me to follow along.

"Living room." His finger twirled in a circle to indicate the room we were already in, and then he quickly moved down the hallway and kept talking. "Kitchen is over there." He pointed to his left. "Bedrooms up there, and downstairs is an entertainment room."

Well, that was a fun tour.

"And," he pushed open a huge door and stepped outside, "this is where I spend as much time as I can." He beamed back at me as I took in what he was referring to.

A small pool, a hot tub, and a full-on functional outdoor kitchen completed a lovely back yard.

"Do you want to swim?"

"No." I didn't miss a beat, not wanting to swim with him. "Thank you, but I think I'll take you up on getting some sleep."

"Your call." He shrugged and led me upstairs to the first bedroom on the left. My palms were sweating, and my heart was unsettled, but the nerves faded away when I realized it was a guest bedroom and not his own.

He checked his watch as he opened the patio doors to let a cool breeze in. The house I had seen earlier glowed like a beacon on the hill above.

"What are your neighbors like?" I tried to fill in the silence.

"They're nice." He turned away and went to the bed and gave the pillow a punch then picked it up and reshaped it. "Sienna," he paused in what he was doing, "I am sorry for today."

I appreciated that he finally had addressed the elephant in the room. "It wasn't your fault. I still can't believe what happened, and I have so many questions."

"I know." He came closer. "But I am sorry. I can't

tell you much more except that my men are looking into it."

"Thank you," I answered in a small voice, pleased he was trying.

He suddenly leaned in took my hand and kissed the back of it. I blinked and stiffened at his touch.

When did we cross this line?

"I like you, Sienna." I forced a smile, unsure how we got to this point. I remained polite and gave his hand a slight squeeze.

"Did we just get to first base?" he teased, and a small part of me tugged in the opposite direction to leave. Being broken was never something I wanted to be, and when someone joked about it, I pulled in tight to hide my scars from view.

"Well." He cleared his throat. "Get some sleep. We have some things we should talk about, but we'll wait until morning."

"All right." I dropped my hand away and spotted the driver at the door trying to get Mariano's attention.

"Sir?" He held up my bag.

"Leave it there," he ordered and walked toward the door then stopped as he reached for the handle. "I've never met someone quite like you before," he said without turning.

"And what is it you see?" I felt how tired I was.

"Sexy but tame at the same time." He shrugged at his wording. "It's an interesting combination, but I don't know how to steer you."

"Steer me?" I nearly choked back.

"I mean steer around you." He realized how he sounded and turned to face me. "Your body tells me you're interested, but I think your head stops you."

Does it, now?

"I need to get to know someone for more than a few weeks before I let my guard down." I tried to follow his sudden swing in our relationship.

"There's always tomorrow," he said with a sardonic smile.

"True."

"Good night," he said briskly, and I gave a small wave as the door closed.

After a hot shower, two aspirin, and a warm bed, I tried to process the evening. As sad as it was to even think about, I was able to compartmentalize the shooting and tuck it away. Yet another trick the streets had taught me.

At seven a.m., my phone vibrated around the table, and I answered it, knowing he wouldn't stop.

"Where are you? Don't lie. I know you're not home."

"Morning, Wyatt." I yawned. "I'm…" I stopped to think where the hell I was. "Somewhere."

"Are you stuffed in the back of a trunk? What do you mean you don't know where you are?"

"I'm at Mariano's house."

Silence.

"Did you?"

"No, God, no." I rolled on to my side and stared at the house on the hill whose lights were a dim glow now.

"Sienna." His tone changed. "Please promise me

you'll relax and let yourself have some fun while you're working on this article."

"I am." My mind flashed back to last night and the bang of the gun, and a sudden chill went through me. I wanted to tell him about it, but Mariano's words found me. I couldn't bring my best friend into what I witnessed. "I promise I am."

We spent the next twenty minutes talking about his sister's wedding and how he would give anything for me to be there.

I felt tremendously better after my call. I forgot how much I missed his storytelling, and his hilarious view on the groom's family, who apparently were one hundred percent hippy, had me laughing after I hung up. At least he liked the actual groom and was happy for his sister. His parents were often absent in his life, so I was pleased his new brother-in-law was great.

The smell of something yummy drew me to the kitchen, where I found Mariano on the phone in front of the window. As he spotted me, he pointed to the espresso machine.

I watched as he toyed with a file on the counter, and after another ten minutes, he ended the call.

"So," he massaged the back of his neck as though he was stressed, "are you hungry?"

"I could eat."

"Let's take breakfast out back and talk."

I followed him out and took a seat by the little table and looked out over the pool.

"Well, first, here." He handed me a file and waited

for me to open it. I flipped it open and read what was basically a summary of things he'd been sharing with me over the past few days. "I thought it would be easier for you instead of taking all those notes. You can just be there with me in the moment and experience it all."

"That's very thoughtful." I looked up at him, completely blown away with his gesture to help me. I skimmed another page and noticed there was more information there than I would have remembered. "This is fantastic."

"So, that makes you happy?"

"Yeah?" I laughed at his wording.

"Well, good, because I have a favor to ask you."

"All right." I tucked the file under my plate, so I could pick up my muffin again.

"I have this party for work tonight, and I really don't want to go dateless. Would you come along as my escort?"

"Oh." My mind flipped through the items in my bag. "How fancy is it?"

"Fancy, but," he held up his hand, "I have a friend who owns a shop in town and will have everything you'll need if you want to join me."

I shifted my gaze away from him and took a deep breath. What the hell did I have to lose?

"All right, I think that would be fun."

"Good." He leaned forward for his phone and answered a call.

Here we go...

Chapter
ELEVEN

Elio

"What exactly do you know?" I held the blowtorch a foot away from the head of the man who worked for me. He had been seen somewhere he shouldn't have been. He was the third man of mine that I knew was holding something back from me.

"Nothing, I, I, I can't!" he stammered and broke out in a sweat while I grew annoyed. The howl of the torch echoed through the basement walls of the warehouse where I handled most of my *business*. It was hidden deep within the property of my dockyard, and the basement was built like a bunker so screams could not be heard, and any odor would blend in with the surroundings. It was a necessary place where we could deal with the darker side of things that was out of the public eye and well away from our homes. Our ammunition and other specific items were stored here in bunkers below ground, and a huge walk-in safe held the overspill of cash from the gas stations and casinos we laundered through.

"You dare withhold information from me after I took you in and gave your family a good life? You would be living on the streets if it weren't for me."

"It's not like that." He tried to buy time, but I was not having it. I leaned forward and melted away the side of his skull. His screams were deafening, but I didn't care. I'd learned over the years to tune them out. I didn't have time to play the *who done it* card. Something was happening here, and I knew something worse was coming. The body found at the dockyard was shot execution style, and I had no goddamn idea why.

"Elio." Niccola, my cousin, called me away from the others. With a quick, emotionless glance at the man's charred face, he turned his back to it as he spoke. "Martin said the few who were around didn't see anything."

"Let me guess, no one will talk?" I swiped my hand through my damp hair, confused as to what was going on at the docks. Maybe I needed to spend more time down there myself.

"No," he mirrored my movements, "but there's something else."

"Go on."

"There might have been a witness to the hit at the dockyard."

"Our hit," I had ordered Donatello, my other capo,

to deal with a problem last night, "or someone else's?"

"Not ours."

"Who the hell used our territory for their goddamn hit?" Off hours, you would need a code to get in, and we had many cameras.

"I'm looking into it."

"Good." I sighed, tired of more shit happening on my property. "Did you check the cameras?"

"They were turned off."

"Why do you think there was a witness?"

"There was a woman's bracelet found only a few feet away."

I ran a hand along my bottom lip as pure, white-hot rage smothered my blood and took over any sane thought I had left in me. I stepped closer to him so only he could hear me.

"Find them, bring them to me, and I will decide if they live or die."

"Of course." He went to leave, but I stopped him.

"What about the rest of the footage leading up to and afterward?"

"We're still looking into it. They were down for twenty minutes, and others around the parking lot were just flickering."

"Of course they were."

He nodded to show he understood my train of thought.

"I need to go to my parents' to get ready. I have a date that I need to mentally prepare for. Come on." I barked some orders to the others, then we hurried to the parking lot.

"Good afternoon, Elio." Mama's friend batted her long eyelashes at me. "We may have found you the perfect woman. She's new in town, just arrived here from America."

"Come on, now." Mama shook her head at her friend, pushing her hand down to dismiss what I'm sure was a photo on her phone. "This isn't the right time."

I turned away to reach into the refrigerator. I tried to ignore their almost weekly setups.

"As much as I appreciate that you want to find me love, I'm good. Why don't you entertain the idea of finding Niccola love?"

"Don't drag me into your hell." Niccola whisked by, shooting me the finger with pure delight that this conversation didn't include him.

"Niccola would have to stop in one place long enough to meet someone," my mother shouted after him. "His time will come."

"No, it won't," he called back.

"Lucky bastard," I muttered. "The last woman you set me up with had more cats than any human should own and an odd obsession with holding my hand even when we ate."

"Fine." Mama huffed and took pity on me. "Maybe another time." She smiled warmly at me. "You should get ready. We don't want you arriving late."

"Thank you, Mama," I whispered as I leaned over the marble island and kissed her cheek. I knew she was giving me an out away from her friend.

An hour later, I stood in front of my parents' house, greeting guests in my three-piece jet-black suit my father insisted I buy. It was worth every penny. It was the softest fabric I had ever worn.

"My, don't you look handsome tonight." Aurora appeared at my side in a chocolate brown dress with peacock feathers across her bust area.

"You look lovely." I offered her my arm, and we headed inside and down into a massive party area that spilled out into the back yard.

Two bands were hired tonight, given the size of the property and the number of guests who were to attend. Though the party was really a cover for a meeting we were having with the Milani syndicate, we also wanted to show the power our family had within Northern Italy. Everyone and anyone who was part of our lives would be here.

"Drink?"

"Yes." Aurora scanned the crowd while I nodded to the server, who I knew would attend to my every need tonight. "Impressive."

"Indeed." I spotted my mother privately chatting with my father. Something seemed off.

The hairs on the back of my neck stood at attention, and I did a quick scan of all the faces around them.

"Want to dance?" She didn't wait for my answer and pulled me out onto the floor. She pressed her breasts into me and rested her head on my shoulder.

I couldn't absorb the melody of the song as I led her in the dance. A strong gravitational pull had me in its clutch. I found myself looking around, curious as to what had my compass spinning out of control.

"Elio?" Aurora placed two fingers on my cheek to pull my attention back to her. I pushed her away in a firm movement. I seemed to know that whatever had me on high alert was about to reveal itself.

I spotted Mariano speaking to some friends who were laughing loudly. I moved my glance away from him to the door and waited.

For what? What was I missing?

My mother started walking toward me, and then I noticed Francesco heading in my direction as well.

The band pulled back on their instruments, and only a soft piano and guitar filled the room. Flora Cash's *You're Somebody Else* made me whirl around, expecting to see someone there, but it was just guests moving about.

"Elio, dear, I think you and I need to talk."

"About?" I barely heard my mother when Mariano broke through the crowd and I zeroed in on his date. She had her head turned, talking to someone else. *Familiar?*

"Later, perhaps." Mother disappeared from my side while I studied the woman. She had on a skintight backless black dress that hugged her curves, and her long, dark, glossy hair tumbled down her back in huge, loose curls.

Damn, what was it about her?

"Elio, you need to know something," Francesco said from behind me. "I found some new footage from the parking lot at the docks. It's the woman. I have the guys working on her ID right now."

"Good." The woman had disappeared from sight.

"Hey," Mariano shook my hand as a greeting, "what's wrong with you?"

"Nothing," I said, even as irritation at his absentmindedness with our business lately flashed through me. I wanted to snap his neck for some of the things he had not remembered to do.

"Where are our drinks?" Aurora questioned behind me.

"Well, hello, there." Mariano reached across me to shake Aurora's hand. He obviously wanted to be noticed by my date. "Elio," his grin told me he was really excited by something, "if you could pull yourself away for five minutes." He eyed Francesco, who had stepped back and left us alone at Mariano's comment. "I wanted you to come meet my date."

"Welcome, ladies and gentlemen." My uncle stood at the microphone, and I knew I was due to be up there any moment. "I hope you're enjoying yourselves, and if not, the bar is that way." The crowd laughed, clearly having a good time.

"Sorry, she'll have to wait," I replied and whispered to Aurora that I needed to be on stage and worked my way through the crowd.

Chapter
TWELVE

Sienna

"Thank you. I'm unsure how I can breathe at all." I laughed along with the lady I was chatting with, who had pointed out how tight my dress was. She wasn't wrong. If I wasn't used to dressing this way, I would have heaved over.

"Well," Mariano huffed by my side, "I wanted you to meet my business partner, but he needs to do his part up there first." He nodded toward the podium.

"That's all right. I can wait." I sipped my drink, enjoying myself in a room full of high fashion and good times. It had been too long since I'd let loose and done something that wasn't calculated to the tenth degree.

"There he is." I followed where he was pointing and

did a double take at the man with a killer smile onstage.

The crowd whistled and cheered. They obviously loved him, and even the men seemed to be under his spell.

"Welcome." He smiled, feeding off the room's vibe. "I could stand up here and thank you all for coming, but I think my uncle did that already, so instead, let's have some," his gaze swept across the crowd and suddenly landed on me, "fun…" His word trailed off, and I nearly dropped my glass. "Ah." He struggled to find his words while I struggled to breathe.

This couldn't be real.

He couldn't be real.

No one had said his name yet. Maybe it wasn't really…*Elio*. "I'm sorry." His eyes were locked onto mine, both of us stuck in a strange point in time. "Please be sure you eat lots, that your drink is never empty, and that you bid on anything here that might pique your interest. After all, all the proceeds are for St. Paul's Church. Cheers!" The crowd went wild as he hopped off the stage.

"That was odd." Mariano shrugged and sipped his drink.

"Mariano," my throat was dry as sand, "what is your friend's name?"

"Elio Capri."

A puff of air escaped my lungs, and I felt the Earth tilt slightly. Then something strange passed through me. I knew he was there. I could feel his presence deep in my chest, sending it into a dangerous chaos of butterflies. It was like an addiction. The craving was starting to spread, and my will to stay away was being tested.

I scanned the faces in the crowd, eliminating them one by one, while my heart played tug of war with itself.

"Are you all right?" Mariano leaned down too close, and I struggled not to jerk back. "You seem nervous."

"No," I barely breathed, "I think I just need some air."

"I'll take you outside."

"No." I froze as I spotted his dark eyes at the bar. I blinked to see if he was real, and he was gone.

I can't do this.

"Would you mind if I stepped away alone for a moment? I think the wine may have gone to my head."

He seemed uncomfortable with me leaving by the way his jaw flexed.

"Of course." He lowered his eyes and waited for me to leave.

"Thanks." My exit couldn't happen soon enough. I needed to get out of there. Gathering my dress in my hands and utilizing the high slit in my skirt, I rushed for the door.

My heart thumped so hard it made me lightheaded.

I felt disoriented and bumped several shoulders as I made my way out, desperate to find some space. I stumbled backward and turned when I was suddenly face to face with *him*.

"You're not real," I barely whispered, sure he was going to disintegrate into the air.

The dark eyes that had held me prisoner since I was

very young seemed to carry many secrets. Time had been good to Elio. Just as time had in its turn slowly picked away at my core, reminding me that I had been left alone in the wake of his existence. He seemed uneasy.

I shook my head and tried to ignore how dangerous and sexy he had become. His dark suit and crisp white shirt that stretched across his broad shoulders gave him an elegant look. His light beard suited him and matched his jet back hair that he wore slightly long and was gelled back.

"Sienna," Mariano handed me a glass of water, "I thought you could use this."

"Thank you." I turned to take it, and when I turned back, Elio was gone.

"Did you still want to go outside, or do you feel fine now?" I couldn't help but hear his annoyance that I left him on the dance floor.

"Let me use the powder room, and I'll meet you back at the table."

He nodded and leaned in for a kiss. I tensed, and I knew he felt it.

What was he doing?

"Are you always this tightly wound when you party?" he whispered, drawing away.

"I think I'm confused with what you were about to do." I nervously forced a laugh. "I just need a moment." I hated that I felt the need to justify my feelings to someone.

"Well, I'll be over there when you return."

He left, and I let out an unsteady breath on my way

down the marble hallway. Arched windows provided a beautiful view of the Olympic swimming pool that was lit with a thousand floating lights. I couldn't help but recall the last time I saw a setup like this.

Stop.

I pushed open the powder room door, only to find it was crowded inside. Girls were spraying a boatload of hairspray and some God-awful perfume.

No, thanks.

Instead, I turned on my heel and headed down another hallway, hoping to find a quiet place to digest my thoughts.

Three turns later, and I thought I heard Piero's voice. My feet moved in that direction, knowing that if I saw him, I would know this was real. Huge double doors were at the end of a hallway, and I stopped outside, unsure what I was going to say. What if he didn't want to see me? Or what if it wasn't him?

"That's not how he should die!" someone yelled, and my hand retracted from the handle. "He deserves to feel the pain of all those he tortured."

"I think a little trip down to the beach wouldn't hurt anyone," another voice chimed in.

None of this was meant for my ears. I stepped back then heard someone heading in my direction.

"Damn." I spotted a small restroom and slipped inside, only to have someone come right up behind and press against me as the door clicked shut. The light was off, but the glow from under the mirror was just enough to know it was *him*.

"Sienna." My name sounded like velvet. My knees trembled, and I locked them in place.

"Elio," I whispered back, "how…" I trailed off when his lips brushed over the back of my shoulder and one hand slowly slid down my dress to the top of the slit, brushing it aside. In a moment of weakness, I gave in, closed my eyes, and allowed my head to fall back against his chest. His hand brushed the inside of my thigh, skimming my thong. My breasts strained against the fabric of my dress as his finger commanded my chin to turn to look up at him.

"Is this real?" he whispered.

"No," I answered, caught up in his spell.

"Kiss me," he hovered over my lips, "so I know it is."

I snapped out of the moment, and I tried to move, but his muscles locked, trapping me in his hold.

"Elio…" I shook my head and pushed on his arms to free myself. I slipped around him and escaped the little room. Once around the corner, I held on to the wall.

"Holy…" I took a moment then started the hike back to the party.

"There you are." Mariano stepped away from his friends. "Come, I want you to meet a few people."

What? I was spinning.

Names went in and out of my head. I plastered on a smile and tried to be as polite as possible, which was hard because I could still hear Elio's voice in my head as he said my name. It repeated over and over and nearly brought me to tears.

"Wow, son, she's just gorgeous." I blinked back my thoughts and tuned in to who was in front of me.

"Sienna Giovanna, this is my father Roberto."

His father? I wasn't in the right headspace to meet his father right now.

"Lovely to meet you." The very large man smiled approvingly at his much younger wife.

Roberto set his drink down on the table and stepped closer to me. "I'd really like to have a few moments alone with you, if you wouldn't mind."

"Sure," Mariano answered for me.

I wanted to protest, but Roberto took me by the elbow and steered me out of the party room. He didn't say anything as he escorted me outside to the opening in the garden that led to a giant water fountain. I fought not to trip over my feet. I was caught up in a storm inside my head at the very worst of times. The noise inside became consuming, and I tried to silence it, but it took a tremendous amount of effort.

"I can tell my son likes you," he finally said. *Yes, I discovered that tonight, too.* "How long have you known one another?"

"Just a few weeks."

"Has he shared anything with you?"

"Ah," I tried to pay attention, "such as?"

"Such as what he does for a living?"

I squinted confused. "Well, yes, that's how we met."

He smiled like he was happy with my answer.

"I read the article about you in *Fab Magazine*. I understand your past, and I think you would have a place here in our lives."

"Okay…" I still felt that I was missing half the conversation.

"A beautiful woman, with a difficult past, and no family. I feel that you could perhaps use some love in your life?" He stepped closer, and I felt my walls flinch to shoot up. "If our son likes you, that means we like you, Sienna. Will you join us for dinner tomorrow?"

What if I don't feel the same way about your son? As the thought ran through my head, given the present company, I thought it might be best to be polite and go along with the invitation.

"I would like that, thank you." I tried to catch up with all that was coming at me this evening.

"Wonderful." His smile was as wide as he was. "I'm looking forward to getting to know you better."

"Me too."

"We should get back." He pressed his freezing hand against my back to direct me ahead of him. I cringed at the contact.

"Do you mind if I take a moment? I'll meet you inside."

"Certainly."

I waited a beat and let the events of the night wash over me for a few minutes. I decided I had better get back to Mariano, but as I hit the bottom of the stairs, I felt *him* before I saw *him* and looked up to see Elio with his hands in his pockets watching me from one of the balconies.

Breathe, Sienna. Breathe.

Chapter

THIRTEEN

Elio

The party was in full swing, and I did a quick scan to see if I could spot Sienna. My father came up as he greeted people and handed me a drink.

"Are you all right?"

Not in the least. I felt like I was twenty again, standing at the edge of the pond staring at the most beautiful girl I had ever laid eyes on. I read once that when your soul meets its match, they connect in a way that can never be undone. I knew this was true because there had never been one day since I left that I hadn't thought of Sienna. Every day, I had to face the painful reminder of the sacrifice I had made. Francesco promised that he had people watching out for her but never once shared any details about what she was up to or where she was. He said it was for the best, and he made sure I knew that they didn't share any of those details with him either. We needed to make sure we cut as many ties with her as possible, for her own safety, yet here we were.

"Did you know she was coming?" I sidestepped his question and referred to the mandatory guest list.

"Of course not, son. I would never put you in such a difficult situation." He turned to look at me, and I saw he was being honest. My father might be the boss of our syndicate, and had the power to make a lot of things happen, but he was always a father first. "I had no idea. We made a very difficult family decision back then, and if I had any idea that she was coming, I would have handled the situation very differently. Francesco was just as blindsided." He took a moment to sip his drink. "Mariano had someone else's name down, and we did our usual background check, and she was cleared. I plan on having a chat with Mariano myself. We have rules for a reason."

"He's slipping," I confessed.

"I know."

"And now she's here, and…" The heavy weight on my chest left me feeling exhausted, "I'm not sure how to navigate this."

"How deep is she?"

"I don't know."

"We'll handle this, son. We always do."

"That is true. We do."

"Remember, Elio, time may have passed, but that

doesn't mean the threat has lessened. It is still very dangerous, perhaps more so. But she's here now, and if you want her—"

"I know." I cut him off, not needing a reminder of why we had left her years ago.

"Very well." He dropped the topic and exited just as Aurora approached me, holding up something.

"Have you seen Mariano?"

"No, why?" I was curt.

"I want to take a photo with his date."

"Why?" I was becoming very unamused with Aurora, or maybe it was because the only woman I truly loved just appeared at my parents' party on the arm of my best friend.

"Why?" Her tone drew my attention. "Because she's famous."

"What?"

"You can have this copy because I will be buying more." She handed me a rolled-up magazine. "Now, where did he go? I have a zillion questions for her, starting with whether her breasts are real."

I shook my head, trying to get her words out of my brain.

"My friends are going to lose their heads when they see me with her."

Resting my drink on the piano, I unrolled the glossy magazine and took in the sexy cover with Sienna draped in a red silk sheet staring into the camera with such raw pain I felt her gaze burn right into my soul. The headline read, "Abandonment, living on the streets, to success."

So many questions swam around my head, but the biggest one was what were the odds that she and Mariano would ever have met, let alone be here on this very night.

"Elio," Francesco appeared by my side, and by the look on his face it wasn't going to be good, "a word?"

With an inward sigh, I turned the magazine face down and let him speak quietly about what was going on.

"Gain and Brando are here and asked to speak with you now."

"Is that so?"

"Yes."

I downed my drink, and we headed for the door. Taking the stairs two at a time, I motioned for them to start talking.

"We thought you might like to know who *S* is." Gain reached over my shoulder and handed me a photo, and I felt my mouth go dry.

"Are you sure?"

"Yes, boss." He nodded, handing me another photo of Stefano Coppola talking to one of my men at the dockyard. "He has stepped in for his father, who apparently became ill a couple of months ago. He is creating quite the shitstorm with his new power as head boss."

Great, a new young mob boss with control over our biggest rival syndicate. *Let the storm begin.*

FOURTEEN

Sienna

"You look like you saw a ghost, Sienna." Mariano sat next to me in the car as we headed back down the hill to his place.

"I think I just got a little overwhelmed with all the people," I lied and felt guilty about it. I certainly wasn't ready to share that I was once in love with his business partner.

By the time we reached his front door, I felt pure exhaustion, and it took a great effort to keep the tears at bay.

"Would you like something to eat?" He moved into the kitchen and started to dig through the refrigerator.

"If it's okay with you, I think I'd like to go to bed."

"That's fine." He closed the door and glanced at me. "I have some calls to make, anyway."

I nodded, knowing I couldn't speak. I nearly ran to the stairs, and once I was inside the safety of the room, I leaned against the door, covered my sobs, and let my dam break. Sinking to the floor with the weight of the situation pushing me down, I fell apart just like I had years ago.

I wasn't sure how long my heart bled into the night, but I woke in a puddle on the floor. I blinked my swollen eyes open and waited for the blur to come into focus. The room was sideways. I must have wriggled out of my tight dress sometime in the night, as it lay beside me like evidence, and the memory of last night came flooding back. My arm felt heavy as lead as I reached for my purse with awkward fingertips and shimmed my phone free. I pushed Wyatt's name.

"Shit, girl, it's hotter than an Alabama jock strap out here. Remind me again why I'm not there?"

Just hearing his voice made me homesick. A silent sob ripped through me, and I was lost as to where to start.

"Sienna? Are you there?"

I nodded as though he could see me, and when I finally took a deep breath, a cry escaped.

"You need to tell me what's going on. Did Mariano hurt you?"

"No," I managed to get out.

"Then what happened?"

I shifted to sit up and leaned against the door.

"He's here." I hiccupped.

"Baby girl, you need to give me more. He who?"

"Elio."

The phone went silent.

"Elio Capri? The man you fell in love with, the one who broke your heart and turned it to dust?"

"Yeah." I struggled to breathe.

"Not to sound like I'm questioning you, but are you sure?"

"Very."

"Holy shit."

"Wyatt," I cried harder, "I don't know if I can do this anymore."

"Sienna," his voice changed to a more serious tone, "when I met you, you were in the worst state I ever saw someone in. When you got yourself right, what was the one thing you promised you were going to do for yourself?"

"I know, Wyatt, but I never thought it could hurt this much."

"You promised you would never let a man stand in the way of your career." He ignored my excuse. "I don't doubt that the hole in your heart didn't just get deeper. But you've worked your ass off to get to where you are. So," he took a second to make sure I was listening, "where are you now?"

"I'm on the floor. I fell asleep here."

"Well, you are going to pull yourself together, get up, have a shower, and write the best damn story that no one has been able to do yet."

I used my arm to dry my face and leaned my head

back against the wall. He was right. I couldn't let this swallow me up whole again. I could look him straight in the eye and not let him have the satisfaction of knowing he had destroyed a major part of me.

"Yeah." I let out a heavy breath.

"Good. Now, aren't you glad you called me?"

I laughed at my best friend. He always knew the right time to be funny and strong.

"Yes."

"That's right."

"How're the groom's sisters?" I did manage a smile as I said it.

"Well, I dug a hole in the woods yesterday, you know, just in case I need to dispose of them quickly."

"Smart." I sniffed.

There was a long stretch of silence, as we both needed to be together in the best way we could.

"How does he look?"

A flicker of pain stabbed my stomach when I pictured his face.

"You remember the girl who used to work the copier for us last summer?"

"Oh, yeah, I do." He chuckled.

"Times that by ten."

"You know what you need, then?"

"What?"

"You need to get some."

"What?"

"It's a proven fact, Sienna." He cleared his throat. "Part of your problem is that you're sexually frustrated.

If you could calm down your *thunder-dunder,* think how well you could straighten out your head."

"I could use some thunder," I joked back.

"Coming," he yelled out to someone. "I have to go, but I'll call you later."

"Thanks. I needed this."

"You know I'm always here. Well, in one way or another." As he laughed, he hung up.

I closed my eyes with a chuckle.

"Okay." I took a deep breath and dragged my tired body to the shower.

Chapter
FIFTEEN

Sienna

I found Mariano outside at his little breakfast nook by the pool.

"Hungry?" he asked, not looking up from his phone.

"Yeah, I am." I took a seat and helped myself to a scone. He pointed to the espresso machine while he typed away on the screen. Carefully, I poured myself a cup.

"Are you feeling better from last night?"

"Yes, I think the wine went right to my head."

"It'll do that." He finally set his phone on the table, but when he went to speak, it rang again, and he held up a finger, stepping away from the table.

Turning away from him, I sipped my espresso as

I admired the grounds. My eyes went up to the grand house on the hill where the party was held. It was all very private. There were a few homes around, scattered in a circle pattern. I wondered who owned them all and why they chose to live there. One neat thing that Mariano had pointed out to me was if you stood on either the west or east side of the house, you could see a car coming miles away, so no surprise visitors.

I finished eating and pushed back my chair as I brushed the crumbs from my fingers then relaxed and continued to sip my espresso. I couldn't deny it was a lovely place to be.

"A meeting came up that I can't get out of," Mariano reached for his keys, "so if you want to get out and look around the town, it's not too far from here."

That actually sounded like a great idea. I knew my head could use it.

"Sure. That sounds nice."

"You're so easy to get along with." He grinned. "Oh, and dinner tonight with my parents?"

"Should I cook?"

He laughed. "No, we are eating at the Hill House. They have all the cooks we'll need."

"Oh." I looked around, thinking it was a shame for such a nice kitchen not to get used.

"I'll be back later. You have my number if something comes up."

And just like that, he was gone, and I was alone in his house.

Wyatt: You are near a local market. See

attachment.

That was just another of the reasons I loved my friend so much. He knew I would want and need to get out. I tapped on the attachment and was delighted to see the market was already open. I hurried to get ready.

"Keys." I searched the bowl on the table in the entryway. "If I were keys, where would I be?" I opened the little drawer and spotted them. "There you are."

I couldn't help but notice a copy of *Fab Magazine* underneath them. My stomach twisted at my face on the front. The photographer had captured the depth of all the pain I held inside, and there it was for the world to see. Not to mention it opened me up for people to come to their own conclusions about who I was. It was exhausting to think about. I noticed that one of the pages was turned down, and I quickly flipped to it. Circled in pen was the line about me moving from Sicily to Florence and that I had gotten a job at the paper. Strange. Closing my eyes and feeling a little guilty for snooping, I tucked the magazine back in its place and stepped outside.

"Good morning, miss." I jumped about ten feet in the air. "Sorry." The driver from the party the night before smiled at me. "I didn't mean to startle you, but would you like me to drive you somewhere?"

"Oh," I was pleased to see Mariano hadn't left me completely alone, "yes, actually. I'd love to go to the market if that's not too much trouble. I was going to drive myself, but it would be nice to go with someone who knows where things are."

"I don't mind at all." He opened the door. "I never

miss an opportunity to get some of Miss May's pastries." I happily climbed in as he chattered about the delicious *bomboloni*.

"Do you live around here?" I enjoyed the small talk, and as there was only the two of us, it was easy.

"Yes, ma'am, I do."

"Any kids?"

"No, I've been too busy driving to settle down and start a family."

"Have you been working for Mariano for a long time?"

He paused for a moment then looked in the side mirror. "I don't normally drive for Mariano, but I have been known from time to time to drive for the boss."

"Boss?" I asked, but his phone rang, and I went back to my thoughts to give him some privacy.

I was suddenly glued to the window, marveling at the massive sunflower field that lined the opposite side of the hill. Nestled in next to it were rows and rows of grape vines. It was just like the postcard Cara had given me. True excitement coursed through me, and I could hardly contain it.

"Do you like sunflowers, miss?"

"I do. I really do," I smiled wide, thinking of how long I dreamt of this very thing, and it was finally a reality spread out before me.

"You're welcome to explore that property if you wish."

"Really?" I couldn't wait.

"Yes, and there's a bicycle in the garden house next

to the driveway if you'd like to pedal around." His eyes lit up, feeding off my excitement. "Just let me know, and we can go there, and if you get too tired or too hot, I'm only a phone call away."

"That's very kind of you…" I waited for him to say his name.

"Vinni."

"Vinni, thank you."

I leaned back in the seat and made plans to visit there before I left the area. I was pleased I brought my camera on this trip. I couldn't wait to share it all with Wyatt. Not long afterward, we arrived at the town, and Vinni handed me a cloth bag to collect my things in.

"I'll wait here. Take your time. I'm not due to be anywhere else."

"All right. Thanks."

I wove in and out of each little display. Each was packed with fresh fruits, vegetables, and miles and miles of cheeses and wines. I laughed when a kid tried to steal one of the ladies' cookies. When she turned her back, I handed one to him and winked, watching his eyes bug out. He quickly jammed the entire thing in his mouth and ran away.

"I'll take one, please." I pointed at the loaves of bread on the table near the cookies and paid her double the cost. I knew how hard it was to make a living. I wasn't hurting now, but there was a time when I would have been willing to sell an organ just to get something to eat.

"It's too much."

I shook my head and smiled then moved on to the next section, soaking in the culture that came with a market. People earning their living by working hard and standing behind their products. There was something to be said for that.

I stopped when I came to a stall that carried my favorite wine. I picked up the bottle and studied the label.

"I'll take two bottles, please." I couldn't believe it was here. I knew it was local to the area, but I had no idea it would be at the market.

"Have you tried this before?" the girl asked as she took the money.

"Many times. It's one of my favorites."

"He'll be happy to hear that."

"Yes, please do pass that along," I smiled, but her gaze shifted over my shoulder.

"Good evening, sir." She stood a bit straighter.

I turned with my arms full of treats and saw Piero, Elio's father, standing behind me, looking impeccable in a business suit.

"Oh, my," I whispered in disbelief.

"Hello, sweet girl." He called me by my old nickname.

"Hello." I felt my cheeks grow pink.

"Would you take a walk with me?"

"All right." I wasn't sure if I wanted to, but I would never be rude.

He nodded at someone who took my bags, then he tucked my arm through his and urged me to start walking.

I hesitated, but when I saw my driver, Vinni, take the

bags from the other guy, I felt a bit better.

"It's lovely to see you, Sienna." He gave me that warm smile that made me feel like I hadn't lost him years ago. "I'm sure the past two days have been a bit overwhelming for you." When I didn't respond, he kept going. "I'm sure you're very confused and have a lot of questions, but Elio—"

"Not really." I cut him off, not wanting to cave in public.

"Oh." He gave me a quick glance, no doubt trying to read my mind. "Well, when or if you do have questions, I would hope you would come directly to us rather than speaking to Mariano. We like our privacy, and he doesn't know everything, and we'd like to keep it that way."

"Privacy," I repeated as the word bounced around inside my chest, playing ping pong with the sides of my heart. "You wouldn't want someone getting too close. I understand." I couldn't help my clipped tone.

He stroked his chin as he watched me intently.

"You really surprised Elio yesterday."

I raised an eyebrow to express the feeling was mutual. He stopped and motioned for us to sit at a table near a fountain. He stared at me for a moment, and I felt my feisty side kick in because that was all I had for a defense system.

"How did you and Mariano meet?" He waited for me to answer and studied my face when I didn't. "Sienna, please, put aside everything that has happened for one moment. Can I just say how much I missed you?"

Damn, that put a creak in my heart.

"You weren't the only person who lost someone that day, Sienna." He paused to gather himself. "I lost a daughter, too."

I pressed my fingers to my lips to stop the quiver that threatened.

"Hate us if that helps." He cleared his emotions from his throat. "I hate us too sometimes, but there are reasons for what happened. Just know that we never once stopped loving you." He reached for my hand.

"Please." I pulled away, not wanting to hear it. It was too much.

He reached out again and took both my hands in his and squeezed them gently.

"Sweet girl, I know we're not worthy of it, but can I ask you for one favor?" My tear-filled eyes found his. "Please don't let Mariano know your history with Elio or our family."

I tugged my hands away when I realized they might be ashamed to be associated with me. The poor little orphan girl who fell in love with the rich boy was back, and perhaps it would screw up their image. I quickly dried a pesky tear.

"I need you to be careful, Sienna. He isn't who you think he is."

Confusion and hurt swept through me, and my backbone went up at the conversation. I stood quickly, and I knew he caught my mood.

"I have dreamt of the day I would once again see the man I considered my father." I paused to choose my words carefully. "Never did I think he would ask me to pretend I didn't know him." I had more to say, but that was enough to make my point.

"It's not like that." He tried to explain, but I was done.

I turned on my heel and rushed away from him to where I knew Vinni was waiting.

"Ready?" he said as he opened the car door for me.

"Yes, I'd like to go back to the house now."

"Of course." He squinted at me then looked over my shoulder and gave a nod to someone.

I hated that my market trip was ruined, but I hated even more that after all these years of trying to make something of myself it was still not enough. Well, that was fine. It was enough for me, and that was all that mattered.

"Would you like to stop and see the sunflowers?" Vinni drew me from my thoughts.

"Perhaps another day." All the joy the flowers had brought me had vanished.

"Very well." He glanced at me and seemed to want to say something but thought better of it, and we drove in silence.

When we arrived back at the house, I put the food away and decided to forget about doing any work. Georgio could wait. I wanted to take an afternoon for me. I changed into my bikini and headed down to the pool. I spent the afternoon floating on the air mattress and reading one of my favorite books. I was completely swept away as the love story took over my mind. I was so absorbed in the characters, it took me a moment to hear the voices.

Using my hand as a paddle, I made my way over to the side and eased out of the pool. The tiles were hot, and I was thankful I'd packed my sandals and a silk robe and not something heavier.

I was curious to hear how Mariano's day went, and I wanted to tell him I had bought ingredients to make us a dinner, perhaps for tomorrow night. Cooking was fun for me, and over the years it served as a stress reliever. Wyatt and I had taken cooking classes together, and we became quite good. Besides, I thought it might be a nice gesture since I was staying here for free.

I heard the voices and followed the sound down a long hallway. They became louder as I entered the library, and I came to a halt and took in the three men yelling at Mariano.

"His body was dug up! What were they looking for?" one man yelled.

Body?

I covered my mouth with my hands when they all turned at once, and I froze as they stared at me.

"I'm sorry." What was happening here?

The man closest to me whirled around and pointed a gun to my forehead.

I screamed and tried to back up.

Oh, my God! My gaze jumped to Mariano for help.

"Stop moving, Sienna," he ordered and looked at the man with the gun.

"How important is she to you?" The man's voice was menacing.

"Come on," Mariano laughed and eased himself onto a desk, "are we really doing this right now?"

"Mariano?" I felt like I was rooted to the floor or stuck in some nightmare. How was he so calm when all it would take to kill me was a flex of a tiny muscle.

Mariano sipped his drink like this happened every day. "Move the gun away."

My panic took over, and I went to run, but the man with the gun lunged forward and wrapped his arm around my bare waist and pressed the hard steel to my temple.

My blood was like ice, and my heart pounded in fear.

"What were they looking for on my brother's body?" The gun twitched as he spoke. "He was never a part of this!"

"I don't know." Mariano held his hands up. "Let's just all relax and have a drink."

"A drink?" The guy who was holding me laughed and smelled my hair like a snake taking in its prey. "I say let's play with her instead." His free hand started to move down my stomach.

"Don't touch me." My skin crawled under his touch.

"What did you say, pretty young thing?"

"I will chop off your sorry excuse of a penis and jam it down the barrel of your gun." I tried to keep the fear from my voice.

The man laughed as I wiggled in his hold.

"It wouldn't fit," he whispered into my hair, and I wanted to vomit.

"That's not what your sister said last night!"

His buddy smirked while I clamped my mouth shut in fear more garbage was going to fly out. Damn Wyatt for making me binge watch all those American movies.

The click of the hammer echoed in my ears as it was pulled back, and I knew it was time. I squeezed my eyes shut and waited for the tiny bullet to wedge inside my skull, ending my hell of a journey in this life.

Suddenly, I was spun around and into a different pair of arms. It took me a half a second to know exactly who it was.

"Whatever the hell this is, it ends now," Elio barked over my head while he held me protectively close to his chest. I saw that he held a much scarier looking gun in his free hand. "Get out."

"Elio." The man who had held the gun to my head spoke up with his hands in the air. "You need to control your friend." He nodded at Mariano. "He's stepping on dangerous territory by digging up my brother."

"I won't ask twice," Elio snarled as the guys stared at Mariano for a beat longer.

"We know your face, and we know your name, little lady," the creep said directly to me. "Let the games begin."

SIXTEEN

Elio

I had one of the steadiest hands out there. It took a lot to cause it to waver, and it was why I was good at my part of the business. But seeing someone threaten Sienna nearly brought on the shakes.

She closed her eyes and turned her face into my chest, and I glared at my friend who had almost got her killed.

"It was just a misunderstanding." Mariano sounded irritated. "I had it under control."

The gun twitched in my hand. He was incredibly stupid at the worst of times.

"Sienna, the guy who is holding you is my business partner." He then looked at me. "They wouldn't've hurt her."

Sienna was molded to my chest, and it brought back memories of her lying next to me on the lounge chair, looking up at the stars.

"Hey." I rubbed a hand down her back and spoke gently. "Are you all right?"

"Yes, I'm fine." Her voice betrayed her words, and her body trembled beneath my touch.

"Just focus on breathing." I coached her through the shock. "What the hell was that about?"

Mariano shrugged like it was an everyday occurrence that these men were in his house threatening him.

"It was a misunderstanding, Elio. Don't pull the rank card just yet." He poured himself a drink and handed Sienna one from the table. "Drink up, dear." She reached to take it, but I could see she didn't want it and her hand shook as she held it. Who would want a used drink poured for someone else, perhaps the man who almost killed her? "It will help with the nerves."

I took the glass from her and tossed it in the bar sink, shattering the glass.

"You're slipping, Mariano. Everyone sees it!" I shouted, and as Sienna stepped back, I pressed her into me again.

"Sienna," Mariano pulled her attention to him, and I slowly let her out of my hold, "you're good, right?"

She nodded, but her raised shoulders told me otherwise.

"Why is she even here?" I saw red with him for involving her in this whole thing. I had sacrificed my own happiness to keep her out of this hell.

He started to grow annoyed with me and rubbed his face with a groan. "I thought she was in the pool."

"Sienna," I addressed her myself, "what did you hear?"

"Nothing." She answered too quickly and continued to avoid eye contact with me.

"See, nothing to worry about, boss." He smiled at me, and I wanted to drill my fist into his skull.

"Has he exposed you to anything else, Sienna?" I had to know, but I also knew I was asking in the worst way.

She glanced at him then lowered her gaze back to the floor.

"No, nothing."

I licked the inside of my mouth and fisted my hand to control my temper that was about to blow.

"I'm tired of cleaning up your messes, Mariano." I kept my voice calm. "But if you don't smarten up, you're going to ruin what we all have worked so hard for."

"Thanks for the pep talk." He snickered but stepped back when I stepped forward. "I need to make some calls." He left us alone in the room, and everything suddenly became very intense.

Sienna's gaze was still glued to the floor, and I wondered if what just happened was too much for her to handle.

"So," she said slowly, "he knows my face?"

I closed my eyes and cursed Mariano.

"I won't let anything happen to you, Sienna."

Her head shot up, and I saw I struck a chord.

"Forgive me for not believing you."

Ouch. "Believe it or not, I kept my promise."

"Right." Her face scowled, and my rage bubbled up even further in my chest. She was the only one I would allow to speak to me like that.

"It's true."

She held up a hand and started to walk by me, but I blocked her path and steered her back against the wall. I used my height and weight and curled myself around her, trapping her so she couldn't escape.

A light pink blush kissed her face just like when we were younger, when she was turned on.

Interesting...

I admired her toned skin and plump breasts that were half covered by her pink bikini. She smelled like coconut and fresh shampoo.

She tilted her head up, and I spotted her necklace. Using the tip of my finger I traced the thin chain from her shoulder, to her collarbone, down her chest, and to the side of her smooth breast to finger the two pendants. I was immediately tossed into the memory of giving it to her.

I couldn't believe she still had it, let alone still wore it.

"Elio." Her warm breath shot up at me, and I was instantly aroused.

"You still have this..." I stated and slipped my hand in between her robe and across her bare hip.

"I keep the things I love close." She looked away.

"I can't believe you're here right now." I missed being lost in her. I leaned down and ran my nose along her earlobe and into her hair like I used to do. "I missed this."

I felt her body go stiff, and I knew I went too far.

"Whose fault is that?" Both her hands went to my chest and gently pushed me backward. I allowed it, as I knew this process would take baby steps. "I'm not yours to touch or play mind games with anymore."

"I'm not playing mind games, Sienna." I purposely reached out and hooked my fingers through hers to show I could still touch her.

"I'm not like you, Elio." She wiggled free and ran a frustrated hand through her hair. "I can't just turn that switch back on."

"It's not a goddamn switch." I pointed to my chest. "It's us, Sienna, it's what we've always had. An unexplainable connection, love."

"Love." She laughed like I was mad. "You have a pretty horrible way of showing love, Elio."

My phone rang, and I knew who it was. I cursed and pulled it from my coat pocket.

"What?" I almost yelled into the phone as I kept my eyes on her, not wanting to look away.

"We found another rat."

I rubbed my forehead, beyond frustrated.

"Get him ready. I'll be there in ten."

"Sure thing, boss."

I tucked my phone away, and when I looked back over at her, she was watching me. Lord, she was gorgeous. Her perfect lips that were meant for me had turned into a scowl.

"You better go."

"This isn't over." I waited a beat then kissed her cheek and peeled myself away, rounding the corner where Vinni and Niccola were waiting for me. "I don't care who, but one of you needs to watch her at all times. She is not to be alone here. Ever."

"Sure thing, boss," Vinni answered for both of them.

"Good." I whisked past them and out the door and into my car. I spun out of the driveaway and floored it down the hill on my way to the dockyard. Her scent was all over me, and I tried to focus on what I needed to do, but I was hard and tightly wound. I hadn't felt this out of sorts since the day we got the call to leave the island.

My patience was gone as I skidded to a stop and slammed the car door. I slipped my gloves on as I walked up to the man who waited for me.

"He won't say anything, boss." Donatello folded his arms, clearly as annoyed as I was. I pulled back my fist and started to pound on his face then his body. I lost count how many times I punched him, but when he couldn't hold himself up anymore, I pushed him to the ground.

"Are you sure you don't want to talk?" I held up a container of gasoline and a box of matches, but when he rolled his head to look away, I doused him, threw a lit match, and watched as his body burned.

"Why are you taking out your own men?" Donatello stood next to me as I lit a cigar. "It just seems kind of backward to me."

"Or brilliant," I hissed and blew out, letting the smoke rise to mingle with the smoke and screams from the man who lay writhing at our feet.

He nodded, but I could see he wasn't sure where I was going with that. Nothing like forcing me to do the dirty work to remove my own men. I felt like I was plucking them off one by one, leaving an open trail for whoever was behind this.

"I want you there tonight, I'm tired of this shit."

"Yeah, boss." He snapped his fingers, and two men came closer, waiting to dispose of the body.

"Hey!" I ran my tongue along the inside of my teeth. "Take a photo and let it circulate as a warning to the others."

"Will do."

Slowly, I made my way back to my car where I finished my cigar then tossed it in the trash and headed for my parents' place. The entire way, my mind flipped from the one woman I'd ever loved suddenly being here, to the faces of the men I'd once known and trusted, who I considered an extension of my family. It drove me mad. There were too many unanswered questions. The worst part was when I turned on the cooling system, Sienna's smell swirled around the car like the smoke from my fine cigar. As I pulled into the roundabout driveway, my mother greeted me in the entryway.

"Did you see her?"

"Yes." I kept walking to the kitchen.

"And?"

"And what?"

"Elio Capri." I stopped with a sigh and turned around to find my mother with her hands on her hips. "That girl was like my daughter for years. Your father saw her, and now you have, twice. I want to know how she is…now!"

I slipped out of my gasoline-smelling suit jacket and draped it over the maid's arm. She whisked it away without comment. I rolled up my dress shirt while I thought about the right words to use.

"Elio," she snapped impatiently.

"She's Sienna, still gorgeous and has a new bite to her personality. She's pissed and hurting, but…" I paused, remembering how good it felt to have her in my arms again.

"What?"

"She's still wearing the necklace I gave her with the two pendants."

Her hands went to her mouth as she let out a breath. "That's something, isn't it?"

"We'll see." I wasn't getting too excited yet. We had a long way to go first.

"Do you…" She came closer. "Do you still feel the same way?"

"Yes." There was no denying it. I was still captivated by her.

"Little steps, my son. You'll get there."

"What about Mariano?"

"We don't know exactly what, if anything, they have between them. Besides, Mariano doesn't share a past with her. Elio, you and she have deep roots in your relationship. She loved you once, and she'll find her way back to you again. Just give her a little time and help her remember what you had."

"Agreed." I rubbed my head, thinking it was possibly the worst time for her to show up.

"Besides, Mariano is a selfish man-whore who doesn't think about anyone but himself. She's smart and will see that quickly."

I grinned at her choice of words, but she was right. He was self-involved, and over the years he had gotten worse.

"Now, go get cleaned up." She turned away. "You have twenty minutes to get that smell off of you."

I headed upstairs to my old room where I had the convenience of a second wardrobe.

"Son." My father stopped me at the bottom of the stairs. "Another one?"

"Yeah.

"Has it been dealt with?"

"Yes."

"By you?" I nodded. "Why don't you let someone else handle it?"

"Fear is a weapon, Father. You taught me that, remember? It can't be seen, you can feel it, you know it's there, but it's faceless until…" I held my arms open as if to say *until they see me.*

"Very well, then."

"Oh!" I turned back around. "How was she when you spoke to her?"

His face slipped, and I could see it hadn't gone as well as he had wished. "She's hurt and angry, son. We just need to figure out what Mariano is up to. Give it some time."

"Clearly, I'm not a patient man…but a few more weeks won't kill me, I suppose, though I can't promise Mariano's fate."

"You and me both." He nodded and left as I rushed to get ready for dinner.

A black dress shirt with my sleeves rolled up with a pair of dress pants was normally as casual as I got when we were hosting a dinner. Especially when it was a dinner with Mariano's family.

SEVENTEEN

Sienna

"Hey." Mariano tugged on my arm as I was about to climb the steps to the Hill House. "I just wanted to make sure you were okay with what happened in the library today."

"I'll live." I shrugged, annoyed. Why was he bringing it up now and not earlier when we were getting ready at his place? It took three hours for me to get my head back on straight and the shakes to stop. I was a strong person, but not as strong as I wished I was. "I would prefer not to have another gun pointed at my head."

"Me too." He stepped closer. "That really frightened me."

"Did it?"

"Of course it did." He pulled back, confused.

"You just seemed unfazed."

"Look, babe…"

I cringed. "Babe?" I shook my head. "When did we start to use nicknames?"

"It's cute, and it suits you." I started to laugh, but he held up a hand. "I know those guys well. I knew that if I flipped out, you'd have a bullet in your head right now. They're ruthless."

I didn't comment that earlier he had said they wouldn't have hurt me. "Elio did," jumped from my mouth, and I wished I could rewind the moment I saw his face flicker with anger. "I mean, he got them to leave."

He rubbed his nose and cleared his throat. I apparently hit a nerve.

"Elio is a different breed, Sienna." He shifted his weight from side to side and his eyes widened, and I knew he was holding back something. "He doesn't care like I do. He's a shoot first and ask questions later guy. That man has killed more people in the worst ways. He would make your worst nightmare look pretty."

I flinched at the comparison, but it really didn't sound like the Elio I knew.

"It's no secret that we carry guns and deal with lowlife scum in our business. We are in an industry that runs side by side with organized crime. I was playing it cool so they would leave. So," he brushed my wavy hair off my shoulder and left his clammy hand on my skin as if I wanted it there, "you need to be careful, Sienna. Elio dresses as dark as his soul, and he's always watching."

"And on that note…" I muttered as he left me and ran up the stairs and opened the door.

"Good evening, sir and miss," a woman at the door greeted us and waved us in. "Everyone is in the living room."

"Thanks." Mariano forged onward while I fought to catch up in my heels. We passed a games room before he finally slowed, and his shoulders went back as he entered the room.

"My, my, Anna, don't you look pretty tonight." He greeted a woman with a kiss on the cheek and stepped back to study her little dress, while I stood awkwardly in the entrance.

"Mariano, you didn't call." She batted her eyes at him, and when he smiled, she continued flirting. I stepped back out of the room and decided to look around.

I wandered into the kitchen and watched the staff fuss over the appetizers. One of them looked over at me and smiled.

"You must be Sienna." He wiped his hands free of flour and offered one to me.

"I am." I shook his hand. "And you are?"

"Donte."

"This all looks amazing." I let the delicious odor take over my senses and felt my stomach grumble.

"Nothing but the best for the boss." He winked.

"Do you like working here?"

"Best job I've had yet."

I eased onto a stool at the massive island and watched Donte roll out the pasta dough.

"That's nice. Can I help with anything?"

"Well, if you like." His smile grew as he handed me a roller and some dough. "But one moment." He came behind me and draped an apron over my outfit. "It's not often that we have guests wanting to help."

"We all eat the food," I tied the apron around my midsection, "shouldn't we all help make it?"

"I like your mindset, but we really don't mind working here. These are good people and treat us well."

"You don't hear that often." I laughed and wondered what it would be like to actually like my boss and want to spend more time with him. "So, who lives here, anyway?" I was interested to know.

He glanced over my shoulder at someone. "He does."

I twisted around and saw Elio leaning against the wall, hands tucked in his pockets, dressed in a jet-black dress shirt, staring at me.

The fact he was wearing black wasn't lost on me.

Jesus, my body went into hyperaware mode. My nipples strained against my bra, and I had to shift my stance to relieve some of the ache below. Flashes of the other night burst their way through.

"Evening, boss." Donte grinned as he sprinkled more flour on the counter. "I think I may have found you a new cook." He winked at me again and laughed.

"Mm." He kept his dark gaze on me, and I nearly licked my lips as it dropped down my white blouse, to the black leather skirt that peeked out behind the apron. My black leather heels wobbled as I stood.

"I didn't know you lived here." My voice was all breathy.

Seriously, Sienna, snap out of it.

"Yes, ma'am, and he owns the winery too. You should try a glass." Donte reached behind him for a bottle of red wine.

"Wait." I twisted the familiar bottle around to read the label. "You own Sunflower Field wine?"

Elio nodded as he pushed off the wall and joined me at the island.

"You've heard of it?" Donte beamed proudly.

"Heard of it?" I chuckled. "It's my favorite wine."

"You hear that, boss?" Donte hit the counter, excited. "Your guest is a fan. Now, for marketing reasons, I need to know why you tried this wine." Some of the other staff laughed at his excitement, which was quite contagious.

"Because of the label. It looks exactly—"

"Like the postcard Cara gave you years ago." Elio finished my sentence for me, and I couldn't help but be stunned that he remembered. "You always wanted to lay in a bed of sunflowers and watch the clouds float by."

"Yes," I whispered as he looked down at me, and I felt my body heat up. "Did you really name your wine after that?"

"I did."

"Why?"

"Why do you still wear your necklace?"

I shook my head, thrown by his question, and when I didn't answer, he just smiled and poured me a glass then did the same for himself.

I dusted the flour from my hands and swirled the wine around the glass, allowing it to breathe.

"Cheers." He gently tapped my glass and watched me take a sip.

I closed my eyes for a moment and savored the smooth, full-bodied wine. I swirled my tongue around, making sure each taste bud had its turn sending the divine taste to my brain. When I opened my eyes, Elio's jaw was locked and ticked as he stared at me intently.

His thumb came up and brushed my bottom lip, catching a drop, and my stomach flipped.

"I missed you so much," he whispered, and I wanted to give in, but…

"There you are." Mariano came into the kitchen with the Anna girl right on his heels. "Hey," he snapped his fingers at Donte, who was wrist deep in pastry, "two glasses."

"Donte," I said before anyone could make a move, "where are they, and I'll grab them."

"Thanks, but you don't have to do that."

"Nonsense." I tossed an unimpressed look at Mariano. He barely noticed and caught sight of the wine glasses on the counter behind him. Plucking two from the lineup, I set them in front of Mariano.

"Who are you?" Anna addressed me after a fit of giggles from something funny Mariano said. "And why are you wearing that?"

"This little ace…" Mariano wrapped an arm around me, and I gave a strange look at his nickname for me. I was no ace; luck was never on my side. "…is Sienna.

She's a journalist."

"Oh." She scrunched her nose, unimpressed. "What are you doing here?"

"She's a guest." Elio spoke up next to me as he knocked Mariano's arm off my shoulders. "Show a little respect to the lady."

"Are you here for long?" Anna ignored Elio and gauged my involvement with the men.

"No." I wanted her claws to retract. I had no interest in being in someone's firing line.

"I'm hoping to change that." Mariano boldly kissed my cheek, wrapping his arm around me again with a laugh as he looked directly at Elio. I felt the tension and didn't like the idea that came to me that I was a pawn in some twisted game of power and sexual tension. That was just another red flag for me. The moment his arm moved, I shifted to the far side of my chair, wanting to create some distance between us.

"Mariano," Piero came in the kitchen looking just as handsome as his son, "your parents just arrived."

"Great, where's the bourbon?" He laughed in a poor attempt to be funny.

"Shall we go greet them?" Anna pushed her wine glass away. "And get something stronger to drink on the way?"

"Excellent idea." He smirked at me like he thought I would enjoy his silly college banter. "I'll be back." He made a show of giving me a wink and a light pat on the bottom.

My face heated.

I watched them leave and tapped my fingers on the island, unsure how I was supposed to act around anyone anymore. Tugging the tie loose from around my back, I slowly removed the apron.

"Hello, my sweet girl." Piero smiled.

"Good evening, Piero."

"You look lovely tonight."

"Yes, she does." Elio nodded.

"Thank you." I draped the apron on the back of the bar stool as I looked at Piero.

"I don't like the way things ended so suddenly at the market." Piero leaned down to see me better.

"Funny how things end like that around your family." I hated how much my pain ran out of my mouth.

Piero pulled me into a hug and kissed the top of my head.

"I know, and it pains me."

Once he let me go, I knew I needed to get out of the kitchen. It had become suffocating. A flash of green caught my attention, and I spotted her in the doorway. My hands flew to my mouth.

My heart squeezed. There was no pain or betrayal when I saw her wonderful face. There was just uncontrollable love.

"Hi, there." Andrea's hands were on her cheeks, and tears filled her eyes. "Look at you, all grown up."

I flew into her arms like a child.

"Oh, Sienna," she cooed and squeezed me tight. "I missed you so much!"

"I missed you, too."

We cried and let all the hurtful feelings wash away because we both needed one another. I needed a mother, and she needed a daughter. I knew the hurt would return, but in that very moment at the house on the hill, in the middle of this crazy life, I felt free for half a moment.

Chapter
EIGHTEEN

Elio

We left to let the girls have their moment alone and headed to the living room to wait for them.

"If nothing else, your mother needed that." My father glanced down the hallway at the DeSimones.

"Mariano is acting strange with her, but I'm not sure why."

"I don't trust his motives, Elio. Be sure to keep an eye on Sienna."

"Trust me, Papa, it's taking all my will not to hurt him. Who does he think he is, touching what's mine?" I was nearly vibrating with the need to fix the situation.

"I wouldn't mind taking a swing or two myself," my father's voice rasped.

Sienna stepped into the hallway and looked down the hallway toward Mariano then down to where my father and I stood.

She took a deep breath and brushed her hands down the sexy skirt that accentuated her toned legs. She seemed to hesitate then made the decision to come toward us, and as she did, Mariano came racing down the hallway. It was clear he had been into the bourbon, as his voice was loud and over the top.

"There you are!" He leaned down grabbed her face roughly and kissed her cheek twice. He made sure he made a show that she was *his* to kiss.

"Take a breath, son," my father warned as my grip on the wine glass came dangerously close to snapping off the stem. "Whatever is going on here will soon show itself, and we will deal with it accordingly."

"I don't know how much more I can take."

"Mama!" Mariano waved his mother to follow us as he led the way outside. "It's time to feast."

"Hello, Sienna," Bria greeted her. "Let's find out what's on the menu tonight."

"I already saw, and it will be amazing." Sienna made sure Donte heard her compliment.

"I'll be the judge of that." Bria rolled her eyes toward the kitchen.

My mother opened the back door, and we all headed out to the garden where paper lanterns hung in the trees, their light casting shadows across the beautiful table every time the wind blew the branches.

The rustic wooden table was set to perfection. Long

gray napkins folded in half draped over each place setting, and cream dinner plates rested on top. Next to each plate were individual loaves of bread with rosemary twigs on top wrapped in twine. Fresh greenery from our fields was displayed in glass jars with a gorgeous sunflower wedged in each to give the table a pop of color.

"Wow, *bello*," Sienna breathed with a sigh as she came out and admired the work that had been done. "Have you ever seen anything so pretty?"

"Yes." Bria shrugged, and I shot my father a death-look. He rolled his eyes, just as irritated as I was with them all.

Mariano was already seated next to Anna with his napkin on his lap, so I reached forward and pulled out Sienna's chair.

"Thank you." She eased into the seat.

I took the seat across from her so I could read her body language. I planned on digging a bit tonight.

Niccola glared at Donatello when he approached from behind us. The *capos* often joined us for dinner when they could.

"What?" Donatello looked at me, wondering what was wrong.

"The next time," Niccola pointed his fork at him, "you ask to borrow my car for a date, don't."

"It wasn't for a date." He brushed him off.

Niccola looked like he might be sick. "Care to explain why your undies were wedged between my back seats?"

My mama snorted and tried to recover quickly.

These two were always at each other for something, and then add in Vinni, and the entertainment grew. We were one big family, and we loved each other, but we also gave each other a hard time whenever possible.

"Are you sure they aren't yours?"

Niccola shot me a look before addressing him. "We all know you are the only one who wears the tight ones that go up on the sides like a woman's."

Papa burst out laughing, and the rest joined in.

"First, I like the way they feel. They tuck and hold me in, and second, I lost another pair, so if you don't mind digging around more, maybe they're there."

"Nope." Niccola tossed his napkin on the table as he stood, making Mama turn red in the face from laughing. "Let's go, move it. You owe me a full detail cleaning, and you just lost any chance of coming on my next trip."

"Excuse me." Donatello kissed Mama on the head and started to race down the hill as Niccola bolted after him.

"Never a dull moment." Mama grinned at Sienna, who had her hand over her mouth in pure enjoyment.

After the main course was served and most were halfway through their meal, I decided to dive in headfirst to catch Mariano and Sienna off guard.

"You know," I wiped the corners of my mouth, taking a moment for the chatter to stop, "I never did hear how the two of you met."

Sienna waited for him to start, but he motioned for her to speak.

"Ah," she cleared her throat, "I had done an exposé

about my life story for *Fab Magazine,* and I guess Mariano read my article and was inspired by it. A few weeks ago, I got word that one of the owners of Ricco Oil wanted me to tell their story, and here we are."

"A story?" My father sent a pointed look at Mariano. "Maybe that should have been something you ran by us?"

"I was inspired, Piero." He leaned his elbows on the table, which showed disrespect to my mama, who had spent the day making sure this dinner was perfect. "I didn't think showing her the basics of what we did was something you needed to approve."

"Careful." I shot a warning his way, and he shrugged, annoyed I had spoken to him that way in front of everyone.

"Mariano." Sienna, to my surprise, spoke with a warning tone.

"What?" he snapped at her, and I bit the inside of my mouth.

"Maybe we should just enjoy this delicious food and keep things light? The Capris were kind enough to make us this meal, and look at this table." She smiled at my mother. "It's beautiful."

"Thank you, Sienna." Mama, always the gracious hostess, smiled back.

"You think we were allowed to have dinner anywhere else but here?" Mariano cursed under his breath.

"Our rules are in place for a reason," my papa reminded him.

"Regardless, Mariano," Sienna's tone had a clip to it, "perhaps this discussion should wait for another time."

"I don't think so."

"It's uncomfortable," she shot back.

"It's not for me." Anna giggled as she reached for her bourbon.

Mariano ran a hand through his hair and leaned back.

"It's simply an 'on the surface' story, one which I hope will help Sienna build a name for herself at her company. She won't be in any danger—"

"Really?" I corrected him.

"That was a simple misunderstanding, Elio."

"Perhaps, but you did put her in danger, and what was said should never have been said in front of her."

"All right," Sienna tossed her napkin next to her plate, "please forgive my bluntness, but I never asked for any of this. I appreciate the opportunity that Mariano was trying to give me, but clearly it wasn't a wise move to make, and I will not be the reason for an argument. I promise I won't write the story. Only the start of it has been sent to my boss, and the rest will be deleted. As far as what I heard or didn't hear, I can promise you it will never be repeated."

"I think that would be for the best, Sienna." Papa gave a relieved nod, and she nodded back, understanding there was a lot more to the story. "Thank you."

"Sienna," Bria broke the silence, "why don't you tell us a little about yourself?"

"Yes, entertain us in the little time you have left with us," Anna piped in and hiccupped from her drink.

"Anna," Mama scolded her, "maybe you should have some water."

"Well, I was hired right after I finished school and have been working as a journalist ever since."

I listened to her speak and couldn't help but notice how vague she kept her story.

"What made you get into that line of work?" Roberto, Mariano's father asked as he cut into his second serving of dessert. The man was huge and one day soon would keel over if he didn't stop eating the way he did.

I nudged the pie closer to him.

"It allows me the opportunity to travel, but also allows me access to certain public information that I couldn't get on my own."

"Oh, and what sort of things are you looking for?" he asked with dessert falling out of his mouth.

"I've spent my life looking for my mama." She played with the corner of the napkin.

"For someone who seems pretty reserved," Anna interrupted as she bit the top of a bread stick, "what made you do that article? I mean, that cover was pretty revealing."

"Doing that story gave me a lot of reach, so I took the opportunity to put myself out there in hopes that she might contact me." She addressed her politely. "I thought maybe if I put myself out there, she would show herself."

"Did she?" I found myself engulfed in her story.

"No." She shook her head, and her gaze fell to the table.

"There's still time." Mama tried to give hope.

"Or maybe she wasn't meant to be found."

"Well, this seems depressing." Mariano poured

himself more wine and handed her the bottle when he noticed her glass was empty. I reached across the table and took the bottle from her hand and filled her glass.

We retired to the sitting room after dinner, and I noticed Sienna had slipped away.

"Piano room." Francesco read my mind, and I waited for the right moment to duck out.

I had no idea what I was going to say, but I really wanted to see her. I stopped when I heard my father's voice.

"The Capris date back to the fifth century here in Italy. We come from strong roots."

"What does the crest symbolize?"

"As you might know, crows are all about family." I watched as he pointed to the crest on the wall. "The crow represents family, the crown represents strength, and the shield represents the protection we provide for those loyal to the family. Family, strength, loyalty, and protection." He caught me watching and kissed her head. "I'll leave you be now, my dear." As he turned to leave, she reached for his hand and gave it a squeeze, and his face softened. He left and quietly closed the door on his way out.

I watched her admiring our family photos in the semi-dark, one hand wrapped around her stomach and the other on her hip. The reflection from the lamps danced across her slender body, and the way her eyes glinted revealed the depth of her emotion. The wind had picked up and rattled the windows of the house.

"I love your parents so much." She must have felt

me standing there. "Sometimes when I tell people about my past, I lie and pretend they were my parents." She swiped at her cheek.

"You mean the world to them, too."

"Please don't," she sniffed.

"Don't what?" I moved a few steps closer.

"Act like I matter."

"You matter. You always have."

"Have I?" Heavy tears leaked from the corners of her eyes. "I don't think so."

NINETEEN

Years of painful memories rushed to the surface, and I knew it was time to open the forbidden door that had been under lock and key, guarded by what was left of my soul.

"Tell me something, Elio." I turned to face him dead-on. "If the one person you trusted with your entire heart used your worst fear against you, would you be as understanding as you want me to be?" I tried to push away the vague memory I had of my mother's back to me. He closed his eyes, and I slowly turned back to the photos on the wall. Each happy face secretly nipped at my core. The Capris welcomed me into their lives and made me one of their own and just as quickly disappeared without a trace. "I didn't think so."

"I never wanted to abandon you."

"But you did. Any way you spin it, I was left in the dust with only memories that over the years made me question if you were even real."

"You think it was easy on me? You don't—"

"No," I cut him off, "at least you knew why you left me, and you had people to lean on." Tears burned painful paths down my face. "While I cried for years, wondering what I did wrong to make you leave me."

"No, Sienna." The heartache written on his face told me I was getting through to him. Good. "You did nothing wrong."

"Don't." I put more distance between us, and his eyes narrowed in on me. "Unless you can tell me the true reason for leaving." He opened his mouth but snapped it shut, and so did the door to my heart. "Right." I shook my head as I walked by him. "We're finished here."

"Like hell we are." He snagged my arm and held me close. "Answer me this, Sienna." His jaw flexed, and his pupils dilated. My chest fought to keep up with my lungs. "Has anyone ever made you feel whole or right again?"

When I didn't answer, he finally broke eye contact, and I sagged in his hold.

"I just need to let go," I said, more to myself, and felt my temper lash out. "Maybe Mariano can do that for me." I instantly regretted the words as they leapt from my tongue. I hated that I wanted him to hurt as much as I did. I didn't even want Mariano.

"He's too selfish." He waved off my comment, which ignited the flames inside me.

"Selfish!" I nearly screamed. "Selfish like leaving without even a note. You broke every single piece of my soul, Elio. God!" I pulled back, feeling my words wash over me. "I'm dust inside, empty, and hollow." I wailed my pain. "Do you get that? I'm broken, and I hate that I was weak enough to let a man do that to me. Christ, I'm only human…or at least I was."

He stormed up in front of me, his hands clasping and unclasping at his sides.

"Well, if I broke it," he boomed, "then I'm the *only* one who can mend it!" His growl echoed across the marble floor just as his mother stepped into the room.

"Elio," she said calmly, "your father needs you."

His shoulders lowered as his intensity slowly subsided. He turned on his heel and left the room.

I wrapped my arms around my stomach and turned away from Andrea.

Her heels clicked as she approached, and I gave in and flew into her arms.

"There's so much more you need to know, dear, but for now, understand it wasn't his choice to make. We grabbed the few things that meant the most to us and left."

I sobbed harder, not having the energy to express how much her words just tipped me over the edge.

"Come on, sweet girl." She walked me out of the room and away from everyone else and up the stairs. "Let's give you some privacy."

She led me to a bedroom that looked over the winery, and as I tucked into a ball on the big, cushioned window seat and stared out the window, the weight of it all exhausted me. She snuggled up next to me and started to run her fingers through my hair.

"Tonight, it's just you and me, Sienna," she whispered in her motherly voice. "Get all your tears out. You'll feel so much better when the sun comes up."

"I feel like," I tried to speak calmly, but it took a great amount of effort, "life is punishing me for something, Andrea. What did I do wrong? Am I a bad person and don't know it?"

"No way, and you did nothing wrong." She tried to soothe me.

"Then why is it, when I finally let my guard down after all these years and attempted to let someone in, *he* shows up." I pulled myself into a smaller ball, hoping I would disappear.

"Maybe it was for a reason." She brushed my hair back and with her other hand pulled a soft quilt over me. "Maybe someone somewhere knew I needed my daughter back."

I squeezed my eyes shut, feeling how much I needed her to say that.

She kissed my head and let me cry my heart out until my fight with my heavy eyelids won, and she leaned down and whispered, "Do you still love Elio?"

I dug deep, past all the darkness, pain, and doubt, and gave her the last bit of me I had left tonight.

"Does it matter?" Seconds later, I gave in to sleep.

The effort it took to open my swollen eyes to let the sunlight in was almost unbearable. Three attempts later, I lifted my heavy head and took in my surroundings. There was a note on the night table with my name written on it. I had to blink a few times to clear my vision.

"Mariano stayed the night. No one thought anything about you disappearing early. The bourbon took care of that. Everything you need can be found in the restroom, including a clean dress hanging on the inside of the door. Take your time. We are all home today. Love, Andrea."

A long shower made me feel better. I let my hair air dry and slipped into the blue dress that was left for me. I didn't want to know why they had a dress my size hanging around, but her face popped up, and I pushed aside the thought of Elio and Anna together. I passed on the shoes and slipped on my beloved leather heels, impressed with how they looked with the dress.

"Good morning, Sienna," Francesco greeted me as I walked into the kitchen.

"Francesco." I kissed his cheek, beyond happy to see my old friend. "How have you been? No, first, how are your children?"

He pulled out his wallet and shared some photos of his grandbabies.

"Look at those sweet little cheeks," I gushed over how adorable they were. "They have your eyes."

"They do, don't they?" he agreed.

Someone came running into the kitchen and almost collided with one of the kitchen staff.

"Sorry!" he apologized as he steadied her by the elbow then whirled around to us.

"Oh, Sienna, have you met Vinni?" Francesco waved between us. "He's Elio's cousin."

"Cousin?" I questioned. "I thought you were the driver?"

He grinned and snagged a pastry off one of the pans the girls were walking by with.

"Not normally, but the boss wanted to make sure you were taken care of."

"Oh." I was shocked by that, but I waved my hand, trying to place everyone. "Don't you have better things to do than cart me around?"

"And miss a chance to drive around a pretty lady?" He smiled.

I smiled back and paused to let his words sink in. "Thank you."

Donte emerged from the walk-in refrigerator just as Vinni left again, talking about something he had to do.

"Last night was interesting." Donte gave me a wary look as he set two dozen eggs on the island.

"I went to bed early."

"That explains why the boss paced the bottom of the stairs for hours."

I shifted on my stool and glanced at Francesco, who kept very busy and pretended not to listen.

"So?" I spun an egg on the counter. "What happened? Someone fall in the pool or skinny dip?" I held up a hand.

"You know what? Given the company that was here last night, don't answer that."

He laughed, and to my surprise, so did Francesco. "No, we had some visitors, friends of Mariano, to be exact. The boss wasn't happy, and he shut it down quickly. Mariano has a death wish not to mention he was running his mouth about you."

"Me?" I leaned forward, interested to know what was said.

He glanced at Francesco, who gave him a nod to go on. "He was running his mouth about you and him and how close you've gotten. You know, intimately. The boss lost it and punched him straight in the nose."

"What?"

"Yeah, I don't think I've ever seen those two be like that toward each other."

"Oh, my God." I stared at him, wondering what the hell I was doing to their family.

"I think the boss has eyes for you, Sienna." He tapped his nose. "The kitchen staff sees more than you would think, and my senses are telling me you caught his attention."

"Well, years of love will do that," I muttered before I slapped my hand over my mouth, completely shocked I said that out loud.

"I knew it was more than love at first sight." He pointed a handful of basil at me.

"Oh, my God, Donte." I circled the island and held on to his shoulders and looked him square in the eye. "Please never repeat what I just said to you."

"Under one condition." He beamed with excitement.

"What?"

"You stay."

"What?" I was completely thrown by his comment.

"I've been working for the boss for nearly six years. Girls have come and gone, and never once have I ever seen him throw a punch for one of them."

I threw my hands in the air and looked up at the sky. "It's as if someone tore the pages out of a fairytale and stuck them back in without any order."

"Come on, now, Miss Sienna," he laughed like I should be getting his humor, "surely you know this is no fairytale. You're wrapped up with the—"

Francesco cleared his throat, and Donte pressed his lips together.

"So, am I keeping my mouth shut?" He wiggled his eyebrows, which made me laugh, and I let whatever he was going to say go. It was most likely not meant for my ears.

"I don't know." I reached for my purse and pulled out a train ticket I bought before I left in case I needed to leave on my own terms and showed it to him. "After last night, I'm not sure what I should do."

"May I suggest something?" Francesco spoke up behind me. "As someone who has been around from the very start, maybe stick around for a few more days. It couldn't hurt."

"Am I really welcome? Because last night—"

"Wasn't what you thought it was," he cut me off. "Perhaps some alone time with Mr. Elio would put your mind at ease?"

I let out a shaky breath and tried to get my thoughts in order. "Do you know where he is?"

"I was actually just heading his way right now. We can go there together."

Elio

I was sick of this mess, sick that my own people were being used. Their lack of loyalty hurt, and hurt deeply, but there had to be a reason. These people had been with me for a long time. I hurried into the warehouse that was heavily protected by my men.

The smell of dirt, cement, and blood rushed to my senses, alerting me I was close.

"All but one won't talk." Niccola stepped out of my way as I raised the knife and slashed one man's neck, clipping his artery. He was new and had already sidestepped on some of his duties, so he was on his way out anyway. Blood sprayed, and I felt some of it splash my face as I watched him drain white. I felt no empathy for him whatsoever.

The others who watched were like family, so I when I turned my attention to them and dabbed my face with my handkerchief, I hoped they'd remember where their loyalty lay.

"Are you sure you want to keep your silence?" I shrugged.

"Please, sir," the oldest spoke up, "we'll talk."

"Good." I glanced at Niccola and flicked my wrist. "Separate and question them."

"Yes, boss. The other one is in there." He pointed down the hallway, and I glared at the others, daring them to lie before I left with a hiss.

My shadow loomed over my shoulder and followed me, flickering in and out with the gaps in the lighting. It was as if my soul was unable to make a full connection when I was here. It allowed me to do my job without a conscience. I didn't always handle the kills myself, but with how far out of hand all this was getting, I wanted to use my presence as a tool to get them to speak up. These men were my family, their families were my families, and hurting them wasn't something I wanted to do but had to do.

I nodded at Donatello as I stepped inside the round room. No corners to cower in, no shadows to hide within, just a place that left nowhere to go. Before we got started, I needed to make my point. No matter how you looked at it, he had betrayed me and the family. I stepped forward and rammed my fist hard into his stomach, then I stepped back and waited for him to catch his breath.

"You want to talk, Antonio?" I took my time and fixed my tie, drawing his eyes to my pristine attire. It was a necessary reminder as to who he was dealing with.

"I-I," he stumbled, "I need you to promise my family won't be harmed."

"You should know I have no interest in hurting your family." I had never and would never hurt women and children. That was a line my father and I stood firm on.

"When the man in white asks you to do something, you have to do it." He tried to stand, but his knees nearly gave out, and he used the wall for support.

"Who is this man, and why do you feel this way?"

"I don't know who he is, but when my brother said no to him, they took my niece, and she hasn't been seen since." He stiffened when I stepped closer. "He doesn't just hurt us. He hurts our babies."

"They have Val?" It was the first time I'd heard of this. "Why didn't you come to me?"

"I wanted to. I was so afraid for her, but when I tried to protest for her life, he did this." He pulled up his pant legs and showed me his battered kneecaps.

"Antonio," I sighed and rubbed my tired eyes. "Bucket and water," I ordered Donatello, and he rushed to retrieve the items, returning a moment later. He turned the bucket upside down and handed me the jug of water.

"Sit," I ordered Antonio, who wasted no time easing his battered body to sit. I handed him a plastic cup and watched him down the water. He needed to see that I wasn't a monster like the man in white. He needed to be reminded of the protection I offered. He had been honest with me and had provided information, and in turn, that deemed a reward.

"Thank you," he huffed in relief. "I'm sorry, sir." Tears pooled in his eyes, and I could see his sincerity. "The dockyard is not what it used to be. The men are scared to go to work there because of him."

"You have no idea who this man is? What does he look like? Tell me everything you know. How is he getting past all our men?"

"He's tall, wears a white suit, white tie, white everything. Like he's impersonating an angel, but he's anything but." He squinted, and his mouth turned down as he took a minute to think. "You never know when he will appear. His men leave messages on our windshields and then follow us until we are off your territory. They wait until we stop at a stoplight or something and then pull up on their motorbikes and force us to follow them to a location where he will order us to do things for him."

Stefano.

"What location?"

"It's always a different place."

That was smart. It made it harder for us to track him.

"What did he want you to do?"

"I was supposed to deliver something to the market." He nodded to Donatello, who held out a stained envelope. "I didn't look at it. I didn't ask any questions, I just took it, but before I could drop it off at the entrance of the market, I was picked up and brought here."

I nodded once and tucked the envelope into my jacket pocket.

"I know, what I did was wrong." He shifted with a grunt, clearly hurting from his injuries. "But I couldn't risk Val's life. She is so smart and beautiful and so young. She's going places." His tears flowed, and his hands shook as he wiped them away.

"Antonio." I leaned back and tried to remember that fear sat in everyone in different ways. I would drill a stack into Stefano's heart, my hatred of him was so strong, while Antonio was an old man trying to do his job and live a life with little to no violence. "I'll get my guys to look into Val, and in the meantime, Niccola will take you to the hospital and get your knees checked over."

"You're such a good man, Mr. Elio." His mouth dropped open when he realized he had used my first name. I cleared my throat and waited a beat then let it slide. It was a slip of the tongue, and he had been with the family since I could walk.

"Is there anything else you can tell me about him?"

"He did ask about someone." His hands shook on his lap, and I knew I wasn't going to like this.

"And?"

"He wanted to know where Miss Sienna was living."

"Sienna?" I played dumb and felt a layer of sweat break out along my neck. How did he know her name?

"Yes, the young lady with Mariano."

"And what did you say?"

"I said that she was Mariano's girlfriend. He wanted to know if they were in a serious relationship."

"And?"

"I really wouldn't know." He shook his head. "I've

only seen her once with him and twice with you. She seems very nice, but I wasn't about to offer all that to him." He groaned, holding his knees. "I've learned less is more."

"Good. Any idea why he was asking about her?"

"I think he likes her. He has a woman by his side sometimes, but she's got nothing on Mariano's girlfriend."

My mouth went dry with his answer.

"All right." I motioned for Donatello to help him to his feet. "One last thing." I pivoted to look at him. "Have you mentioned this to Mariano or anyone else?"

"I tried," he shrugged, "but he doesn't listen very well to people like me."

"Antonio," I thought for a moment, "this is your one and only pass with me. If I ever find out you went behind my back, no matter what the reason…"

"You have my word."

I turned on my heel and left with Niccola hard on my heels. "Well?" I demanded.

He spent the next ten minutes filling me in on the other two men's stories. They were all the same, which meant we really had a problem.

"All right." I turned my head away from the others. "Get the body cleaned up, and make sure that you personally escort Antonio to the hospital. I need a minute to think."

"Sure, boss."

With that, I left for home.

Three hours in the ring with my best trainer and

fifty laps in the pool helped subside the urge to hurt my best friend for dragging Sienna into this nightmare. I dried my hair with my hands as I made my way to the refrigerator for some water. My body was still hot from the workout, and my jeans hung low on my bare hips, which was a blessing as the cool air from the refrigerator swirled around my stomach. I eyed the envelope on the counter, still unsure my temper could take it if there was something about Sienna in it. Instead, I slipped it into my back pocket for later.

The doorbell rang, and I checked the time. I knew it was Francesco here to give me my daily briefing. I hit the buzzer, but when he didn't come in, I headed for the door on the chance he had someone with him who I might have to take care of first. It seemed to be that kind of week.

"Fran—" I paused when I saw Sienna standing there. "Hey."

"Hi." She flipped her hair out of her face as her gaze swiped down my body. "Um, maybe I should have called."

"No," I stepped back, "come in."

"Are you sure I'm not interrupting anything?"

"Come on." I waved for her to enter.

She looked around, no doubt looking for a female.

"I won't stay long." She fidgeted with her hands. "I, ah, just wanted you to know that I meant every word I said, but I don't want bad blood between us."

"Okay."

"Okay," she repeated and headed for the door.

"That's it?"

"Yeah." She reached for the handle, but I pressed my hand against it to keep it shut.

"You're telling me," I gently turned her around, pushed her back into the door, and held her chin with one hand, "that you came all the way down here just to tell me you don't want bad blood between us?"

"Yes."

"Why don't I believe you?"

"Elio."

I loved how my name sounded as it passed her lips. My entire body coiled, and my muscles became steel.

"Tell me you don't feel something for me, Sienna, and I will step back and let you leave."

"I…" she started but stopped herself. She looked panicked and trapped. "I just…" She closed her eyes as I bent down and ran my lips along her temple, breathing in her scent.

"Tell me." I licked her earlobe and gave it a nibble. Moving my hand to her side, I slid it down the fabric of her dress and around to her bare thigh. "Tell me you hate me."

"I do," she whispered as I relished her scent.

"Tell me," I pressed my lips to her slender neck and slowly inched down to her collarbone, "why you still wear my pendant."

"Because." Her hands flew to my sides as she lost her footing, and I took the opportunity to push my knee between her legs, holding her in place.

"Because?" I coached her, loving the fact that I

had my lips on her sexy skin and the heat of her arousal warmed my thigh.

I leaned back when she wouldn't speak and looked into her deep, dark eyes that flipped between a deep blue to a dark navy.

I gently dragged the pad of my thumb along her lower lip. Leaning down, hovering my lips above hers, waiting for her to initiate the rest. I saw a million things run through her expression, but she wasn't making a move to leave.

"Why are you still wearing my pendant?" I repeated and made sure my lips touched her once so she could feel the spark.

She closed her eyes again as I broke down more barriers between us. "It's the only thing I have that proves you were real."

"Sienna," I whispered so she'd look at me, "kiss me so you know I'm real."

"I want to," she confessed, and I moved in closer, only to have her stop me with a hand on my chest. Her fingers flexed over my bare skin as she caught her breath. "But I can't."

"Because of Mariano?" Were they dating?

"He did bring me here, but—"

"Mariano doesn't do relationships, Sienna. I think last night can be testimony for that."

"That's not what I'm saying." She leaned in and kissed my cheek, lingering there for a moment as her breath brushed underneath my ear. "He brought me here, and out of respect for him and until I can understand myself, I need you at arm's length."

I stepped back, running a hand through my damp hair, frustrated that although so much time had passed, whenever I was near her it felt like no time had passed at all. That she was still mine, to love and touch.

"He's not right for you."

She shook her head then quickly glanced back with an angry glint. "Then, who is?"

"Me!" I nearly yelled.

"You had your chance." She shrugged sadly.

"Give me another." I took her hands in mine and kissed her fingers.

"How can I trust that you won't leave again?"

I switched gears. "Sienna, I'm nervous what he might expose you to."

Her face slipped, but she recovered quickly, and something dark fell over us.

"Has he?" I licked my dry mouth. "Exposed you to something?"

"I should get back."

I let her go, more because I knew my temper might scare her away.

"Elio," Francesco made me whirl around as he approached from the back door, "I think we should talk."

"Yeah, okay." I reached for my shirt, and we both headed to my office.

"I never thought we'd see her again, let alone here." He put his files on the desk so he could settle in for our daily meeting. Francesco was our eyes and ears, and over the years he had been at my father's side, even before he met my mother. He was one of the best *consiglieres* I had ever known. He had also proved to be excellent at hunting down people for us.

"Kind of like seeing a ghost." I sighed, remembering how true her statement was about whether we were real or not, because many times the photo was all that kept things real to me. A thought popped into my head, and I frowned.

"What is it, Elio?"

"I hate that she's searching for someone who clearly doesn't want to be found." I was referring to her mother. "Do you think she's still out there?"

He chewed the inside of his cheek as he thought. "Sienna put herself out there with that article. If her mother is out there and wants to be a part of her daughter's life, she'll show up. If not..." He gave a sad shrug. "Sometimes things are better left in the dark."

"Yeah." I glanced outside and shook the feeling away. "What do you have for me?"

"Well," he opened his leather-bound notebook, "Stefano and his two cousins are staying at the La Tegolaia villa. They checked in three days ago and apparently packed enough to presume they are staying for a while."

I had learned that Stefano had been appointed the head seat in the Coppola syndicate in Rome when his father got sick. His father had stepped in as head boss for his brother, who had vanished years ago. There had been many theories on what might have happened to Teo Coppola, but nothing concrete. The Coppola family had been trying to rule the north for decades now, and when we made the quick move from Sicily to Florence and joined forces with my uncle's family, we became extremely powerful and untouchable. Up to now, Stefano had been very quiet, but his power suddenly seemed to go to his head, and he had become more and more aggressive. He wasn't hiding the fact he'd been encroaching on our territory.

"I have a tail on them and will report any findings."

I leaned forward and removed the envelope, handing it to him filling him in on what happened.

"And you haven't opened it?" He seemed to still be reeling from what I'd shared. "May I?" I nodded and watched him open it and scan the paper.

"It's just numbers." He handed it back, and I let go of the breath I was holding. Rows and rows of numbers lined the page, each seven digits long. "A tracking log maybe?" He shrugged.

"Whatever it is, it must have been important enough to use one of my men to deliver it."

"Or maybe he was testing him?"

"Perhaps." I rubbed my head, trying to make sense of it all. "If he is threatening our people to force them to do things," I held up the numbered sheet, "or testing them, then we need to get Niccola to do some more digging." I flicked a pen through my fingers.

"You don't think that's risky?"

"Niccola is always on the move, and he's the only one who has spent more time out of country than in. Since he's been back and has grown out his hair, he's barely recognizable."

"True." He scribbled in his notebook. "So, if Stefano is sniffing around our men to do his grunt work, then why the hell is he hanging around the dock? Your men are everywhere, and normally that place is under intense surveillance."

"I have no clue, but I don't like that he has eyes on Sienna."

"Let them continue to believe she's with Mariano."

"Yeah."

"In the meantime, I'll get more trusted eyes on the dockyard."

I leaned back in my chair and stared out the window, studying the windy road.

"As one of your oldest friends, Elio," I heard the pages of his notebook close, "may I offer you a bit of advice?"

"I'm listening."

"Sienna is old fashioned. It's part of her appeal. Trust and loyalty are as huge in her eyes as they are for us. She's hurting but hasn't run yet. Maybe hit the reset button and try a different tactic with her. Show her that you're still you, even after all these years."

"And what about when she discovers what we actually are?"

"I don't know," he shrugged, "but what I do know is that she suspects something more is going on. She's smart and is figuring it out quickly on her own. You either get ahead of it and soften the blow, or she runs."

"True." I sighed, trying to get my head on right.

"Would you like to see the numbers from last month?"

"I would." I turned back around and spent the next two hours combing through a sea of numbers, all the while running possibilities of what the other numbers meant.

Chapter
TWENTY-ONE

Sienna

Le Logge del Vignola restaurant was insanely busy. Mariano explained he knew the owner, and whenever he dined there, he got the best table. Perks of the oil business, I guessed.

"I noticed you were packing this morning." Mariano leaned back as the waiter poured his wine. I couldn't help but notice the waiter seemed a little nervous. "What's with the bags?"

"Well, um," I fumbled on my words, "I figured since I'm not writing your story, I should get back to my life and my job."

"Oh." He checked his phone that was glued to his hand then rubbed his chin. "But can't you do your job from anywhere?"

"Yes, but I don't have a story that keeps me here, and you've been kind enough letting me stay with you, but—"

"What if I gave you one?" he interrupted.

"Mariano, I don't want to step—"

"Not my story, but a different one?"

I tapped my fingers on the tablecloth as I thought.

"Look." He quickly pulled my attention back to him. "I'm sorry the first idea didn't work out. I really think Piero got the wrong impression of what I wanted to share with you." He paused then glanced at the server who was talking with the kitchen staff. "Have you ever heard of the Santoro Brothers?"

"I believe they were two brothers who executed a family in the south."

"That's correct, but do you know any more about them?"

"Not really. My projects are not often crime related."

"What if I agreed to set up an exclusive interview?"

"Impossible." I lowered my voice as the plate of Il Gran Fritto Toscano was placed delicately in the center of the table. I waited until I knew no one could hear. "From what I do remember about them, after they massacred that family, they were never heard from again."

"Huh." He leaned forward and helped himself. Leaving me to wonder what he really knew.

"I call your bluff." I waited to see what he'd say while I shifted in my seat.

"Would you be able to stay if I gave you such an

opportunity? I know the guy who helps them find their people. He's nice, friendly, he just knows how to find people." He lifted an eyebrow as though there was a lot more to say. "Seems to me you also spend a good part of your life looking for missing pieces, so perhaps he can help."

I stared over his shoulder and studied the wine bottles tucked up along the ceiling in the corner. It was spectacular here, and there was a part of me that wasn't ready to say goodbye to Elio yet. As uncomfortable as it was staying at Mariano's house, it wasn't lost on me that he wanted more from us than I did. They were both so different for being best friends.

I knew this could be something huge. I wasn't stupid. I knew these guys were tangled up in something dark, but that could also work in my favor. Journalists dreamed of moments like these, and here I was staring at another big break, and since the other story had fizzled out...

"Sienna." Mariano broke through my thoughts and covered my hand with his. "You have my word there is no danger. This man always kept his identity hidden from the brothers. They simply spoke over the phone, and that was it. I want you to stay." He paused a moment. "Of course, I'll go with you to the interview."

My nerves flickered, telling me to tread carefully. I'd been living with that feeling for so long now perhaps it was time to relax a bit and take a little risk to see what was beyond that.

"Okay." I nodded, knowing I had been putting off

that call to Georgio, but if I could pull this story off for him instead, it would blow his mind.

"Really?"

"Yes, but, Mariano, I need you to understand I'm not looking for a relationship with you. If you want to get to know one another as friends, I'm okay with that." I held up a hand when I saw his eyes flash with excitement. "But that's where it ends." I waved between us. "You should know there is someone else in my life who I apparently still have feelings for."

"I figured that, and it's okay, because a little more time with me and you'll see what a great man I am."

I rolled my eyes. "Just remember there is someone else."

"A little competition never stopped me before." He winked, and we went back to enjoying our evening.

With the air cleared with Mariano and a new story to pursue, I felt all-around better than I did two days ago before my dinner out with him. It took a bit of convincing, but Georgio came around to the new story idea. He was upset over losing the Ricco Oil story, but his disappointment evaporated once he heard me out. He told me to take my time but that he wanted an outline before the end of tomorrow.

I woke early and went for a walk through the sunflower fields with my Mac. Mariano had given me some articles to research on the Santoro brothers, and I hadn't meant to wander quite as far as I did, but it was a wonderful place to let your mind go.

There wasn't a lot of information in the newspaper

articles, but I did learn that the Santoro brothers killed thirteen people in total. The heads of the family were executed. The women and children had been rounded up and locked in the root cellar while parts of the family's farm were burned to the ground. It was a sign to all that the brothers had been there. After that, they started plucking off anyone with the last name Rosario. It was said that the city was still stained with their blood.

By the time I found my way to the road, I had dictated the outline and the first part of my writeup.

"Hello, there." A man who was waiting by his car in Elio's driveway came over to greet me. "Lovely day for a stroll through the fields."

"I thought so." I shaded my eyes to see him better. He was dressed well and looked like he belonged here.

"I couldn't help but notice you have a laptop."

"I do." I looked down at my hands, thinking of how much of my heart was poured into the document that was stored in there under a password.

"Do you always carry a laptop when you go for a walk? Would you care to share what's in there? I'm a sucker for a mystery."

I laughed at him, trying to see into my notes. I held the laptop close like it was a masterful secret.

"As a matter of fact, I do often carry it, and some secrets are not meant to be shared."

"Who are you here with?" He stepped closer. "I've never seen you here before."

"Who are you?" I knew better than to open my mouth until I knew who I was talking to.

"The boss doesn't like people on his property, let alone with a camera," he pointed to my phone, "and a laptop."

"What?" I laughed, thinking how absurd he sounded. "Do I look like a spy?"

"Let me see your laptop, and I'll let you go on your way."

"No." I stepped back, and he reached for my arm and yanked it hard. "Ouch."

"Hey!" Elio boomed from the doorway and marched up to the two of us. "You touch her again, and I will drive my fist through your forehead."

Porca merda.

The guy let me go and held his hands up as he leaned back against his car like the threat didn't faze him.

"Sorry, boss," he muttered.

Elio had his hands on my shoulders as he leaned down to see my face. I saw many emotions flicker across his, and all looked haunted.

"Are you okay?"

"I'm fine." He waited a beat, as if trying to read my mind.

"Okay."

"Didn't know she was with you," the guy muttered.

"Do I look like a threat?" I challenged and grew angrier.

"You think she would be here if she was?" Elio snapped then took a deep breath to calm his nerves. "Everything is fine. We're good here."

"Understood. I'll wait down the road until you are

ready to talk." The man disappeared behind the blacked-out windows and drove off, leaving the two of us alone.

"Who is he?" I tried to figure out what had rattled Elio so hard.

"He works for me."

"He seems, ah, nice." I tried to lighten the mood with a little sarcasm, but when he didn't relax even a little, I reached up and cupped his face, slipping back into old habits. "Hey, I'm all right. I'm not that fragile."

He closed his eyes, taking a moment to let it go, and covered my hand with his.

"What's wrong?" I asked softly.

"Having you here," he whispered, "is unnerving."

"Oh." My stomach dropped.

"No." He shook his head like I misunderstood him. "If anything was to happen to you because I…" He dragged my hand to his mouth and kissed the palm. "Can I ask you something?"

"Sure." I was immediately swept into the spell he so easily cast.

"Will you come to dinner with me tomorrow night?"

I pulled my hand away, feeling the amor click tightly around my heart.

"I don't know." My head spun as the fog lifted from the mental hold he had on me. "Why?"

He stood a little straighter and leaned his head to the side and frowned like he realized he was coming at it all wrong.

"Sienna," he said quietly, "I'm not used to having someone question me like you do."

"I haven't changed, Elio. I'm still the girl who wanted to stab you at the dinner table for making me meet your parents soaking wet."

He dropped his head back and laughed, and I saw the old, carefree Elio I remembered. "You were scrappy at times."

"Right, so…" I lifted my chin and fought a smile.

"Well, I would like very much to take you to dinner tomorrow night."

"I don't know if that's a good idea." My lightness faded away.

"And I disagree."

"Of course, you do."

"No, look." He stumbled, and given his flustered look, he wasn't prone to being thrown off his game very often. It was kind of sweet. "You told me I hurt you, and I know I did because I hurt me in the process, but for some reason fate has brought us back together again, and I think we should listen to it."

I folded my arms and continued to make him sweat this one out. When I didn't answer, his eyebrows pinched, and he stared into my eyes, no doubt trying to mentally break down my walls and read my mind. By the way his stance shifted and how he rubbed his face I could tell his temper was rising. I would never purposely play mind games with any man. I wasn't like that, but Elio hurt me, and as much as a night out with him sounded intriguing, what would it mean if I simply said yes?

"I want the chance to prove I am worthy of you, Sienna. I just need the time with you to do it. Please."

Well, I wasn't expecting that.

"I feel I need to check in with Mariano to see if he has plans."

"He has plans for tomorrow night." He cleared his throat as though he was uncomfortable talking about him.

"Oh?" He had mentioned something about not being around, but nothing was set in stone.

"He and Anna have plans."

"Oh? All right, then." I nodded, not sure I believed him. "Let me talk to him first, and then I'll let you know."

Chapter
TWENTY-TWO

Elio

"Everything okay?" Niccola tossed two cards aside and signaled to Francesco, who sent two new ones flying across the table.

"Yeah." I glanced at my cards and saw I had a full house, and my thumb flicked the corner of the card, covering a small symbol at the bottom. "Just taming the pit bull."

"Ernesto met Sienna today. It didn't go so well." Niccola filled in Vinni's grunt of confusion.

"If he touches her again, I will kill him." I directed my comment to Francesco, so he knew where I stood.

"Get in line," he responded.

Reciting my cards in my head, I took note of the

pot on the game board. The ace and king of hearts was currently the biggest pot. Now I just needed the chance to play them before anyone else did.

Once a month, we took turns hosting a game of Rummoli. We played for high stakes and took the game seriously but had a lot of fun. It was really more of an excuse to shoot the shit while we discussed things as a family. My father called it our *family meetings*. We were a modern syndicate, but a few old-school roots still ran deep. We knew we had to move with the times to continue to stay on top, but things like the Rummoli game went a long way back in the family and kept us focused.

"So," Vinni started in, "how long are we going to let this prick rule the dockyard?"

"Until I know exactly what Stefano is up to." I sipped my sidecar and, with my free hand, removed my tie.

"Fair enough." He cleared his throat like he wanted to say more. I sent my glance his way and waited. "So, are we going to talk about the elephant in the room?"

"I'm not following."

"The hot little number who has you in a twist?" He laughed. "I've never seen you in such a mess before."

"I second that." My father muffled a laugh, and I shot him a glare. We normally gave each other shit when we played, but we all knew when we left the room, that was where it ended. It was the main reason Mariano stopped being invited.

"I mean, I knew you two had a history," Vinni went on, "but you've dated lots of women, and none of them have ever made you this uptight."

"Is it because she doesn't fall for your charms?" Harris, Niccola's long-time best friend and basically family, chimed in with a laugh.

"She does," I admitted. "She's just a very stubborn woman who knows me all too well."

"That's the best kind, son." My father laughed. "Women should make you work for their love."

"Agreed," Francesco, to my surprise, spoke up, "no matter how hard the work is."

"Care to share, old friend?" I lifted an eyebrow at him. He didn't often talk about his personal interests when it came to women.

"No, this conversation is about you." He chuckled.

Everyone started to play the game. We usually began with the poker round. I tossed my chips in the center and waited for my father to go. He eyed me and leaned back, tilting the corners of the cards up.

"I'm in." He tossed his chips into the center, and we waited for Niccola.

It came down to Vinni and me, so I showed my cards and won the pot. Now I led and played my lowest card.

"Ten of hearts." I tossed my card down and waited for the others.

"Jack of hearts." Niccola kept the game moving.

The dockyard hit was consistently playing in my head, and I thought it was time we discussed it.

"I think we need more cameras at the dockyard," I started. "How was it that someone was killed on our territory, there was a woman witness, and the cameras were turned off?"

"It's not more cameras that we need. It's that they should be run on a separate WIFI network that only you and Piero can access." Harris moved his hand to declare the suit was dead. He tossed out his lowest card. "Three of spades."

"I like that." I nodded. "Make that happen."

"Will do."

"My question," Niccola puffed on a cigar, "was how did they get in with their mark? Did he pop him over a thirty-five-foot fence then jump over after him?" He pointed the lit end of his Cohiba at me. "He had help."

"Not one of our guys would risk such a thing." My father shook his head.

"Yet this happened." Niccola shrugged. He had a very valid point.

"We have twenty-nine cameras and eight more in the parking lot." Francesco cleared his throat. "Did we check all the footage? Because one of those should have picked up something."

He was right, and we knew it. We went back to playing the game and kept the conversation light for the rest of the evening. Every so often, I'd check my phone, but there was no word from Sienna.

I lasted until a little after eleven before I couldn't get my head off the tapes. I gathered my winnings and left for my office.

I fell asleep on my couch that night, running through the endless footage of my dockyard, and woke to someone shaking my shoulder. In a heartbeat, I jammed my weapon in that someone's face.

"Easy." Mama pushed my hand to move the aim of the gun away from her. "Why are you here?"

"Jesus, Mama, I could have killed you."

"Why are you on the couch?"

"I fell asleep watching the footage."

She gave me a worried look as she clicked off the TV on the wall.

"I want to talk about Sienna."

"Okay." I sat up and massaged my sore neck.

"I'm really worried about her being with Mariano. He's reckless, and from what your father said last night, he was out with some woman, and then Anna told me she is going out with him tonight? Do you know if they are…?" She trailed off and waved her hand. "I need to keep remembering she's not ours anymore."

The cold rush that burst through me was chilling.

"I'm working on that, Mama."

"Good." She kissed my forehead and stood with a smile. She seemed pleased about how the conversation went.

I sighed, leaning back into the couch, not at all sure I could do anything about Sienna.

"Son, we had to push her away, but somehow someone had other plans. You either fight for our girl now, or you will lose her forever this time. Third chances are like finding the end of a rainbow."

"I know, and I am working on it."

I flopped my head back when she left and knew I needed to get myself together before I headed out for the day.

It wasn't until three in the afternoon that she finally called me.

"Good afternoon, Sienna." I quickly moved away and held up a hand to silence Donatello. The man in his hold wiggled and bucked, which only excited Donatello more, but he caught my drift and pulled the guy back toward the far wall and stuffed a rag in his mouth.

"Hi." Her voice seemed off.

"Are you all right?"

"Yes," she cleared her throat, "and if the invitation still stands, I would be happy to join you for dinner this evening."

I couldn't help the smile that raced across my lips, and I kept my back turned away from the men. I felt like I was a young boy again standing on the edge of the pond waiting for her to agree to visit my home.

"All right, I'll pick you up at six?"

"Sounds good. What shall I wear?"

"Something nice." I grinned harder, loving the idea of being alone with her.

"That's incredibly helpful. Glad I asked." Her sarcasm made me chuckle.

"Wear a dress."

"Thank you." She sighed with relief. "I'll see you at six."

"It's a date." I couldn't help myself.

"It's dinner," she reminded me, but I could tell I was working my way through her barrier.

I was tired of what was happening here and gave

Donatello the word to finish the man off himself. I needed to get home. As I strolled across the dockyard toward my car, I fell into a deeper thought.

I seemed to be killing off a man a day. Since this hit was linked to Stefano and not one of my own, it wasn't a hard decision to make. Still, I wasn't any closer to learning why my dockyard had suddenly become attractive, and I still hadn't figured out what the hell the numbers meant. My ships were arriving on time, and none of my oil was being touched or tampered with. Were they trying to distract me by driving my attention there so they could make another move somewhere else? That was a very real possibility that worried me.

"Elio." Niccola addressed me as I came into the kitchen. He wore a pissed off expression as he looked up from the newspaper.

"What's on your mind, Niccola?" My oldest cousin was just shy of two years younger than I was, and we had become quite close since we moved to Tuscany.

"Mariano and Anna are already into the grappa, and they haven't even left for the evening. I don't want to be a witness to your mother's actions, so here I am."

I rolled my eyes and bet my parents wished they never implemented the open-door policy for their house.

"Lucky for them, I hid the pistols from her."

"Mm," he chuckled, amused. "Where are you off to?" He peered at my signature black attire. The jet black with a pop of gray just spoke to my soul.

"I have a date." I dropped my wallet in my breast pocket.

"With who?"

"Sienna."

"Oh, please, let me be there when you drop her back off at Mariano's place?" He laughed darkly as he pulled out his phone. "Vinni needs to hear about this."

"I don't think Mariano will even notice she's gone."

"Either way, text me, and I will pull up a chair for the performance."

My phone rang on the counter, and I flipped it over to see the caller ID.

"Dammit." I took a deep breath, not wanting to deal with work shit right now. I answered it quickly. "What?"

"I think I may have something for you," Donatello grunted.

I squeezed my eyes shut and cursed again. "It will have to wait." I hung up and rushed out the door. I was certainly not going to be late.

"Vinni." I pointed to the car, not wanting to drive tonight. I didn't want to be spotted in the city any more than necessary. I didn't need to tell him why I was leaving; his brother had already filled him in. "Mariano's."

"Yes, boss." He opened the door for me, and I slipped inside. Vinni was a lot younger, but he was a damn fine shot and always had my back. He loved to drive and had worked his way up from being my driver to a *caporegime*. However, I don't trust anyone else behind the wheel, so he still continues to drive for me. Cousin or not, we all earned our place and our keep here. Plus, Vinni was the last person you'd ever think would have ties to the Mexican Cartel. The fact that he did had come in handy a few times.

"We will be eating at the E Lucevan Le Stelle Bar Bistro," I let him know as we pulled up in front of Mariano's house. As she stepped out, she nearly took my breath away.

A silver silk dress clung to her body, and when she took one of the steps, I saw her long leg reach out from the slit in the fabric. My hands twitched to feel that skin. Her breasts were half tucked into scraps of fabric, and her hair was long and wavy. I pressed my hands against my thighs to settle my legs then gathered myself and stepped out of the car.

"*Ciao belle,*" I whispered as she came closer.

"Elio." She gave me one of her sexy smiles as she looked up with hooded eyes.

Be good, I had to remind myself as she walked past me and I caught sight of the thin ties that zigzagged across her back and joined in a bow at the bottom.

Vinni mouthed a "wow" as I climbed in behind her.

"Hungry?" I nodded at Vinni to get moving.

"I am." She smiled up at me, and memories started to flood my head. I had to chase them away so I could focus on the here and now.

My phone rang, and I saw it was Donatello again. I wondered if the news was good.

"Please don't let me stop you from taking that." She glanced at the ringing screen.

I tucked it away, not wanting any interruptions.

"He can wait."

I noticed her lips twitched. She was happy with my

comment.

"Andrea came by this morning." She filled in the silence, which she was always so good at.

"Oh, did she?" I lifted my arm and rested it behind her, wanting to be closer.

"Yes, she asked me if I wanted to come stay up at the Hill House for a while."

I couldn't help but chuckle at Mama's attempt to make sure she had her *daughter* back under our sole protection.

"And your response was…?"

"I can't impose on your family again." She kept her answer light, but I knew she was holding us all at arm's length.

"You were never imposing, Sienna." I curled her hair around my finger.

"Well, I still couldn't. You have so many people there as it is."

"We're Italian." I chuckled. "If the house wasn't full of people we loved, we'd be lonely."

"Still," she shrugged, "her offer was kind, and I appreciated it."

"It was."

When we finally arrived at the restaurant, she reached for the door handle, and I quickly reached for her hand, holding it in a firm grip. I smiled, wanting to explain myself.

"Please wait a moment. Allow me to get out first."

"Why?" she challenged me, and I blinked back at her words, still not used to a woman questioning me.

"Because I would want to take the first bullet." I smiled to try to lighten the moment.

"What?" She laughed, but it trailed off when I didn't join in on her laughter. "Um, all right."

Vinni opened my door, and after his quick scan of the property, I joined him and did the same. I leaned down and offered my hand to her. Gracefully, she exited and glanced at both of us.

"Where are we?"

"One of my favorite restaurants." I placed my hand on the small of her back and urged her inside as two other cars arrived.

"Mr. Capri," the host greeted me and said a pleasant hello to Sienna. "We have your table ready for you."

"Thank you." I let Sienna walk in front of me, and I couldn't help but drink in her curves as she moved. Some of the staff glanced her way in appreciation, and I fought the need to keep one hand on her.

"Oh, my," she gasped as we stepped out onto the balcony that boasted a stunning view of this part of the city. The downward sweeping vista drew the eye, and the expression on her face was worth every penny.

"Your waiter is ready whenever you are." The hostess placed our menus on the table and let us be. The orange glow of the evening sun picked out the subtle highlights in her hair as I came up behind her.

"Where is everyone else?" She didn't turn around, but I knew she could feel me behind her, and her shoulders relaxed as I found my lips ached to kiss the delicate curve of her neck.

"When I dine here, I get the patio to myself."

"Why?"

"Because," I brushed my lips by her ear, "I can."

"Must be nice getting everything you want."

"It comes with a cost." I pulled away, knowing if I kissed her neck it would be my undoing. "Would you like to have a drink before we order?"

"Sure." She waited a beat before she joined me.

TWENTY-THREE

Sienna

Everything inside tugged me in Elio's direction, everything but my heart. I wanted him to work for it. He pulled out my chair, and I eased onto the velvet fabric.

"Would you like a glass of wine to start, or would you like an *aperitivi*?"

"Either is fine, thank you." I pulled my napkin on my lap and hesitated with the menu.

"What's wrong?" He picked it up and started to read, and I hid my delight that I was allowed to order on my own, unlike when I was with Mariano.

"What's good here?" I avoided his question.

"Everything, so order anything that interests you."

"Mr. Capri." An older man came over and offered a

hand. "It's lovely to have you back. I do hope everything is up to your standards?"

"It always is." Elio glanced at me. "I would like you to meet my date for the evening, Sienna Giovanna."

"*Ciao belle*." He offered me a hand. "I'm Gusto."

"Lovely to meet you, Gusto." I returned his warm smile.

He suddenly snapped his fingers, and a young sommelier who looked nervous but excited held up a bottle of wine.

"A new batch just arrived, sir, and when we heard you were coming, we thought we'd offer you some."

"Would you like to try it?" Elio asked me, and the sommelier turned the bottle so I could see the label. *Gattavecchi Vino Nobile Di Montepulciano.*

"I'm sure it will be wonderful."

Elio motioned with his hand, and the young man opened the wine to give us both a taste to make sure we were happy with it. We both agreed it was delicious, and I did notice they both sighed with relief as it was set aside to breathe. We soon placed our food order, and as Elio thanked Gusto, I leaned back and let myself relax.

I found myself watching Elio. He had two very strong sides to his personality. One was the boy I had fallen madly in love with, and the other was much darker and commanding. I was pleased to see that for the most part he was the same boy I once knew, but oddly, his dark side piqued my interest in the most arousing way. One I hadn't seen coming.

"What are you thinking?" His raspy voice shot right

to the center of my stomach. While I blinked, trying to recall his words, he tilted his head and smirked. "You have a face when you're thinking naughty thoughts, Sienna."

"Is that so?" I licked my lips and reached for my water. He watched me, and his eyes wandered down to my throat and dipped low on my chest. He fingered his cufflinks, looking relaxed as one hand absently stroked his chin. Not wanting to give away my private moment, I decided some answers were going to have to be given tonight if I was going to be okay with Elio being in my life again.

"Is Gusto the owner?" I changed topics.

"He is."

"And you get the entire patio whenever you bring your dates here?"

"Whenever I come here, yes."

"Seems like a lot of lost revenue for them."

He looked away for a moment. "I make it worth their while."

"Do I want to know what you do, Elio?"

His gaze darted over to mine, and I felt my stomach tighten. He held me in his gaze until I finally broke his hold. "I'm not sure yet."

"Fair enough." Why wasn't I running away? Normally, there would be a burned path out the door, but for some reason I just knew I was going to be okay, because it was Elio. I absentmindedly reached for my necklace and rubbed the pendant he had given me.

"Why did you leave without a goodbye?" came

flying out of my mouth, and I could see the fear that raced across his face. "Wait." I held up a hand, feeling a sudden panic sweep over me. "Don't answer that."

"I will answer that question, I promise you, Sienna, but can we address that one another time?" His face told me it wasn't the time or place. I gave a curt nod, hating that I wanted to run from the answer.

"Can I ask you a few questions?" He kept his voice soft.

"All right." I swallowed hard and wondered where he would go with this.

"Tell me about your life now."

That was not what I was expecting.

"Yes." I shook off the unneeded stress. "I share an apartment with my best friend, Wyatt. He's from the States."

"What part?"

"New York."

"Lovely place." He nodded at me to keep going.

"He's there right now. I was going to join him, but I'm here, so..." I trailed off and quickly realized that might have sounded bad. "It's his sister's wedding, and, well, that's just pure entertainment if you knew the groom's family." I laughed as I thought about them.

"Tell me about Wyatt."

I found my face stretching into a huge smile as I thought about my crazy friend.

"How much time do you have?" I chuckled. "We met when I was living on the streets. He helped me get a job, and later we moved in together. We are both journalists, work at the same company, share basically everything. One would think we'd be in constant competition chasing down stories and leads, but it was never like that. Instead, we work together and co-write a lot." I smiled to myself. "He's crazy, wild, fun, exciting. He's really the polar opposite of me."

"Seems to me you weren't always tame, my *belle*." Elio made a dive motion with his hand as he arched an eyebrow, and I knew he was referring to the time I jumped off a thirty-foot bridge on a dare one summer.

"Things change." I lowered my voice as the waiter returned with our food.

"Yes, they have." He cleared his throat and thanked the waiter. "Do you enjoy your job?"

"I do. I can't stand my boss, Georgio. Oh, don't get me started on him." I laughed. "I've met some interesting people, which has been fun, and I get opportunities like this."

Elio took a moment to sip his wine and music suddenly started to flow from below us.

"I love this song." I closed my eyes and listened to the sweet melody of *Primavera,* by Ludovico Einaudi. We ate in silence, listening to the music and enjoying each other's company, not needing to make a lot of small talk. When dessert was served, I was almost too full to take another bite, and I was swept up in the music and the thousand twinkling lights below us.

"Do you really think Mariano is right for you?" He finally spoke, and I kept my gaze on the scenery, trying to place my true feelings.

"No," passed softly over my lips.

"Then, what are you doing?"

Slowly, I swung my gaze over to him. "Living." I felt my shoulders stiffen. "I'm trying to let myself live. I want to let go a little, have some fun for a change."

"Have you kissed him?"

"It's interesting to me that you think we're dating."

"It sure seems that way. I just wanted to know if when he kisses you, do you burn to kiss him back more deeply, or do you feel like you want to pull away because it doesn't feel right?"

I had felt that with every man I'd ever dated since him.

"Because that's how I feel when I kiss another woman."

"Please stop." I held on to the sides of the table as my gut churned in confusion.

Giuliano Sangiorgi's *E penso a te* flowed up and surrounded us with his bleeding words. Elio stood, dropped his napkin on the table, and offered me his hand.

"I don't dance." I didn't do romance that well either. I loved it, but I'd never allowed myself to feel truly intimate with anyone…but him.

"Yes, you do." He pulled me into the middle of the patio. "Remember what I said." He gave me a smile, referring to our childhood at his parents' place. "Form to me, and I will do the rest. I promise."

I glanced down as my heart battled my head, then slowly lifted my hand and slipped it into his and stepped closer to let my body surrender to his. His warm hand pressed against the small of my back, and I rested my head against his chest and began to sway with him to the music.

"Mm," he purred as he kissed my head with contentment.

Slowly, I closed my eyes and relaxed, and with the release I let go of the tight hold on my memories and allowed my mind to drift back to our past.

"Come on." Elio lifted me by the waist and hauled me onto the dance floor where at least a hundred other guests were slow dancing to a live orchestra. I had borrowed a dress from Andrea but still felt completely out of place as he insisted I dance with him.

"Dancing is the perfect way to be with someone without any need for words, without a care in the world. It's just two people listening to music intimately. I want to experience everything with you, Sienna."

"Elio." I loved that he wanted my firsts to be his, but... "I want to, I just don't know how to."

"Lucky for you." He stood straighter and gave me his famous sexy smile. "I'm an excellent teacher."

I looked around, feeling awkward. I didn't belong there. I didn't belong anywhere, it seemed.

"Hey." He held my chin. "Form to me, and I will do the rest. I promise."

"Can I ask you one last question?" I was immediately plunged to the present as he whispered into my hair. His hand gently rubbed my bare back.

"Mm?" was all I could say as I fell deeper under his spell.

"Do you still love me?"

I knew he felt the waver in my step, but I quicky regained my composure. Carefully, I leaned back to look at him. I was sure a thousand and one emotions were evident as they danced across my face.

The fact was I had never stopped loving him, and I was scared, so damn scared to be hurt again. I wasn't sure if I could ever recover from another heartbreak.

"Can we address that one another time?"

He nodded and removed his hand from mine, running the backs of his fingers down my cheek, then he tipped my chin up and hovered over my lips.

Giving in to my heart, I pushed up on my toes and pressed my lips to his, letting the world drop away. His kisses were gentle and tame, and I moaned, loving his taste. The hand on my back slipped low into the back of my dress and touching the top of my lacy thong.

"Oh, Sienna," he groaned painfully against my mouth, "there's so much you don't know and so much I want to share." His hand moved to my heart and rested there a moment then slid down between my breasts to finger the pendant. "To think a part of me has been sitting right here all these years."

I held on to the lapels of his jacket, needing an anchor.

"I hate how scared I am around you," I confessed. I felt like my heart might burst if I didn't share what was happening inside. "I hate how much I ache for you when you aren't there, and then when I'm with you I ache in a different way. Like an addiction that feels so good and makes everything seem right, but deep down inside you know that drug might run out and leave you in its terrible wake."

"I'm so sorry, Sienna." He pressed his forehead to mine. "You must know that I never, ever wanted to hurt you."

I nodded. I knew he was telling the truth, but sadly, the damage was already done.

"We'll just take it one step at a time, okay?"

"Okay." I settled back into his arms, needing to be held.

TWENTY-FOUR

Elio

Ten minutes into the drive home, I felt her starting to slip away from me. Her eyes were locked on the window, and I could feel the wheels turning in her head. Our secrets suffocated the quiet moments we shared unless we were tangled in one other. I brushed my fingers down her arm and watched as she blinked away another memory.

"What are you thinking?"

"Nothing." She smiled through her lie.

"Sienna." I fingered a piece of her hair as I drank in her beauty. "I want you to know—" Suddenly, the partition dropped, and Vinni's worried eyes told me something was up.

"Sorry, boss, but…ah." His eyes shifted to the mirror, and I spotted a car behind us.

"Shit." I shifted to pull a gun out from under the side bar and twisted on a silencer.

"What's happening?" She looked around.

"We have company."

"Shall I call it in, boss?" Vinni waited for me to answer as I assessed the situation.

"No, but let's visit the festival tonight. Get the plate," I ordered so we could see who the vehicle was registered to.

"Yup." He took the next exit, and I reached for Sienna's seatbelt and unclipped it.

I glanced down at her shoes.

"Any chance you can run in heels?"

"Most likely, I could outrun you," she shot back, and I grinned at her quick wit and appreciated her lack of questions.

"All right, Vinni?"

"Next turn, boss."

I checked the clip and loaded one in the chamber. "No matter what happens tonight, if we get separated, you head to any restaurant and tell them my name. They will know how to reach me. Got it?"

"Yes." She looked out the back window at the headlights that were disappearing quickly.

The car came to a screeching halt in front of a massive parade as I swung open the door and pulled Sienna out of the car behind me.

"Stay close." I linked my fingers through hers and dove into the madness of the crowd. Careful to hide my gun, I wove through the sea of bodies, gently asking people to move without making too much of a scene.

"Shit." I realized as we started to move out of the spectators and into the actual entertainers who were dressed in Medieval cloaks, we stuck out like beacons.

Sienna caught on to what was happening and started to whirl around looking for something to help us.

"Elio, wait!" She unlocked her hand from mine and approached a younger couple and whispered something to the girl. Her face dropped as she listened then turned into a small smile as she removed her cloak and nodded at her friend to do the same. I scanned the crowd, hating that we had slowed. "Here." She handed me a cloak and quickly tied hers around her neck, covering her dress.

"Flip up your hood." Once she did, I took her hand again, and we started moving more in sync with the rest of the crowd.

Every so often, I would glance up to see if I could spot them. I couldn't, but I knew they were there by the way the hairs on the back of my neck stood at attention. My sixth sense had never let me down so far, so I knew they were close.

Just as we approached an opening to an alleyway, I spotted him, Stefano's right-hand man, sniffing along the sidelines of the parade. Three other men joined him, and they whispered together.

"I see them," I said, answering my vibrating phone.

"If you can duck under the display and head down the alleyway, it drops you off at the cemetery." Vinni, who was watching our backs from somewhere, huffed like he was running.

"Have you been spotted?"

"No, but I did have to ditch the car."

"Good. I'll call when we've stopped."

"Yeah, boss."

While Stefano's men had their heads turned in the opposite direction, we skirted across the rows of people and ducked into the alleyway.

Once we were out of sight, I whirled around and held her face between my hands and checked her over. "You good?"

"Yes." Her chest heaved, and her hands shook, but all things considered, she was a champion.

"No matter what, don't let them see your face."

"Who?" She tried to keep up.

I heard a noise, and my head shot up, trying to locate the direction it was coming from. Footsteps became closer, and I weighed my options. We didn't have enough time to run the full length of the alleyway, and there was nothing to hide behind.

I threaded my hand through her hair, dipped down low, and caught her lips with mine. I used one hand to hide the side of her face, and the other slid up her leg and around her bottom with the gun hidden by her cloak. I knew she could feel it against her skin, but she didn't react.

"Whoo!" Some boys cheered us on, and I opened my eyes to spot one of the men coming up behind the boys. I kissed Sienna deeper. Part of my head relished the moment, while the other half waited for the boys to leave. Once they did, I whirled her around so her back was to him and pointed the gun from beneath her cloak and fired, sending a bullet straight into his gut. I swallowed her scream, pressing her body to mine and holding her tight.

As terrified as she was, I could tell she was turned on by the way her body rubbed against me. I fought to keep focus.

Between Sienna's reaction and the smell of gun powder, I wanted to rip her clothes off and sink deep inside her.

Once I knew the second man wasn't on our heels, I pulled away with all my might.

"Come on." I motioned for her to follow me, and we headed deep into the dark alleyway to the cemetery.

I checked the gate, and it was locked. I backed her up and used the handle of the gun to hit the lock sharply, breaking it off.

"Now what?" She huffed as she glanced around and wrapped the cloak around her chilly arms.

"Now we hide."

"Here?"

"I don't think they'll mind." I used my head to point at the tombstones and motioned for her to follow.

The grass was wet, indicating the sprinklers were just on, which wasn't in our favor. The grass would give away our footprints.

"Sorry, sorry, sorry," she apologized to the graves we walked over.

"They can't hear you, Sienna." I took her hand and tugged her along.

"You don't mess with the dead, Elio. Damn." She brushed mud from her high heels.

I chuckled, and as we made a sharp turn, I pointed down at her heels.

"Think of it as aeration."

"Ha!" She laughed darkly. "Sorry." She cringed when she missed her footing and used a stone to catch her fall. "Sorry," she mouthed again with her eyes shut.

"We've got to keep moving."

"Elio." She lifted her heel that was stuck in soft mud of a fresh-dug grave. "As of right now, I might be joining them, so a little respect can't do any harm."

"Any bullet coming your way has to go through me first. Besides," I scanned the tops of the tombstones for any sign of company, "you're not the one they're looking for."

She stood straighter, and her chin rose with a questioning eyebrow.

"Then why can't they see my face?"

I hesitated, and I knew she caught it. I'd never been more off my game than since she arrived.

"Another time." She mirrored my words as I spoke, and I shook my head trying to get it on straight.

"There." I pointed to a row of mausoleums, and we rushed over, happy to finally find cover.

I tugged hard on the first few doors, but they wouldn't open. These were smaller and probably independently owned. Therefore, they weren't open to the public.

"Elio," she whispered, and I kept moving. "Elio," she hissed, and I finally looked over at her pale expression.

"First row, three stones down, I think there's someone there."

Scanning the area, I couldn't spot anything, so I went back to trying the doors.

"Do you know how to shoot?"

"I can manage a weapon, Elio." It wasn't lost on me she said weapon, not gun.

"Good." I took her hand and pushed the gun into her hold. "Push that down, aim, and squeeze." I turned to move on but swung back to her. "And don't kill my cousin."

"Of course." She raised the gun and started to watch my back. "I like him."

I wanted to curse for bringing her into his shit storm, but I couldn't go there yet, not until we were safe. Finally, the fourth door opened, and I turned back to see her like stone, barely blinking, the gun gripped tightly, waiting for the worst to happen.

"Hey," I whispered, "it's open." Slowly, I removed the gun from her hand and tugged on her arm to guide her inside.

She paced the tiny room while I found a lighter and lit a few candles that hung low on the wall. It gave just enough light to show what we were next to. A single tomb with a flat surface sat in the center of the room that held a single thick paned window. That was it.

Removing the cloak and my jacket, I used the sleeves of my jacket to tie the doors shut the best I could. I couldn't tell if she was disturbed by being in a crypt, or if the gunshot in the alleyway was too close. I draped my cloak over the single tomb in an effort to camouflage it a bit.

I heard footsteps and placed a finger to my lips while I leaned against the wall and carefully peered out the murky window.

Sienna covered her mouth and pressed against me, and I could feel her trembling against my back.

I spotted him as he stepped out of the shadow of a tombstone. Raindrops started to fall, making it more difficult to see him through the tiny window. He lifted a cell phone to his ear as he scanned the backs of the crypts, then he slipped behind one of them and disappeared from view. I pulled back from the window.

"Is he gone?" she whispered then jumped when a door creaked a few crypts down.

"Stay down." I motioned for her to get her body low beside the tomb, and in three strides I had a grip on my coat, tightening the fabric around my fist as much as I could. I hoped like hell the knot I made plus my own strength would hold against any attempt to open the door.

The door next to the crypt we were in creaked loudly, and a moment later I felt a hard tug and held tightly to the fabric of my jacket as it strained against the pressure.

"They're all locked," he yelled at someone nearby, or maybe he was on the phone. All I cared about was the fact that he thought we weren't there. "All right, heading there now."

Footsteps raced off and were soon drowned out by the sound of heavy rain as it played loudly inside the concrete box we were in. I slowly released my hold and let the knotted sleeve slip out of my fingers.

"Elio?" Sienna whispered from behind me, and I moved close to her.

"Yes." I swallowed back my desire to confess everything to her as I realized just how too close for comfort the past hour had been. I grasped the top of her arms tightly as her wild eyes found mine.

"I—" She stopped then flung herself at me, kissing me passionately.

Years ago, something terrible had happened to her at the house, and I remembered how she had raced to my place in the middle of the night to fling herself into my arms. My mind immediately went back to the crazy, wild sex we had that night on the balcony. I knew she needed it, as it was her way of letting me ground her, and I had no problem a decade later doing the same for her now.

"Hey." I ripped myself away from her and held her head between my hands. I looked past those hungry eyes and saw her vulnerability and the pain that smothered her heart, and I knew it was all because of me. Leaning down, I brushed my lips across those trembling ones and felt my own heart pound along with hers. "I know it's way too late but," I felt again the pounding of my ribcage, "I'm so sorry, Sienna."

She blinked back her tears and looked away for a moment, and when her gaze returned, I saw my words had hit home. I gave her a moment then felt her press a little harder against me, giving me permission to continue.

I reached down and hooked my arm under her knee,

hiking her leg to rest on my hip. The slit in her dress made everything easier. Running my hand down her bare thigh to her smooth curves nearly made me lose my mind. I used her hips to turn her away from me then kissed her neck from behind. One hand gently slid across her collarbone and up her neck to her chin, turning her to look at me, while the other fingered the bow that kept the front of her dress up. Feeling confident that we were alone for the night, I let my guard down a bit.

"Do you still love this?" I licked her bottom lip. "And this?" I eased her along and tried to be gentle. She began to breathe hard and urged me to move faster. "Oh, so, you want things the way they used to be, do you?" I referred to our old style of making love. She nodded, and I grinned and allowed myself to relax and take her the way we both wanted.

The bow fell away, and the thin ties loosened, falling down her shoulders to expose her bare, plump breasts.

I swirled my tongue around her neck as I licked her favorite spots.

She moaned and used her backside to grind into my erection. I dragged my fingers down her spine and pushed her dress down to her ankles, slipping between her cheeks and massaging her swollen bud, coating my finger in her arousal. With my other hand, I freed myself from my pants and let it hit the top of her ass.

Her back bowed and her head fell onto my shoulder as she let out a hard puff of air. She was just as hungry for me as I was for her.

"Wait." I took the horrible piece of latex from the

package and quickly rolled it on, hating that I had to place even that thin barrier between us. "Lean forward, Sienna."

I eased her back over the cloak that covered the tomb, lined up, and gently fed myself into her. She shook beneath my fingers as they skirted up her back, into her hair, and grabbed a fistful.

"Home," I whispered without thought.

Leisurely, I pulled out and dragged my erection over her swollen bud, giving it the much-needed attention it deserved. She was dripping with excitement, and I could barely see straight. For years, I had dreamt of being back inside the only woman who made me crazy. The only one I could let go with and get lost in. So many delicious memories washed over me as I remembered the first time we had ever had sex and how I was so careful not to hurt her, not to push her too far, but it had been a struggle. It hadn't taken her long to show me how she liked it. Who knew she liked it rough but tender all at once? It was all about trust, and even though I knew her heart didn't have any for me now…her body did. That was why, right here, right now, she needed me.

I pulled her back and licked her neck up and around to her lips, needing to kiss her. Needing any part of me I could have inside her.

Just as I pulled out, she whirled around and jumped into my arms, wrapping her legs around me. Pivoting, I pushed her up against the wall and buried my face into her breasts and nipped at her erect nipples.

Her hands combed through my hair, tugging at the roots before I dove back deep inside. Our heavy breathing was all that could be heard, echoing against the concrete walls. The flames on the candles flickered as I ravished her. Her high heels dug into my back as she grew closer to her release.

I wanted to change the angle, so I hooked my arms around her back and laid her onto the tomb, grabbed her ankles, and forced them over my shoulders. With both arms wrapped around her legs, I plunged in and out, not wanting the moment to end. Again, her back bowed and her neck arched as her nails clawed at the cement. She was perfect, stunning, everything I remembered her to be.

"Goddamn, I missed you." I couldn't get enough.

"More," she begged, but I stilled. I wanted her with me mentally. I needed more than her body. I needed her mind.

"Look at me first."

She hesitated but looked me straight in the eye, and I gave a slow nod and smiled as I picked up speed. I wanted to time my release to collide with hers. The sounds of our skin, our lungs both fighting for more oxygen, and the sexy moans that escaped from both of us was too much.

I released her legs and dove into her neck as we both let go and gave in.

She wrapped herself around me like an anchor as she bucked and screamed her way through her orgasm. The power of my own was almost too much for my knees. I pushed in deeper, leaning all my weight into her pelvis, wanting—no, needing—to get deeper. I didn't remember coming down, but somehow, I did.

Chapter
TWENTY-FIVE

A constant dripping sound drew me from a dead sleep. I blinked the fog away and tried to process where I was.

Holy shit!

I shot straight up and looked around the crypt.

"Elio," I whispered, terrified he had left again.

"I'm here." I turned to find him in the corner of the room knees up arms resting on top. His shirt was partially open, and his pants and shoes were back on. "Vinni will be here in ten."

"What time is it?"

"Just after three a.m." He glanced at his watch to be sure.

I nodded and wrapped the cloak around me tighter as I reached for my dress.

"Are you going to tell me who we're running from?" I turned away from him as I shrugged on my dress, but when I reached for the strings, I felt his hands take over.

"This time, Stefano Coppola," he replied as he tied the bow.

I whirled around and held up my hands. "As in the Coppola syndicate from Rome?" I had once chased a story about a young artist that led me to the Coppola family. Only when Georgio got wind of the direction I was going in, he shut it down with zero explanation. By the look on his face, I knew not to question him, and I let it go. I barely found anything on them.

"That's the one." He held my gaze.

"Why? Why would he be after you?"

He licked his lips and turned to gather up the cloaks, and a moment later he pulled his phone out when it lit up his pocket.

"Yeah?" he offered as a greeting and listened. "All right." He hung up as he rubbed his tired eyes. He handed me one of the cloaks. "Put this on."

"Elio." I dropped my tone and put my hands on my hips, annoyed that he wouldn't answer me. He tugged the knot from the sleeves of his coat and released it from the door handles then shrugged it on, the wrinkles a stark reminder of what we had been through.

"Look, Sienna, I'm sorry that you're tangled up in this mess—"

"Don't do that," I warned. "Jesus, we just had sex,

Elio."

"Yes, we did, in a mausoleum." He chuckled darkly. "Never done that before."

"Fine, avoid the topic, then." I wrapped the cloak around me and opened the door to a downpour of rain.

"Sienna," he called after me, but I didn't care. I had opened myself up to him, and now he was holding out on me. I would not be played, and I would not be kept in the dark anymore.

I moved quickly between the tombstones while the rain soaked me to the bone. My breath puffed out mist as I went, and even more mist swirled around my feet, making it hard to see the dips in the ground.

"Hey." He hooked my arm as he caught up with me. He tugged so hard I had to turn to him, and I glared up at him in fury. "I want to share everything with you, but—"

"Then do it!"

"What if you can't handle it!" he shouted, sending rain drops spraying. "What if you can't love me after knowing? What if you lea—"

"Leave you?" I shouted back in his face while tears burst through the dam. "Well, I guess that's a risk you're just going to have take, Elio."

Headlights flashed and lit the stones next to us, proving just how hard it was raining.

"Why is Stefano after you?"

"Because now I'm after him." His chest heaved as he looked around us.

"Why?" I knew we were in danger standing out in the open, but if this was the only way to get some answers, I was willing to risk it.

"It's not clear what is happening yet, but my guess would be it's a fight for power. It always is."

"Over the oil?"

"Yes, and," he stumbled, "territory."

"Territory? What, is your family the mafia?" I dripped with sarcasm.

His gaze dropped to mine, and I felt my stomach roll. Suddenly, a flash of memories came roaring back, and everything clicked into place. The unexplained absences, the smell of gasoline, the secret whispering in the next room, and the list went on and on. How could I have been so blind? I knew they had their hands in some dark places, but never could I have imagined that I had fallen in love with a member of the Mafia.

"Can we leave now?" His jaw ticked his discomfort, and at this point I knew I couldn't blame him.

I turned on my heel, and we made our way toward Vinni.

"Good to see you, boss." Vinni addressed Elio as I shrugged off the drenched cloak and wrapped my frozen arms around my midsection.

"Vinni, heat," Elio ordered and removed his jacket, tossing it on top of the cloak. He angled the vent toward me as I slipped into a memory that insisted on taking over my head.

"You're muddy." I pushed him away when he came in for a kiss. "Elio!" I shrieked as he picked me up and slammed his lips to mine. When I came up for air, he was grinning like a fool. "You're in a good mood."

"I am."

"And why is that?"

"Two reasons. One, I finally beat someone at their own game, and two, which is the most important, I came home to you."

I had to bite my lip from grinning. He was always such a gentleman, making sure I knew I was the most important person in his life. He made me feel like I was worthy to be there in his home with all his love.

"And who did you defeat, my love?" I wrapped my arms around his neck, matching his excitement.

"A villain from the north."

"How mysterious." I kissed him again, feeding my habit, but when I pulled back, I found blood on my hand. "Oh, my God, Elio, you're bleeding!"

"My buddy hurt himself. It's nothing." He shook it off. "But I do need to check in with my father."

"Let me check you over."

"I promise, I'm fine."

"All right, then." I hesitated and stepped back to watch him jog inside. He appeared fine. Once he was out of sight, I looked down at my bloody hand as it glistened in the sun and tried to push aside my confusion.

"Sienna." Elio made me jump. "Sienna!"

"Yeah?"

"I know your head is probably elsewhere, but you will hear me on this one thing. It is very important. I know you probably learned a little about the mafia when you worked at the dockyard, particularly as we later took it over."

I blinked at him, trying to concentrate as the memory I had been caught in fizzled out.

"Please, Sienna, I feel you should know this." He turned to face me to show he was serious, and I forced myself to take in what he was saying. "Piero is the boss, I'm the underboss, Francesco is the *consigliere*. Each syndicate has the same hierarchy. Right now, that's all you really need to know, but the ranks are very important. Okay?"

"All right," I whispered as his words sank in.

"Let's get some rest, and we can talk later." I knew he could see my exhaustion, and his eyes softened.

"Yes, I think we really should." I felt incredibly drained.

"Your place, boss?" Vinni asked through the open partition.

"No, please." I shook my head. "I really need some dry clothes."

Elio cleared his throat but instructed Vinni to do what I asked.

"Boss, Donatello has been trying to reach you." I nodded to tell him it was fine to talk in front of me. "Another man has been found."

Elio cursed and didn't say another word after that.

We remained quiet for the rest of the ride. I needed time to process everything, and I was sure he was doing the same. He reached over and took my hand. I tried to pull it free, but his grip tightened. He was a dominating man, but he was still Elio.

When I stepped out of the car, my grip on Elio's hand

tightened as I noticed the folded note stuck to Mariano's front door. Elio stepped up and tugged it off and handed it to me. I opened the folded paper and skimmed the words.

I'll be out for the night. I hope you remember where I told you I keep the key. – Mariano

"Would you like to spend the night at my parents' place?" Elio's voice had an edge to it.

"No." I shook my head and held up the note. "I will have the place to myself. That's good, really, but thanks."

He cleared his throat and nodded once. "I'll call you tomorrow."

With a turn, I disappeared into the dark house and hurried to my room where I lost no time getting myself into bed, too tired to even shower. I fell into a restless sleep.

TWENTY-SIX

Sienna

Still tired after last night's events, I felt like a robot as I moved around the kitchen, making coffee and burning my third slice of bread.

"Morning." Mariano came in and settled himself at the bar top in front of me.

"Hey." I couldn't look at him, feeling strange about being in his house after having such an intimate night with Elio.

"How was last night?"

"Good," slipped off the tip of my tongue as I forced my eyes to look at him. "You?"

"Eventful." He grinned, and I assumed he didn't know when I actually got home. "I have something for you."

"Oh?" I went to pour my coffee, only to have him slide his cup under the flow, then when my toast popped, he pulled the cream from my hand.

He handed me a piece of paper that had a time written on it. Ten a.m.

"Okay…"

"Wear something nice and maybe show a little." He pointed at my breasts as he hopped off the stool. "Thighs, too," he called over his shoulder as he left for his office.

"Why? Where are we going?"

"To get your story," I heard as the door shut.

"Oh." I toyed with the small piece of paper and felt an excited surge rush through me as I grabbed my coffee and headed to get ready.

When I came down an hour later, Mariano flicked his keys around his finger as his eyes raked down my front. "Wow. You look really good." He brushed down the edge of my dress to my cleavage just the way Elio did. I stepped out of his touch as he lifted my chain to expose the pendants. "Do you ever wear anything else?"

"No."

"Well." He pulled out a thin box and opened it to reveal a gold chain with a large heart at the end. I cringed, hating any heart-shaped jewelry.

"Mariano." I hesitated, unsure if I could go even a few hours without my necklace. "Do you remember our conversation at the restaurant?"

"Yes, but I'm not asking you to wear it every day, but it would be nice if you would wear it at least for today."

"It just feels strange…" I tried to quickly come up with an excuse, but before I could, his hands were on the clasp, removing a piece of me and replacing it with a cold, heavy steel heart.

"Perfect." He smiled wide, and I suddenly felt as if I had been claimed by him. "Come on, we can't be late." He took my arm and pulled me out the door, but not before I took one last look at my necklace on the table.

A marble waiting room was not exactly where I imagined such a meeting would take place. A juvenile part of me expected the *Finder* to only want to meet in a dark garage or maybe a rundown motel. A two-story building that sat in the middle of the city with frosted glass doors, cucumber water, and expensive artwork simply didn't fit. I was glad about my outfit and used the reflection of the glass to make sure everything looked just right. The white dress with purple buttons hugged my body, and my matching purple heels and handbag paired nicely. The only thing that looked off was the heavy, inch-long heart that sat above the crease between my breasts.

"Sienna." Mariano patted the spot next to where he was sitting, but I shook my head and stayed where I was, not wanting to be so close. "Are you ready?"

"I am."

"Good, because here he comes."

A short, bald man dressed in an expensive suit moved toward us. He glanced over at me with a warm smile that widened further when he spotted Mariano.

"You must be Sienna." He came froward and offered a handshake. I slipped into work mode and introduced myself and complemented him on the artwork I had seen as we entered the building, being sure to mention the Teresa Cox original. It showed my attention to detail and that I wasn't afraid to show off my knowledge.

"You know your artists. I do love her paintings." He seemed impressed. "Are you a fan?" He motioned for me to follow him.

"Of some, but I enjoy Lee Herring more."

"I see." He pulled out a chair for me, and I took it as Mariano took one in the corner, his phone glued to his face. "I have to be honest with you, Sienna, I have never done an interview like this before, so I will tread very carefully."

"And like Mariano promised, I will keep my word and will not use your name, or anything that will connect you to this article. You are simply 'The Finder' to me, and that's it. I'm looking more for how you got wrapped up with the Santoro brothers and what it was like working for them."

And like most interviews, if more comes out of his mouth, then fantastic.

"Very well." He glanced at Mariano for a moment then moved his attention back to me. "It was roughly ten years ago. I was hired by the Coppola family to find the person who killed one of their cousins. As you might know, they have a history of unexplained disappearances."

I sat forward in my chair and began to scribble on

my notepad. He sure had started out with a bang.

"The cousin was connected to a mass murder that happened the year before, and the Coppolas suspected the northern syndicate had done it." I shifted in my seat, wondering if he meant Elio's family. "They wanted to know who they needed to go to war with. I started to dig, and—"

"How? Can you tell me where you even start such a process?"

"I start with the murder and work my way backward. First with the bodies, bodies don't lie, unlike the living, and how I see them and where tells me a lot. Then I find out where they were that day, the day before that, and so on and so on. Plus, people tend to be chatty when beer is involved."

"Okay." I urged him on with a quick look.

"It took me about three days to connect all the dots, and it brought me to a local pub in Vasto. I sat down and had a drink to check the place out. I had come up with a theory on who I might be looking for, and rumor had it he hung out there from time to time. Two men soon drew my attention when I realized they were planning something. They spoke in code. Being the man I am," he sat back, wanting me to appreciate his skill, so I granted him a nod and an encouraging smile, "I started to decode what they were saying. I saw a flaw in one of their ideas and pointed it out. A black eye and four drinks later, we got talking, and by the end of the night I was hired to help them plan the takedown of the Rosario family."

"Wait?" I held up a hand, trying to follow. "What

about the Coppola family?"

"I found out who killed their cousin," he shrugged, "and also who was behind the mass murders the year before."

"Did you turn that information over to them?"

"No." He ran a finger along his chin without a shred of remorse. "Instead, I joined forces with the killers." He laughed at that.

"So, it *was* the Santoro brothers who killed the cousin and did the mass murders a year before?" I eyed him as though amazed.

He smirked through another shrug and nodded. "They made me a better offer, and to be frank, the Coppola family are stupidly ruthless and are getting worse as time goes on."

Every one of them is ruthless, in my opinion.

"Was there any blowback from the Coppola family? I can't imagine they would just let you off the hook."

"A little, but part of the deal was that the brothers would protect me and have ever since. Plus, at that point, the Coppola family suddenly went quiet. Their attention moved off me and focused elsewhere."

"Lucky for you."

"Yeah," he nodded in agreement, "it made things easier."

"What do you think happened?"

"There was a rumor that someone from their family had been spotted that they thought was dead, but nothing really came of it. Whatever it was, I never heard. They kept a tight lid on it within their family."

"I see." I scribbled more notes down and drew a quick timeline while more questions bounced around my mind. "So," I held my hands up with my pen balanced between two fingers and my thumb. "So just to clarify, you've now joined forces with the Santoro brothers, and *their* focus is the Rosario family. Not the Coppola family." I tried to move the story forward.

"Correct."

"Did the Rosario family do anything to you?"

"Personally? No."

"Then why help kill innocent people?"

"There's no such thing as innocent people. Everyone has crimes, guilt, skeletons in their closets. The Rosarios were ruthless, showed no mercy to those that probably deserved some. They did terrible things to good people and bad. That's life."

I couldn't help but wonder what Elio's family was considered. Were the Capri family as ruthless, or were they as bad as the Rosarios and Coppolas? Did they kill innocent people to get what they wanted, too?

"Let me explain my involvement with the brothers, as I can only imagine what's running through your head right now."

"Please." I welcomed any more information he could give me to make sense of all this.

"It's not about the power or revenge for me, Sienna. It's the thrill of the game. I got a certain amount of time to find a person. If I didn't come through, the brothers would find someone else who could. I was replaceable, and that meant I was also disposable."

"So, you couldn't just walk away from them?"

"No."

"Because you knew too much?"

"Because of how things work, how you are accepted in."

"Meaning?"

His forehead rested on his hand, and his finger tapped his temple as he thought.

"I can't divulge that."

"Okay." I shook my head, understanding I was pressing my luck, and tried another tact. "Can you tell me anything about the brothers? What they were like?"

"Ah, you ladies always want the personal stuff." He chuckled. "Well, let's see. Tieri is the charming one, takes on any lady who looks his way. He would be the fun one, if you will, while Zazzero is more the brooding type, which, of course, all the ladies love." His smile made me squirm.

"Anything else?" I wanted him off this subject. I didn't like where it might go.

As he leaned back in, the leather on his chair sounded like snow being crunched under a boot. I didn't interrupt him with another question, and a few quiet seconds ticked by.

"No matter what, they won't kill woman or children."

"Killers with a conscience?" I snickered. "How nice."

"We all have a conscience, Sienna, it just lives in people in different ways." He tapped his chest as he said it, almost as though he wanted me to see he had one, too.

I folded the corner of the page with a lingering question I debated asking.

"I couldn't help but notice that you speak in present tense about the brothers." I noticed his eyes shifted to Mariano's. "Would that mean they are still alive, that you're still in contact with them?"

"And if I was?" he challenged.

"Then my story just got a whole lot more interesting."

"Mm." He rocked his chair as he studied my face. The buzz of his intercom had me leaning back and taking a breath for the first time since I arrived in his office.

"You have someone here who wants to speak with you." A voice came through the tinny speakers.

"Be right there." He checked his watch. "Would you excuse me for a moment?"

"Of course." I stood as he did to be polite, and when we were alone, I beamed at Mariano.

"So, do you think you have a story here?" He put his phone in his pocket as he spoke.

"Yes, for sure. How The Finder works and how he met and started working with the Santoro bothers is huge. It's more than anyone else has ever gotten."

"Good, but I think you'll like the next part even more." Just as I was processing his words, the door opened, and in walked The Finder and a very tall man with a very charming smile.

Wait...

"You must be Sienna." He offered his hand, and I nearly blanked on how to move. "You might know me as Tieri."

I swallowed back my fear and somehow shifted my gaze over to Mariano, who simply smiled a smug smile that didn't at all mirror my inner terror. It was one thing to research and meet informants; it was a whole different matter to find yourself in the presence of a known assassin.

"H-hi," I stumbled and didn't care.

"I take it you weren't aware I was to attend this meeting?"

"No, I was not." My voice had a bite to it. "Forgive my manners." My heart was in my throat, and my stomach had left me high and dry.

"No need." He waved me to sit and sat on the corner of the desk, casual as could be, while I sat like a stone, knees pressed hard together and my heart on ultra-speed. "So, Mariano tells me you're a journalist."

"I-I am."

"And that you're writing a story on my brother and me."

"Well, yes and no." I stumbled again. "Yes, I am, but you weren't necessarily my main focus. I was going to focus more on The Finder, as I had no idea you were even still alive."

"I can assure you we are very much alive," he chuckled, "but of course Tieri is merely a stage name, if you will. He has died at least four times now." He laughed again like it was some inside joke. "Also, Zazzero isn't my brother. That was merely to throw the hunters off the scent. I'll answer a question if you have one."

I wasn't sure if I was happy about this at all. I wanted

to murder Mariano for not giving me at least a heads up and for not giving me a chance to say "no way" to meeting a stone-cold murderer.

"Um." I tucked my hair behind my ear, and I knew he saw how shaky I was. "Why?" popped out of my mouth, and my eyes bugged out at how blunt it must have sounded.

"Why what?"

I was in too deep now to backpedal.

"Why did you do it? Kill all those people?"

"*Why* isn't the question you should be asking me."

"I'm the journalist." I shrugged trying to remain calm. "I don't see why that wouldn't be a standard question."

He cleared his throat as he rubbed the button on his jacket.

"Because the why isn't something you could comprehend."

"Try me," I shot back, and I heard Mariano chuckle from behind me. If I could nut punch him, I would.

"In order for you to understand, you need to be vetted. In order for you to be vetted, I would need to take you somewhere and show you some things." He stood and towered over me. "And that could result in a whole new bloodbath." He chuckled.

I thought I might faint with how close he got to me, and I swore I could smell blood on his breath.

"However, Sienna," he leaned closer, and I pulled back, "if you want the *why* answers without the vetting, Zazzero would be the one to answer that." He tucked a small piece of paper inside my notebook.

"Then why did you come and not him?"

Seriously, was I asking to be killed? *Shut the hell up, Sienna!*

"For the same reason you wanted to meet me."

"I didn't know I was meeting you," I reiterated with a sharp tone.

"This is true." He chuckled again. "I guess I should say, it was curiosity."

"Curiosity? I still don't understand." I let my mouth go. "Who am I but a small journalist? A girl with a past not worth remembering. I fail to see the level of curiosity."

He tilted his head as he thought. "It was a pleasure to meet you, Sienna." He seemed to drink me in for a moment longer than was necessary, then he stood and whisked away, disappearing out the door.

I quickly gathered my things, gave somewhat of a goodbye to The Finder, then I rushed outside. I needed to get the hell away from the building.

"Hey!" Mariano came rushing up behind me. "What's wrong?"

"What's wrong!" I shouted, and a man stopped to stare at us. "You set up a meeting with one of the Santoro brothers! Holy shit, do you know how scary that was? How incredibly bad that could have gone and still could?"

"Nothing would have happened to you, Sienna." He caught my arm as I reached for the car door. "I know them, and they won't hurt you."

"How, Mariano? How could you possibly know

that?"

"Okay." He pulled out the paper Tieri had given me and held it up. "I'll prove it."

"I'm not going to meet Zazzero."

"It's not an address, it's a phone number, and I want you to trust me. So, trust me."

"Trust is earned, Mariano." I snatched the number from his fingers in fear he'd make the call anyway. "It's not something you can force on someone. What I want right now is to go home."

His lips pressed together hard, and I could see his anger, but at the same time, I knew he was also upset.

"Fine." He motioned for me to get in the car, and he didn't speak as we drove in the direction of his home.

As we left the city limits, he tried to cover my hand with his. It wasn't a smooth or tender moment. It was one of a man who knew he had screwed up and was now nervous of where my head was.

I immediately pulled away and wrapped my arms around my stomach in hopes it would calm the butterflies that were in a fight to find a way out. My hands still shook. It wasn't only fear, but anger and disbelief at the unbelievable carelessness of his actions that had me in such a state. I wondered if he truly understood the dangerous position he had put me in.

Snap! Snap! Snap! went his annoying elastic band.

"I'm sorry," he called after me as I opened the car door and raced inside his house. Tires squealed as he peeled off back down the driveway.

It took me about twenty minutes to gather all my

belongings and put in a call to Elio's mother. Andrea was always my first thought when I needed someone; sadly, Elio used to be.

"Hi, honey, are you okay?"

"No, I'm not. Not really. Andrea, would it be all right if I spent the night with you and Piero? I'm at Mariano's."

"Of course, I'll send Vinni right down to get you."

"Thank you. I'll be ready."

Within minutes, I was standing in the Capris entryway, feeling like a teen again waiting for Elio to come downstairs.

Andrea took one look at my face and wrapped me up in a hug and rubbed my back.

"Do you want to tell me what happened?"

"I just…" I sniffed. I wanted to share everything with her, but what would that mean? The family had spent years keeping their secrets from me, and if I told them what Mariano had done, would they freak out and make me leave? "I just need a break from Mariano."

"Music to my ears, sweetheart." She brushed a stray hair off my face. "I don't like the thought of you two together alone in his house."

"You are a bit biased." I tried to smile.

"I am." She nodded with her arm wrapped around my shoulders. "Come, let's get you something to eat."

When I lifted a glass of water to my lips, my traitorous hands gave away my nervousness. Andrea's eyebrow arched as she looked into my eyes. There was a time when the shakes were second nature to me. The urge to crawl out of my skin with fear would take over and paralyze me. My friendship with Wyatt over the years had calmed my nerves, and I was much more settled. That was until today.

"Sienna," she sat down and leaned into me, "if something happened, you know you can talk to me, right?"

I nodded, not wanting to lie to her but still not ready to tell the truth of what had happened and where I had been, and—even worse—who I had been with.

The door opened, and I felt Andrea take a deep breath of relief. I knew she must have texted Piero when Dante was dishing up our meals.

"Sienna, did he hurt you?" Her voice broke my thoughts.

"Did who hurt you?" Elio's commanding voice made me yelp.

"Jesus, Elio," I jumped, "you scared me."

"Who hurt you?" he asked again, his voice sharp but much lower in tone.

"Calm down, son." Andrea held up her hands. "She just needed a break from Mariano tonight."

Elio came around to sit in the chair next to me, turning my legs so I'd face him. The look on his face told me now wasn't the time to lie, but it also told me he was on edge, ready for a fight.

"Mama, would you please give us a moment?"

"Of course. I'll be right over there." She squeezed my hand and shot her son a warning to be nice. I missed that look, but it struck me as funny because Elio would never hurt me. Ever.

"*Bella*," he cleared his throat, "tell me what happened."

"No. I can't."

"Why not?"

"Because I can tell your mind isn't in a good place, so no matter what I say, you'll fly off the handle, and we don't need that tonight."

"Sienna," he warned.

"Elio." I mimicked his tone and rubbed the side of my head, feeling worn out.

"Just tell me if he hurt you."

"He didn't hurt me."

"Then," he pressed his hands against my knees, "what happened?"

"He just…" I treaded carefully. "He put me in a position I didn't like. I got nervous, so I packed my bags and left."

"Nervous about what?"

"Elio, please." I closed my eyes, just needing a moment, and I could tell he was growing frustrated, so I changed focus. "What's wrong with you tonight? You seem very edgy yourself."

His dark eyes moved to mine, and I saw something flicker across his face.

"Just a rough night."

"I hear you."

"You could share yours…" His eyes bored into mine.

"So could you."

He nodded. He knew neither of us was going to budge.

"You'll stay here tonight, and we'll figure out the rest tomorrow."

"I think I'm going to go home tomorrow," I whispered, and he shot me a confused look, but before he could speak, I put up my hand to stop him. "I got my story. I just need to write it and turn it in. This isn't my life, Elio, it's yours."

"I want you in it." His voice was soft and raw.

"Elio." I lowered my head, feeling the pain that came along with that topic, and tried to deflect the emotion. "I wouldn't even be here if it wasn't for Mariano. It was a freak accident that I'm here at all."

"So?"

"So, I don't fit here."

"Why are you pushing me away?" He stood and ran a hand through his hair. "Is this because of what I told you at the cemetery?"

"No." I stood on shaky legs and held on to the side of the chair. "That is a whole other can of dark that I need to process. I just need to go home, regroup, and get my head on straight. Between the article, Mariano, and feelings I have spent a decade trying to bury, I think I just need a few days to breathe."

"I can't lose you again, Sienna. I won't."

"Elio…" I stopped when I saw his eyes narrow in on something.

"What the hell is that?" He lifted the heart-shaped pendant off my chest and studied it, his face unreadable.

Dammit.

"It's nothing."

"Nothing isn't heart-shaped jewelry."

"I think he just wanted me to wear it when I met…" I trailed off and bit down on my lip, upset I almost misspoke.

"Met who?"

"It's nothing, Elio. Let it go."

"It's ugly."

"Yes, well." I reached for my dishes and started to walk into the kitchen. "It's not me, but then, I didn't buy it."

"But you are wearing it?" He was right on my heels.

"Yes." I rolled my eyes at Dante, who glanced my way when I reached for the dish soap.

"Why?"

"It was a gift, and I felt bad saying no."

"Why a necklace?"

Drying my hands, I turned around and reached into his pocket and pulled out his phone and handed it to him. "He's your best friend. Why don't you ask him?"

"You drive me crazy," he gritted through his teeth.

"Pot, kettle, black." I spoke each word carefully to be sure he got my point that this was how we used to be. We would banter, we would fight, and we would make mad, passionate love afterward. Whose fault was it that we no longer had that?

I quickly turned around and went back to cleaning my dishes.

"Dante," Elio said quietly, and seconds later the

room was quiet, and I knew we were alone. He came up behind me, pressing his strong chest into my back and locking his arms on either side of me. The smell of him made my knees wobble and my stomach roll up into a tight coil.

"Of all things he could have gotten you," he whispered against the back of my neck, raising goosebumps to the surface. "Of all things to remove." His hands on the counter flexed into fists. "He chose that."

"Elio—"

"Where is it now?"

Damn. I closed my eyes, remembering where it was and how I was in such a hurry to leave that I forgot it.

"At his place."

I barely felt him push away, and when I turned around, I found the kitchen empty.

Needing some time alone, I finished cleaning up and headed for the guest room to be sure I had privacy.

I pulled out my phone and called Wyatt, hoping he'd be up for a chat.

"Hey," his soft voice flowed across the line and made me feel like I was home again. "How are you?"

"Alive," I chuckled, "but I'm getting homesick."

"Homesick or Wyatt-sick."

"Wyatt-sick."

"Well, as much as I love to hear that, I've decided not to come home for a bit. Georgio gave me some bullshit article that links here in New York. As much as I appreciated where he was coming from, it's a joke. The upside is I get to spend a little more time here, though."

"I'm jealous."

"Jealous?" He laughed. "Two men are after you. What could you possibly be jealous of?"

I fumbled with the blanket and pulled it over my bare legs then pushed the pillow further behind my back, getting comfy. Really, I was just stalling for time.

"Come on Si, give it." His tone changed, as he sensed something was off.

"Mariano just pulled a dirty card and put me in a dangerous situation. He didn't see any harm in what happened, and given what I now know about Elio's family, I'm not sure if I should be mad or not."

"Dumb it down for me."

"Let's just say they are not *just* in the oil business."

"I kind of wondered."

"You know how when you do bad things all the time, it doesn't seem bad anymore?"

"Yeah." His voice rose, and I knew he was concerned.

"I think that's what happened with Mariano."

"Bad things are bad things, Sienna. If he can't see that, maybe he's not safe to be around?"

"Yeah." I hated that I understood the situation from both sides.

His phone made a noise as if it shifted against something. "What did Elio say?"

"He doesn't know." I felt funny saying it out loud, which confirmed I should have told him.

"Why not?"

"I don't know. I guess I'm just trying to navigate all the new things I'm learning since I arrived here. It's a mind trip, to say the least."

"That's because this isn't just an article for you anymore. This involves your past and your heart."

"I agree with that one."

"What did Mariano do, exactly?"

I opened my mouth to tell him then wondered if I should. Wyatt would worry even more than Elio would, and I wasn't sure I was ready for another watchdog. I hated to lie, though.

"You know how he helped me get that new article? The one to do with the Santoro brothers?"

"I do, and may I say, lucky you."

"Mariano knew their finder, the guy who helps locate their next hit. And, well, with that interview came a surprise." I swallowed to try to relax my throat.

"I'm literally on pins and needles here. Spill it."

"Let's just say I got to meet one of the devils, face to face."

The line went quiet, and I had to check the screen to see if we were still connected.

"Wyatt?"

"I'm here. I'm just processing that and trying not to pee myself. Which one?"

"Tieri Santoro, and yeah, try not to do that while standing three feet away from him."

"That's fucking terrifying and yet intriguing, and you have the chance to wrap all of that up into one magnificent story."

"Little bit, yeah."

"Well?"

"I handled it and did my job, but I hated Mariano for not seeing how terrifying and dangerous it was."

"What about the other brother? Did either mention him?"

"No, but I did get his number."

"Have you called it yet?"

"And say what?" I laughed and rubbed my suddenly cold hands. "'Hi there. I got your number from your brother,' *who isn't his brother, by the way,* 'and wanted to do an interview.' That would be the quickest phone call ever."

"Yes. But, girl, think of the article."

"Article." I gripped the phone tightly. "Or my life." I held the other hand in the air as I weighed my options. "Not sure here, Wyatt."

"If Tieri gave you his brother's number, it must mean it's fine to call. I really think you should, and here's the thing, you're staying seconds away from Elio's house and his parents. Most likely the safest place to be if you want to risk it."

Oh, he has no idea...

"True." He had a point, and I dwelled over it in silence as he did the same. I just wasn't sure if I should tell Elio. It would be an easy bet that he wouldn't let me if I did.

"You know, that ticket to New York you had from last winter is still valid for another few months. Just saying."

I knew he was right. I did need a break, and I did have to use that ticket soon or it would expire. My work had, as usual, gotten in the way of the trip back then, and I never made it to his sister's for Christmas. I would consider it.

"Just go for it and make the call and let me know how it goes. It's not like you to hesitate on something like this. You'll always wonder if the article could have been so much more if you'd done it."

"All right." I pulled the piece of paper from the book on the nightstand. "I'll call you back."

It was around ten that I heard a car door open and the sound of Elio's voice. I was still debating whether to hit send on the number. I knew Wyatt was right. I never would have hesitated a year ago, but then, he didn't know all the details of what was happening here either. I moved to the balcony and watched Elio. He was on the phone with someone. He leaned against the car beside Vinni, who had his own phone to his ear. Both looked relaxed, their voices level. I saw Elio hold up his hand as he talked to inspect his knuckles, then he flexed his fingers.

I don't want to know.

With a deep breath, I called the number, not caring it was way past business hours. I guessed he didn't have any, anyway.

As the call connected and started to ring. I saw Elio push off the car and pull out a different phone. The gold case caught the porch light.

I watched like a train wreck, not believing what I was seeing.

"Zazzero." His voice made my blood run cold, and

my heart froze on the spot. "Hello?" He held the phone close to look at the screen again.

I quicky hung up and pressed my back into the wall, keeping my hand over my mouth in fear I would out myself.

So many things raced through my mind, including the endless pictures of the bloodshed caused by the Santoro brothers. Articles I had read flipped through my brain like a deck of cards. Small things popped out, like how the press always wondered if they were real brothers or not, and faces of those killed filled my mind with horror. I knew there was hardly any proof of anything, but there were a lot of accusations. Only bits and pieces that were fed to the press gave any hint of who was behind it.

I slumped to the floor, unsure how to process it all, and without even really thinking, I pulled up the airline and re-booked myself that ticket to New York.

Sienna: Sent you my info. See you tomorrow.
Wyatt: Oh, no. All right, see you soon.

My body felt like stone as I sat on the side of the bed and watched the numbers count up each hour. When it finally read five a.m., I grabbed the handle of my suitcase and quietly headed downstairs. I had texted Vinni twenty minutes ago with a bullshit story about work, and he was waiting in the kitchen, finishing off a pastry.

"Morning," he murmured as he took my things and headed outside.

I was glad he wasn't talkative today. I wasn't in the mood and just wanted to get the hell out of there so I could breathe again.

"Sienna." Dante came up holding up a to-go bag. "Something for the road."

"Thank you. How sweet of you." I gave him a hug. "I'll see you soon," I lied. Would I? I really had no idea.

"Let me walk you out." He tossed his dish towel aside, and as we passed by the entryway table, I spotted my gold bracelet I had misplaced a while ago.

"Oh, my bracelet." I slipped it on, happy that it had turned up. It was a favorite of mine.

"Pretty." He smiled politely as he leaned forward and opened the car door for me. I waved at him through the window as we drove away, and I wondered when I would see him again.

"Music, Sienna?" Vinni asked, and I shook my head with a smile. He nodded in the mirror as I leaned my head back and thought about the journey ahead.

Two planes and a small layover later, I touched down on the JFK tarmac. Wyatt didn't say much as he scooped me up in a bear hug and pointed to an Uber waiting outside for us. A little small talk on the ride about what was going on at his sister's place soothed my achy head. I was glad we were such good friends. He totally got me. We'd always had an understanding about knowing when and where to discuss things. Once we arrived at his sister's place and we were out by the lake sipping cocktails, he cleared his throat, and I knew it was time to fill him in.

"Well?" He addressed the subject with an arched eyebrow, daring me to fib.

"I called." I used the straw to move the ice around

in the frosted glass.

"And?"

"And he picked up."

"Okay, we're making progress here." He dripped with sarcasm. "Now, did you take a breath or just hold it in?"

I shoved his shoulder, but when he tuned in to my stressed expression, he eased up.

"Sienna?"

"Elio picked up. Zazzero Santoro is Elio Capri."

He stopped drinking and blinked at me while he processed.

"Yeah." I nodded at his stunned expression. "That was my reaction, too. Although, add heartbreak, utter confusion, and a dash of pure terror, and that about sums up the moment."

"Wait, so you called, and—"

"Hung up."

"And then left with no explanation?"

"No, I told his cousin I had to go to New York for work."

"Oh, that makes it better. Send the hit man to my sister's place."

"Please, Wyatt, tell me what I was supposed to do?" I tossed up my free hand.

"No, you're right." He sighed and scratched his chin. "They wouldn't hurt you, anyway. He's completely in love with you."

"How do you know that? You've never even met him."

"It's guy-dar." He pointed to his forehead. "Like gay-dar but for straight people."

"The shit that comes out of your mouth."

"I know. I'm entertaining." He huffed with a shoulder shrug. "But really, how are you with all of this?"

"No clue." We went back to staring out over the water, watching a duck as it paddled about in the glossy lake. I wondered what my life would have been like if I had disappeared into the wind along with Elio and his family. Would I have been this messed up inside, or would I be at peace and happy with life? Like, truly happy with a heart full of warmth instead of frozen in a layer of frost like it was now.

"Are you looking forward to tonight?" Wyatt split a blade of grass with his nail and held it between his fingers.

"VIP access to one of the best whiskey rooms New York City has to offer?" I playfully flicked my hair over my shoulder. "I am, and I can't wait. I have the perfect dress to wear for it." I smiled over at my best friend. "I really do enjoy your friendship with Leo."

"Me too. He's a good friend." He matched my fun, but like the setting sun in front of us, it soon faded, and we were left wondering what was next. I could tell Wyatt was struggling with something, but I wasn't sure what.

"You okay?"

"Yeah," he answered too quickly.

"Yeah?"

"I just need a little more time before I share."

I struggled to my feet from the deep Adirondack

chair and offered him a hand to join me. "Whenever you're ready, you know I won't push."

"I know." He stretched as he stood and rested his arm around my shoulder, kissing the top of my head as we walked back up to the house. "So, what exactly are you wearing tonight?"

"Let's just say black lace." I grinned at him.

Elio

"Mariano!" I banged at his door, knocking until my knuckles ached. I had called him six times in the past five hours, and I was about ready to kick the damn door down.

I stepped back, cupped my hands around my mouth, and yelled. "Wake your drunk ass up!"

Nothing…

Just as I went for my keys, Vinni pulled up and hopped out of the car.

"Elio," he pointed to my car, "follow me."

"Not now, Vinni."

"Elio." He stood rigid, and his shoulders, like his voice, were stiff. "Please."

I let out a long, frustrated breath and headed for my car, following my cousin up the road and deep into the vineyard. If he wasn't family, I would have suspected something, but I knew better.

"What's going on?" I slammed my door and met him between the two cars.

"Here's what I know. After Sienna came to the house last night, Niccola followed Mariano to a party in the city. He got drunk, slept with a few girls, and started talking about this girl he's seeing and how he's itching to…" He glanced at me and decided not to finish the sentence. "Anyway, he's not home. He's still there."

"Then why bring me here? That isn't out of character for him." I knew there had to be more for him to want this degree of privacy for a talk.

"Correct, but what is out of character for him is to vet her into our lifestyle."

I studied him and pursed my lips, making sure I heard him correctly. "What?"

"I believe Mariano may have initiated your girl."

A wicked shiver tore through me, and I saw red.

"Explain."

"Dante said she saw the bracelet on the table, the one from the murder at the dockyard, and she said it was hers."

I stood very still as everything flickered in front of me. I couldn't get all the chips to lay into place.

"Impossible," I whispered but knew it could still be true. "She never said a thing."

"She hasn't said a lot of things." His comment

brought me back to him.

"Meaning?"

"She's still here. She didn't race home after she witnessed it, right?" I nodded and waited for him to continue. "Do you know what this new lead is she's working on for her article?"

"No."

"Well, it was something big and interesting enough for her boss to let her do it. Maybe we better find out just what it is. After all, the last one she worked on was a little too close to home."

"Shit." I slapped the roof of my car, frustrated that I had been more focused on *us* than what might have been happening behind closed doors. I ran a hand down my face, wanting to kill Mariano, but I knew his time would come once I knew exactly what was going on. "I need to talk to her."

"I'll book you a ticket."

I dropped my hand. "What?"

"She's in New York for work." When he saw my confusion, he went on. "I dropped her off at the airport early this morning, I thought you knew."

"No," I hissed. "Yet another thing she had failed to share with me. Wait. When did you find out about the bracelet?"

"Only an hour ago," he held up his hands, "or I would never have let her leave."

"I know." I gritted my teeth and tried to think straight.

"The woman who has caught the eye of the underboss

of the biggest syndicate, Elio, is quite a bargaining chip if she should fall into the wrong hands."

"I know!" I ran my hands through my hair and glared at him. "Why do you think she hasn't been in my life for the past decade?" I growled and felt as if a rug was suddenly pulled out from under me.

We both knew what it meant to the vultures that circled our lives. If one of us actually fell in love with someone, that person would become a target because they would be our greatest weakness.

Why couldn't she have stayed away? Lived a life free of this?

I wanted to kill someone with my bare hands. I jerked open my door and slid inside. "You and Niccola are coming with me. If what you say is true, someone could be heading her way now." I slammed the door and peeled out of the hidden cover of the trees.

As I packed my bag, I got word the plane was ready to go whenever I was.

"Mama." I raced inside the sitting room where she and my father were enjoying an afternoon drink.

"You look nice," Mama began but stopped when she caught wind of my mood. "What's wrong?"

"I have to go get Sienna." I knew I sounded angry, but it wasn't so much at Sienna as it was the entire situation.

"What happened?" My father slipped into business mode.

"I'll explain later, but if anyone is looking for me, Vinni, or Niccola, tell them we're out on the boat for the weekend. No one is to know we left Italy."

"Elio." Mama stood, and I could tell she was unhappy with my explanation.

"And," I held up my hand, "when Mariano decides to return home, I want him tailed. I need to know who he talks to."

"Son?" My father stood beside my mama, and I knew he needed to know something more.

"The bracelet, it was hers. She must have been the one who witnessed the murder. I think Mariano may have set her up to see the killing." I cleared my throat as my father made the connection to the dockyard murder. "I'm heading to New York. She apparently flew there today for work."

"Oh, no." Mama covered her mouth and looked up at my father, who had grown pale. He placed his hand on Mama's shoulder to quiet her.

"We will want to know everything when you both return."

"Of course. When I know something, you will too."

"You can save me a trip."

"Pardon?" I tried to catch up.

"I was supposed to go to New York next week to complete the deal with Jacob Raine. He's offering us the use of his docks, and we really need those new entry points." I cringed. I hated that snake. "He's better with you, anyway, so you will meet up with him, preferably tonight. I'll arrange it."

"And what about Sienna?" I was shocked he even suggested it.

"Vinni can locate her while you close the deal with Raine. Then you can talk to her. No one can know who she really is to you yet." He held up a hand when I began to speak. "We really need this deal and those docks." He closed his eyes for a moment and let out a long breath. "But, son, find her."

"Papa," I began to protest but hesitated when I looked at his closed face. I knew it was a huge deal, and we needed it in order to get more of our ships moving out of a second dockyard. Plus, he was offering us more protection, not that it wouldn't come with a price. "Fine," I cursed under my breath. "Text me the details." I left, feeling more wound up than I did before.

The flight was far too long for my agitated mind, but I somehow managed a few moments of shuteye on the way. New York City never changed. It was just how I left it six months ago, busy, loud, and full of life. Not at all like my small slice of heaven on our hill in Italy. It was a place I loved to visit when I was younger, and it still provided a getaway when life became too heavy. Now, it annoyed me, especially today.

I stepped out of the protection of the Cadillac Escalade. Careful not to get my Bontoni shoes wet from the random puddles on the street, I shifted back into the bubble our bodyguards formed around my cousins and me. Normally, I wouldn't arrive with such an obvious entourage, but I wasn't sure exactly what Jacob Raine had in store. He wasn't a man to be trusted.

I unlocked my phone to check the message I had received from my father.

Papa: 37 West 26th Street – 7 p.m. EST
Elio: I'll be there.

I rolled my wrist to read the time. It was 6:55 p.m.

My father and I often held business at The Flatiron Room, and we knew the owner well. He was good at making sure we weren't interrupted, and for that, we kept a running tab.

The place had an old-time feel but still carried a classic, modern vibe. It was often busy, but when we were in town, Maxon always made sure our table was free.

"Vinni." I waited for an update.

"Still digging." He held the phone away from his mouth as he spoke. "Her boss says her best friend has a lot of friends who work the nightlife here, and chances are they are out tonight."

I flexed my neck, trying to relieve the idea of her being out in a sea of people. Let alone who she was with.

"Keep me in the know."

"Will do, boss." He stepped through the door behind one of the bodyguards, and I followed.

The inside was long and narrow, with dim red lighting, a fully stocked whiskey bar to one side, and a stage that wrapped around the very back. Deep red curtains framed the stage like a Broadway production. A projector had the FR company logo as part of the backdrop in gold, and a jazz group played softly over the chatter. It was one of the many reasons I loved this place. The music wasn't over the top, just enough to keep private conversations private.

"Good evening, Elio." Maxon greeted me with a handshake. "It's been a while, old friend. How's your father?"

"It has." I peered around the busy tables. "He's well, thanks."

"Happy to hear it." He signaled for a waitress. "Once I got the call you were heading our way, I reserved your usual table in the back. Your guests have already arrived."

"How many of them?" I needed to know we outnumbered them. After all, we were on his territory, not mine.

"Three at the table," he said quietly, "and another four outside. I have one of my staff cleaning the back, so he will be keeping an eye out."

Not great odds, but I kept my voice level. "As always, Maxon, your loyalty is sincerely appreciated."

"You and your father have always shown me and my staff the upmost respect over the years. I welcome any Capri who walks through our door. I wish I could say the same for your guests."

"Have they been a problem?"

He motioned for me to follow him. "Let's just say they aren't as refined as the Capris."

"Is that so?" That would have to be dealt with. "I'll see what I can do."

"Greatly appreciated, as always."

I had always liked Maxon, and our respect for his restaurant, staff, and customers was a testimony to that.

I glanced at Vinni, who was still on the phone.

"Mr. Raine," Maxon pulled back the curtain and

hooked it around a cast iron rod, "Mr. Capri has arrived."

"Elio." Jacob made no attempt to stand or to shake hands as he pointed to a seat across the table. "Punctual, as always."

"I am." I watched as the waitress hurried away with a nervous look to fetch our drinks from the top tier cabinet.

"Cute, isn't she?" He smirked as he shook his head. "Although she's not really my type."

"Mm." I chose not to pull at that thread. Jacob had a reputation with women. "So." I unbuttoned my jacket and took a seat in the red leather chair, thanking the waitress when she set down a wedge glass and the bottle of whiskey they kept here for me.

"Glenfiddich Grand twenty-three." Jacob eyed the bottle. "That's a good one."

"I like it." I poured him a glass and did the same for myself. "Shall we start this meeting, or would you like to discuss our dinner plans?"

"Damn, son." He held up the glass and admired the amber color. "No foreplay? Yikes, that just chafes the head." He reached down and shifted himself crudely.

I licked the inside of my mouth, trying to calm my nerves. It was yet another reason I didn't choose to do business with Jacob and his men. They were vulgar businessmen who had zero concept of professionalism. They were wanna-be gangsters, waving guns and driving ridiculous, souped-up cars, who just so happened to own the one port we really needed access to in order to increase our business.

"It's my understanding that my father and yours

have already come to a tentative agreement on this. There didn't seem to be any issues with the terms and conditions that were drawn up, so I assume we are just here to cross the Ts and dot the Is?" I smiled tightly at him as he spoke.

"That's right." I kept my expression neutral.

He flicked a finger at the man behind him who slid a leather-bound folder on the table. "And since our fathers took care of the hard stuff…" He opened the folder and wiggled the pen between his fingers as he thought, then he scribbled his name on the line above where I was to sign. He pushed the papers over to me then sent the pen on a slide to join it. "Are you always so intense? I hope you'll loosen up a bit so we can have a little fun here."

I looked him right in the eye as I took my own pen from my pocket and removed the cap, never breaking my gaze.

"Ten years, forty-sixty split, with benefits when you ship to our port. Strictly oil, nothing else moves through our channels." I kept my voice even but firm. "Anything that looks out of order is immediately brought to my attention and will be dealt with on my terms." I raised my glass as a toast. "That, Jacob, is my idea of fun."

"Excuse me." A bartender held up a bottle. "This was sent for you, Mr. Capri."

I glanced at Jacob. He shook his head at me and made a show of looking down at the document he now waited for me to sign. I ignored him and took the bottle from the bartender to read the label.

Syndicate 58/6, not a bad whiskey for sure, although

something niggled that the title was meant to mean more.

"Charming," I snickered, handing it back. "And who, exactly, gifted this little treat?" The bartender simply smiled and lifted a shoulder.

TWENTY-EIGHT

Sienna

"So, Blake," I nibbled on the to-die-for seared sea scallop, "how long are you and Spencer in town?"

"I'm not really sure, since you," he smiled down at his wife, "can work anywhere in the world, and I have the next three weeks off, who knows what will happen?"

"Lots of sightseeing?" Gail, Wyatt's sister, spoke up. Gail and Blake had known each other since high school, and he often come into the city to visit his family.

"They just got married." Wyatt rolled his eyes at his sister. "The only sightseeing should be on the inside of a luxurious hotels."

"Yes," Spencer blurted, and the entire table broke into laughter. "Speaking of which, where is Chase tonight?"

Two men in flashy suits walked by and took the booth behind us. Immediately, their scent made my head hurt. I hated cologne, not to mention cheap cologne.

"When did we leave The Flatiron and land in a lousy night club?" Wyatt snickered as he coughed and wiped his eyes at the overpowering stink.

I shook my head at him and tried to clear my thoughts to focus on my friends. Moments later, the low voices of the men came to me, and I found myself listening.

"Do you think he suspects anything?" One of them spoke just as the music was switching over.

"If he's anything like his old man, no. He'll sign it," the other answered with a chuckle. "He'll be none the wiser when Jay's ships arrive at his port. A container is a container."

I couldn't hear the next bit of conversation, but my strained ears caught a comment "scared eyes bring in the biggest paychecks," to which someone snorted and agreed.

"Chase is working." Gail downed her drink and brought me back to the conversation around our table. "Maybe if I had those," she pointed to my cleavage that I knew was tastefully displayed in my favorite black lacy dress, "he would have canceled his meeting." I tried to look like I was paying attention as I strained to hear the words from behind me.

"Like you say, scared eyes bring big paychecks," one repeated, and his tone sent a dark shiver through me. I caught sight of them when a girl turned her phone around and took a selfie.

"Oh, please." Wyatt waved her off and pulled my attention back to them. "You know Chase tried everything to get out of it."

"I know." She pouted as Spencer wiggled out from behind her, needing to use the restroom. As she walked away, I felt the shake of the booth as the guys behind me stood and made their way over to a private booth then disappeared behind a partially closed curtain. "Still, though," Gail went on, "did you get those on demand, or are you just naturally blessed?" She indicated my cleavage again.

I chuckled as Wyatt answered, "Blessed."

"And how would you know that, brother?"

"I live with the *bella*. Trust me, you walk in on a lot."

"What?" I shrugged playfully. "I'm Italian. We embrace what we have."

"You should embrace all of that." Gail bent down and mouthed her straw as she fingered the feathery lace on my capped sleeve. The same lace trimmed the plunging neckline. The dress made me feel good, no matter where I wore it. It came to a wide diamond shape in the front, and a single piece of black tie wrapped around my neck and dangled between my breasts as if it were a long necklace. It was sexy-classy, as Wyatt described it earlier in the evening. He had insisted I sweep my hair up into a messy bun with a few pieces falling down to frame my face. I had to admit it was a pretty look for me.

"Oh, my God." Spencer came up to the table with

her hands over her mouth. "Sorry, babe, but ladies, there is the sexiest man in the private room over there."

"Where?" Gail nearly fell out of her seat.

"Right there. Look over my shoulder, and—oh, my—look at that one." I swung my gaze back over to the private room and felt my body temperature rise.

"You have got to be kidding me," I hissed when I spotted Vinni on the phone, which only meant…I leaned over further and spotted Elio. My heart, stomach, and thighs all clutched at once. "What in hell are the odds they'd be here?" Then I suddenly thought of the men and their conversation and wondered what the hell was going on.

"Hang on." Spencer's face lit up. "Do you know them?"

"I do." I downed the rest of my drink and held my hand in the air to catch the bartender's attention.

"How is it that the foreigner knows the hot mafia men in suits?" Gail chuckled at her joke, but little did she know.

"Sienna?" Wyatt grabbed my arm. "Is that who I think it is?"

"Yes, Mr. Tall dark and dangerous has followed me to New York. But two can play at this game. Hey, Leo!" I smiled up at Wyatt's good friend, and the bartender's sweet face smiled as he served us another round. "I need your help."

We watched as he carried the bottle of whiskey over to the privacy-curtained table. I downed the rest of my wine and poured another then stood with my fresh glass of liquid courage and leaned against the wall, waiting to see Elio's expression. Vinni suddenly spotted me, and his face dropped when he caught me staring at him. He gave a sheepish wave then leaned his head into the room, and a moment later, Elio's eyes were burning through me.

"Sweet Lucifer, he's terrifying," Wyatt huffed while Spencer nearly got knocked over by Gail, who needed a closer look.

"Sit down, you last-week's bride." Wyatt pulled her back down. "Trust me when I say you don't ever want to play in that man's sandbox."

"Why not?" Blake's detective senses started to hone in.

Ignoring them, I pushed off the wall and started a slow-sexy walk in his direction, one foot in front of the other, like a panther to the beat of a song. The white wine swirled around in my glass, which reminded me to take another sip, which I did in what I hoped was a seductive way. I took a quick glance around the room and wondered where Vinni's brother Niccola was. He always seemed to pop up unexpectedly.

Once I reached the small, curtained-off room, I tilted my head and stared deeply at the man who returned it with one that nearly brought me to my knees.

"Mr. Capri, what are the odds?" I lifted a single brow and eyed him up and down, proud that my voice sounded normal. I switched to English and focused in on the man who sat across from him. He looked like the type that should have six gold chains around his neck.

That would pair perfectly with that ridiculous suede suit and deep red shirt he wore underneath. I avoided any kind of eye contact with the two other men who stood in the back corner. "Am I interrupting anything?"

"Not at all." The man in the suede suit smiled wide, and I was treated to a view of his silver-capped teeth in the back. "Funny, I was just saying to Elio that we should get some women in here."

"Oh, really." I eyed Elio. He looked outwardly calm, but I could tell by the giveaway tick of his jaw he was on his last nerve. "Well, please, don't let me stop you."

"You're not. Sit." He pointed at the chair next to Elio.

It wasn't the first time I'd sat across from someone who most likely saw more blood than a morgue. It was all part of the job these days, and a part I did very well, it seemed. In this case, I needed to know if these men were with Elio or not.

"Thank you," I purred and gracefully eased into the seat. I crossed my legs and smirked at the unopened bottle. "I see you got my gift."

"Very amusing," Elio finally said through his tight jaw.

"I thought so." I winked playfully at him, loving my newfound courage. We had a lot to talk about, but for right now, I was going to have a little fun.

"I'm Jacob." His friend took the lead in the conversation. "What's your name?"

I felt Elio tense, and I figured I should tread carefully.

"Anna." I offered my hand, and he took it, holding

it a little longer than I would have liked. "Is this meeting business or pleasure, gentlemen?"

"Business." Jacob patted a leather-bound file folder in the center of the table, then his eyes slid over to the papers in front of Elio.

Oh, Lord…

"How intriguing." I ran my fingertips over the top of the folder. "And how's that going?"

"Better now." He grinned at me, and I wanted to pull back, but I held his look with a smile. "I just need dear old Elio here to give me his John Hancock, and the deal is done."

"How very mysterious of you." It wasn't lost on me that this was probably the signature the men in the booth had referred to.

"So, tell me, Anna, how do you know Elio? Lovers, haters, friends…what?"

I turned my smile over to Elio as I ran my middle finger down the fabric that edged my cleavage, stopping midway before retracing its path. I was buying myself time to think of how I should navigate the situation. Maybe what I heard back at the booth was nothing, or maybe it was something. Either way, I planned on making sure Elio had all the information before signing.

"Just friends." I shifted my gaze back to Jacob, knowing Elio would hate for anyone to know I meant something to him. "A few times, we had a moment, but it just never seemed to stick."

"Mm," Elio growled, and I shifted in my seat, trying to relieve the sexual tension I was feeling. "Maybe it's because you're so stubborn."

"Who wants a woman who isn't a little feisty? It adds to the fun," Jacob retorted, and I clicked my glass to his, enjoying the quick flash of anger that crossed Elio's face.

"A drink, gentlemen?" I reached for the open bottle and poured a double then slid it over to Jacob, who filled his empty one to the brim. I took the bottle back and gave Elio's nearly full glass a splash. "Where I come from, when we drink, we drink doubles. Cheers, boys." I pretended to take a sip and watched as Jacob tried to impress me, finishing off the entire glass. My stomach turned at the thought.

Whiskey was like sex. It was meant to be sipped, savored, appreciated, giving it time to warm you from the inside out. I glanced at Elio, who had his gaze fixed on me. I let my gaze drag across his lap before returning to the man in front of me.

Think, think!

"So." Jacob eyed the contract, and I noticed the two men in the back were staring at me. "Do you think we could end this night on a high note, Elio?"

"I love this color," I interrupted and leaned in to finger the deep-red collar of Jacob's shirt. I could feel his breath on my cheek, and his eyes widened to show he enjoyed my touch. "When I was eighteen, I fell in love with this sexy red Jaguar E-Type S. Oh, hell, she was stunning. Her curves were gorgeous, and her engine purred like a catcall to all men." I chuckled at the memory that came back to me. "When I finally went to buy it, the owner had other plans, and just like that, my dream of owning something so appealing vanished. I guess the deal just wasn't meant to be." It took everything inside me not to look over at Elio as I pulled back from Jacob.

"Jaguar?" Jacob snagged the bottle and poured himself another very large glass. "There's no back seat, where's the fun in that?" He laughed and ran his hand up my thigh as the rest of his men joined in with laughter.

I shook my head at them all and acted completely disgusted at his words.

"A real man would have figured it out," I shot back and hoped for an angry reaction.

"There you are." Wyatt suddenly tugged back the curtain and stood next to Vinni.

"Who the fuck is this?" Jacob glared at him.

"This is Anna's friend, Andrew," Elio said sharply, making sure Wyatt knew not to say anything else. "Nice to see you again."

"You as well." Thankfully, he played his part well. "Ah, Anna, the others left. It's just us now. Are you ready to leave?"

"Nah, she's fine right here." Jacob waved him off, still angry at my words, and I glanced at Elio for help.

"Vinni, take Andrew to my car," Elio said quickly in Italian. "We can give you a ride, and we'll join you shortly."

"Yes, boss." Vinni motioned for Wyatt to leave, and I gave a little nod to let him know it was all right.

"You know," Jacob leaned close and pressed his clammy hand hard against my thigh, "I know a little

Italian myself." He prattled off some dirty words, and I remained unimpressed.

"Just because you know how to pronounce them doesn't mean you should use them." I removed his hand, but he slapped it back down, and I jumped when Elio snagged his hand and twisted it in a tight grip. I sensed the tension and movement from the guys in the corner.

"No touching," Elio warned calmly over my head. "Ever."

"Sorry." He pulled his hand away with a huff, waving off his guys. "She's not even yours."

"Anna," Elio nodded at me, "it's time to leave. Go find your friend."

Slowly, I peeled my body from the chair and leaned into Elio, making a show to kiss him high up on the jaw.

"Don't sign," I whispered and moved away, pulling my mask back down. "Always a good time when our worlds collide, Elio." Once I was free from Jacob's view, I rushed out of The Flatiron Room. I knew better than to test my limits.

The cool night air filled my lungs, and I took a moment to let the adrenalin settle. The last forty minutes had been tense.

"Hey!" Vinni called from across the street where he stood next to a very expensive Cadillac. "Over here."

I waved and looked around for Wyatt. Was he in the car?

"Who the hell *are* you?" Jacob was suddenly next to me. "I've never seen Elio lose it like that before."

I took a step backward as he pulled his gun free.

"I'm just a friend of…of his cousin."

"You just fucked up our deal, little lady." His eyes raked my body, and I felt like I might get sick. "Mr. Big-Shot Italian has no idea what he just did."

"I have no idea what you're talking about." I acted like I didn't care as Vinni slowly pulled his weapon and pointed it at his head.

I only saw a blur as Elio jammed his fist into the side of Jacob's face, sending him spinning into the street. He whirled around, stunned at what just happened, and Elio put his hands up to continue the fight. I kicked his gun under a car as Jacob's eyes whirled, probably waiting for his men, who were nowhere to be found.

"No deal, Jacob." Elio yanked the paper from the file and flicked his Zippo, lighting the corner of it.

"No!" Jacob went to charge Elio, but Vinni used the butt of his gun to smoke him in the temple, and he fell heavily.

Elio dropped the half-burnt papers, took my hand, and whisked me across the street and into the Cadillac.

"Well," Wyatt turned to look at me from the front seat, "so, this is the guy you like?"

I chuckled, mainly to relieve some stress.

"Drive," Elio barked at Vinni as he joined me in the back. He wrapped an arm behind my seat and stared at me hard. "What the fuck was that?"

"The deal was dirty."

"Dirty?"

"Yes, I heard some of his men talking in the next booth saying they wondered if you suspected anything, and another one said if you were anything like your old man you would sign it. Maybe something was added to it at the last minute. Don't be angry with me, Elio. I may have just saved you from something bad."

He held my gaze for a few more intense minutes, then he pulled out his phone and started to dig through his email.

"Wait," I shouted, "what about Niccola?"

"Damage control," Vinni answered. "He'll be fine."

"Where are we going?" Wyatt asked after some time had passed.

"A hotel," Vinni said as he checked the side mirror.

"What? No. I need to get back to my sister's."

"Not tonight, sorry." Vinni's eyes caught mine in the mirror.

Wyatt's gaze flew to me, and I shook my head for him not to protest. Right now, we just needed to clear the air so we could all be on the same page.

I leaned back and watched the city lights as my eyes grew tired. It had been an eventful night, and I wasn't sure what in the world was going through Elio's mind as his fingers flew over his keypad.

"The Equinox?" Wyatt pulled me from my sleepy daze, and I ducked down to read the sign as the valet approached Vinni's door. "Damn, when you said hotel, I sure wasn't expecting this."

"I don't have anything to change into." I looked down at my outfit.

"It's been taken care of," Elio finally said as he moved to exit the car.

"Why?" I followed him out.

"You two are spending the night here."

I folded my arms, growing more and more angry at having my night decided for me. "How nice of you to ask me."

Elio whirled around, and I could tell he was about ready to lose his cool. "You show up out of nowhere years later, you know my best friend, and then you show up at The Flatiron wearing that," his eyes burned through me, "and you have inside knowledge about a huge deal I was about to sign off on. Yes, damn it, you are staying here. So we can figure this mess out!"

I studied his face, and watched it slip for a millisecond. It was his tell, and if I had even blinked, I would have missed it, but it had shown itself a half a beat later than I'd expected. When he showed his true vulnerability, I felt it. I listened. I understood it.

"I know you well enough by now, Elio," I whispered, "to know this isn't like you. You're never rude with me, and the few times you have been, it was for a pretty good reason. You also know I wouldn't do something like that back there without a good reason. So," I started to walk past him, "either I'm in some kind of danger, or you just really missed me." I tried to curb my sass.

"Sienna, you—" Vinni went to speak, but Elio shook his head to stop him.

"Please." Elio closed his eyes for a brief moment before staring at the ground. "Go inside so we can speak in private, because I'm pretty sure I'm a moment away from showing you a side I have never wanted you to see." He nearly vibrated with anger as he waited for me to get moving.

"Okay." I sincerely meant it. I just needed him to see me the way he used to, not blurred with all the distance and lies.

Chapter
TWENTY-NINE

Elio

I watched her sexy backside as she breezed through the lobby and glared at some men who stared, admiring her beauty. I was wound up, frustrated, mad, and knew I could fly off if the smallest thing went wrong. So much had happened tonight, my head spun, and I knew I had to pull myself together, but the loss of control had me doubting myself and fueled the white-hot anger inside me.

When we stepped into the elevator, we were accompanied by a few others who clearly had a lot to drink. The two men laughed as they tried to remember what floor they were on.

"Seven." One man leaned down and tried to push

the button.

"Allow me." Wyatt helped him out while the other caught sight of Sienna.

I was like a ticking bomb as my fingers rolled into fists, ready to make a move. I focused on the elevator door and caught the reflection of my luggage tag that dangled from my

Brunello Cucinelli. The crow from our family crest was midflight coming up on the crown. Written below were two little words that I lived by, *refined darkness*. I tried to use it to control my temper.

"Take a breath, Elio." Sienna glanced up at me with a knowing look.

"What language are they speaking?" one of the drunk men asked Wyatt, who had already spoken in English to them.

"Italian," Wyatt answered politely.

"She with him?" He nodded at me, and I kept my murderous gaze fixed on the shiny steel door in front of me as I swiped out and hooked my arm around Sienna.

"Yes." Wyatt nodded.

"He looks like he just came back from murdering someone." The man hit his buddy as he laughed.

"No, no, he looks like the Godfather or his son."

Slowly, I turned my head and stared directly into the man's eyes, and his mouth snapped shut.

"Sorry," he muttered and hit his friend, who was too oblivious to realize what was happening. Thankfully, the door opened, and they left the four of us to ascend to our floor in peace.

Moments later, we were inside the Equinox Suite where I made quick work of removing my guns and making myself a stiff drink.

"This place," Wyatt sighed as he stared out the floor to ceiling windows that looked over the dark city. "Damn, Si," he laughed quietly, "Georgio needs to step it up."

"He sure does." She joined him and admired the view.

"Our plane takes off at eight in the morning," Vinni said as he mixed his own drink. "Niccola followed Jacob for about twenty before he lost him."

"Figured." I let the smooth amber mingle with my taste buds, desperately needing something to calm me so I could think.

"I'll call my father and fill him in on what happened. Meanwhile, you round up the guys and be ready to go when I text you. We deal with this tonight. I won't risk anything with this contract or with…" I moved my gaze over to Sienna.

"Understood. I'll get Wyatt set up next door. His sister arrived, and all their things are here, so I'll watch for your text." Vinni looked as stressed as I felt.

"All right." I loosened my tie while Vinni explained part of the plan to the others. Once the guys left, I filled my father in on what happened, and all the while, my gaze was on Sienna as she explored the room, running her fingers over various items as she went, she stopped at the sculptures that lined the bookshelf and studied them. When I hung up, she let out a long sigh, and I hoped it was because she was happy to be here with me.

"You still wound up?" she asked over her shoulder.

"Yes."

"How wound?" She peeked over at me, and I moved toward her with one hand in my pocket, careful not to spill my drink.

"Enough to kill someone with my bare hands."

"That's wound." She shifted to sit on the table, and I stepped between her legs and took a deep swallow of scotch. She slowly took the glass from me and took a sip, all the while keeping her eyes on mine.

"I believe this belongs to you." I pulled her necklace from my pocket and held it up. I was relieved I had been able to find it at Mariano's.

Her face relaxed, and a small smile appeared.

"Thank you." She stood as I fastened it around her neck. Her hand ran along the length of the chain, then she fingered the two pendants. Something must have popped into her head because she took my hand in hers and admired my family ring. "You once told me it meant something more than just a family crest."

"It does."

"Can you share it with me?" She was trying to calm my temper that was idling at the surface. However, I didn't mind explaining this to her.

"When your family is the head of a syndicate, you wear these rings to show your rank. There are only three of these in circulation. Mama's, Papa's, and mine. Papa gave me mine, and I haven't taken it off since."

"Really?" She admired the crow in the center of the shield above the crown. "Why not?"

"There once was a time when it meant something to take it off, but now it's a personal thing. It's like your necklace. It's a reminder of who you are and the things you love. The only time I'll remove it is to switch it to my right after we get married." I watched her blink a few times at my words as I tucked her hair behind her ear. "Now, explain exactly what you heard. I need to know what was wrong with the contract."

"All right." She repeated everything she had told me earlier then seemed to remember something else, and her hand flew to mine. "I also remember one said something about Jay's ships arriving or something, and that a container is a container." She handed me back the glass, but I set it aside, wanting both hands free.

"Jay's ships," I repeated, testing the word. "It obviously has something to do with the dockyard. I know something has been going on there. I just wonder what, exactly." My frustration began to build again.

"No clue, but one guy also said something strange like 'scared eyes bring in the biggest paychecks'".

"Is that so?" I wasn't sure what it meant, but I was damn glad I didn't sign that contract and thanked the stars that Sienna had stopped me.

Her hand flattened on my chest, and her eyes moved to mine. "You're vibrating again."

I grunted, trying to process everything. "Well, there's no more I can do about anything until I hear back from my father." I let my gaze drop down to her scrap of a dress and noticed something. "What happened to your heart necklace?"

"I didn't like it."

"Me either." I fingered the tie around her neck, using her body to distract me.

"Elio," she whispered as I ran my hand up her bare leg, disappearing beneath her dress. Hooking her thong, I brushed over her arousal. "We really…" She closed her eyes for a moment. "Need to talk more."

"I know." I rubbed the pad of my thumb over her swollen bud. Then I reached over and pulled her hair free and off to the side before I gently wrapped my hand under her chin, tilting her head to the side. I dragged my tongue along the length of her neck and started to kiss her soft skin. Her hips rocked into my hand.

Before I could think, she pushed me backward and slipped off the table and headed toward the living room.

"Hey." I went after her and hooked her arm to whirl her around. "I know we have many things that need to be discussed, but my head is a bad place at the moment."

"So, sit." She jerked her chin toward the seat facing the window.

I caught her daring eyes and grinned, curious to see what she was going to do. So, I obeyed and undid my shirt and eased into the comfort of the chair. The sound of the rain that pelted the window matched my mood and helped me relax. The light from the opposite building cast shadows across the room and made for a dramatic effect.

Music turned on behind me, and I recognized the song. *Love Is A Bitch* by Two Feet.

Her warm hand touched my shoulder as she handed

me a new glass of scotch, then she reached behind her neck and undid the tie, letting the front of her dress fall forward.

"Jesus," I groaned at the lacy bra that barely covered her plump breasts. A matching thong with a thin gold chain connected the two. Slowly, she lowered to her knees, and my erection jumped with excitement. She crawled over between my legs, unzipping my pants and freeing me. She used one hand to pump twice. She leaned forward and licked the length. I gasped and ran my hand through her hair to pull it out of her way. With her gaze locked on mine, she kissed the tip, and when she pulled back, I saw evidence of my arousal on her lower lip and let out a growl.

She parted her lips and hovered over me for a moment as I shook under her hold. I huffed out a laugh because I was seconds away from taking back the control I needed.

Just as I went to shift, she pushed me into her mouth, taking me straight down to the base. I curled around her, trying to control myself. As she moved back up, she sucked and hummed, and my head dropped backward. I suddenly felt too hot, and I shimmied out of my dress shirt as she continued to suck, hum, and lick. Thunder mixed with the music, the rain beat the windows, and the smell of anticipated climax hung heavy in the room.

She cupped my balls and rolled them over her fingers, and I nearly lost it. Though I kept my calm on the outside, I was thinking of the hundred and twenty ways I was going to make love to her.

"I'm going to come," I warned her, and she sucked harder, so I threaded my hand back into her hair and directed exactly how I wanted her to take me. She moaned and reached down and started to rub herself. My stomach tightened, and I came hard. I waited for her to pull back, but instead she came at me with more intensity, and all I could do was hold on. Once I was finished and she pulled back, I smiled at her swollen lips and smeared mascara. She looked so damn sexy.

She moved to her feet and released her bra and stepped out of her underwear but kept her heels on as she made her way to the refrigerator to grab some water. I felt an erection build once again as I watched her nipples harden in the rush of cold air that reached for her.

When she returned, I hooked her waist, and with her back to me I guided her onto my new erection. She cried out as she adjusted to the sudden invasion, and I cupped her breast and rolled her erect nipple between my fingertips and the other hand found her greedy little bud.

I loved what she'd just done for me, and I loved that she was letting me do this. I would have stopped any other woman from taking control, but I trusted Sienna. I always had. Now I just needed to take it back.

Pushing her forward so she was nearly bent in half, I pressed into her, loving her little squeaks and moans as I continued to thrust. I needed more, I stood and kissed her shoulder.

"Walk forward," I ordered, and we moved to the window where I pressed her front to the cold glass, spread her legs, took hold of her hips, and lined back up.

At a painfully slow rate, I eased back inside her and tried everything in my power to be gentle with her.

"Elio," she growled, "more, please."

I thrusted hard once, and she cried out, and my head went fuzzy. When we were connected like this, it was as if we were one. We were not meant to be separated; we were a package deal.

Suddenly, I pulled out, turned her around to face me, and grabbed her head to smash my mouth to hers. Her leg hooked on my waist, and I slipped back in while I kissed her like it might be my last.

We were lost in that moment. Our animal instincts took over, and we were savages together, both seeking the end result.

Lifting her off the floor to get in farther, I buried my head between her breasts and thrust as deep as I could, giving her my everything. She came screaming my name, and I joined her, relishing in the one moment where our past didn't count.

Only when she went slack in my arms did I finally push off the glass to set her down on her feet.

"Oh, shit." I looked down with a sudden realization, but she shook her head. "I've never done that before."

"Me either, but I'm on the pill." She smiled then disappeared into the bathroom. I cleaned up and tucked myself back in my pants. I wanted to tell her I had never had sex bareback before, not even with her until now.

She returned a moment later in a silk robe and looked a little less wild.

"Now that the edge has been taken off, so to speak,

we should probably talk." She carefully looked over at me, and I knew it was time.

"Agreed."

"Where should we begin?" She reached for a bottle of water from the table and made her way across the room to sit on the oval coach. Crossing her legs, she waited for me to join her.

I grabbed an extra glass and the crystal decanter that held the scotch and set it in front of her. I was fairly sure she might need it.

"Well, that's not a good start." She nodded at the scotch.

"I want to start from the beginning." I pulled on my dress shirt but skipped the buttons and moved to the window, unsure I could sit yet. "How did you go from doing a story on Ricco Oil to a relationship with Mariano?"

"That's pretty personal, and if I answer that, you have to do the same, Elio. No more secrets."

I nodded, knowing it was time.

"Fine." She took a deep breath. "After Mariano approached my boss, we met, and he said he could relate to my story and that he really wanted me to be the one that told his."

I smiled and encouraged her to go on.

"He said to really get to know it from the inside, we would need to spend the next few weeks together. We toured all over Florence, meeting his friends, went on a tour of the oil plant, met some of the mangers and heard their stories. We ate at these amazing places."

She looked up at me then continued. "Though we grew closer as friends, he gives me the impression he wants more, but I don't." She hesitated and blushed. "Then he says some really off the wall comments, and I'm left wondering where he could think we could possibly go. Elio, we haven't been intimate," she repeated as though she wanted to assure me.

"But then one night," her tone went low, and a frown creased her forehead, "he took me to the dockyard." My face dropped, and I knew what was coming. "I waited outside for him while he went to do something up in an office. That's when I heard what sounded like someone calling for help, and it drew me right into the scene of a murder." She paused to take a deep breath. "I saw a murder—an execution, really." Her eyes widened at the memory. "Elio, I saw a man plead for mercy while another man put a bullet into his head."

"Did the killer see you?"

"Oh, yes." She chuckled darkly. I had no doubt that the weight of what she had witnessed still rested heavily on her shoulders. "I was frozen to the spot, and my brain refused to keep up while we both stared at one another, waiting to see who was going to make the first move. Then suddenly, Mariano found me looking terrified as hell and yanked me around the corner of the building. We got out of there after he made sure I was okay." She looked like she had a sudden thought. "I think that's when I lost my bracelet. He must have gone back for it, because I found it at your parents' house."

He didn't. My guys found it. I wanted to break every

bone in his body when I returned home. How could he not have told me?

"I wanted to call the police, but he told me we couldn't because you don't call the police on the mafia." She quickly cleared her throat. "Was that your hit?"

My back shot up. "If it was?"

"I would be slightly relieved." She shocked me with her answer.

"Why?"

"Because you could talk to him, tell him I won't tell anyone."

I downed the rest of my drink as I thought about what my next move should be.

"Living on the streets," she moved on with her story, "you learn how to process the bad things you see. You develop a sort of mental armor, because nine times out of ten, you're witnessing something that could seriously scar you. So, I dealt with the dock situation the way I always dealt with those things and moved on. Mariano checked on me a few times to make sure I was handling it. He seemed pleased that I dealt with it so well."

"I bet he was, but spare me the intimate details on Mariano, please, Sienna."

"There aren't any. We are not a good fit," she shot back. "He needs an Anna, wild, fun, and careless. I think he wants to be with someone like me someday, but he's not there yet. I'm not sure I can ever be an Anna."

"I'm glad you can see you're not compatible."

She ignored that and spoke through a tight jaw. "Anyway, after you and your father shut down the story,

I was going to leave, but then he offered me an even more intriguing story." She looked away from me.

"Which was?"

She stood and walked over to the dining room table then picked up her purse, and after a little digging, she found her phone.

"Was that hit at the dockyard yours?" She tossed her question at me again, and for some reason I couldn't answer her. It wasn't our hit, so why couldn't I just say that? Maybe because I was sure she would run. I wanted to say that my life was too complicated. So, I changed gears.

"What was the new story?"

She shook her head sadly then stared down at her feet. "You say you want me back, but you still won't be honest with me."

"You've been keeping things from me, too, Sienna."

"Okay." She shrugged moving her hands to her hips, and I knew more was coming. "Mariano knew from my article that I had been searching for someone. He told me that he was friends with a man nicknamed The Finder, and he could set up a meeting with me."

My blood turned cold as I listened. I felt her eyes burning a hole through my forehead.

"I was nervous, but he told me he would be there the entire time. The Finder was nice enough, told me his story, but the one thing I kept noticing was that he would speak about his history with the Santoro brothers but often mention them in the present tense as if they were still alive." She moved to the window with her back to me. I clenched my jaw, afraid to speak in case my voice would out the raging anger building in my gut.

"When I questioned him about it, he glanced at Mariano, who gave him a nod. Little did I know what that simple gesture meant." Her finger traced the city skyline across the glass as she thought.

"Well?"

"Your best friend then gave me another surprise, an introduction to Tieri Santoro." She turned to look at me. "That was what showed me who Mariano really is."

"You met Tieri Santoro?" Incredulous, I carefully placed my glass down on the table and moved closer to her as if my being near her now could protect her somehow. My anger at Mariano bubbled just beneath the surface. I could feel the burn of it and knew I had to push it down if I wanted her to continue.

"I did, and as charming as he thought he was, all I could smell on him was the blood of all the people he killed."

"What did he say?"

"Nothing much, really." Her tone was still cold and disconnected. "He just seemed to want to meet me."

"Why?"

"That's what I was trying to figure out."

"Did you get your answer?"

"I'm not sure, but he did give me something before he left."

"Which was?"

She slowly pushed a button on her phone, and a second later the familiar ring tone that came with that phone filled the room. Everything went still. The air was sucked out of my lungs like a vacuum. *She knows.*

She slowly turned toward me, and I saw she was crying.

"Sienna." I tried to find the right words, but there was nothing there.

"Just answer me one question, Elio." She sniffed. "Did you give me up to become Zazzero? Are you the other Santoro brother?"

I shook my head, answering only one of her questions, but she just covered her mouth and sobbed harder.

"Then why did you leave me back then? What could possibly have made you disappear so completely from my life?"

"I…" Once again, nothing came out. It was as if my brain couldn't untangle all the things that were coming at me. There was so much she still didn't know. That was such a dark time for me. I was lost, and I had given in to the monsters that held me tight in their grip as they waded me into a bloodbath.

"Let me get this straight." She turned with tears streaming down her face. "I have to be honest, but not you?"

"It's complicated."

"Right." She laughed and tried to dry her tears. She moved over to the table and started to gather her things. Suddenly, my head kicked in.

"What are you doing? We aren't finished talking."

"Seriously?" She made a wry face. "I want to leave,

but I'm assuming that's not an option tonight." She waited for me to answer.

"No," I whispered.

"Look," she let out an unsteady breath, "it's been a really long last few days. Can I just have a few moments to myself?"

"Of course."

Just as she was about to disappear into the bedroom, she spoke over her shoulder. "One thing that I loved about the old us, Elio, was despite whatever was going on, you still talked openly to me. I was your person, and you were mine. It can't be just one way now." With that, she headed to the bedroom.

I ran my hands through my hair, wanting to scream with my inability to get past the mental block I was dealing with. Grabbing my phone, I dropped down onto the couch and called my friend.

"Please tell me you found her?" Francesco asked.

"I did, and she's here, but I, ah…" I rubbed my face, feeling lost. "I could really use your advice."

"Always." I heard him close a door. "What's going on?"

I spent the next fifteen minutes explaining everything to him, and all the while he just listened and let me get my jumbled thoughts out.

"We will have to meet as soon as you get back, I assume you have filled in your father about all this. There is a lot to digest after what has happened over the contract." He went silent for a moment. "Mariano has a lot of explaining to do."

"Yes, I filled my father in, and I suspect he'll be calling you at any moment." I glanced at the time. "And yeah, Mariano does. What the hell was he thinking? How the hell could he possibly think any of that was all right to do with her? He's losing it, Francesco, and now look where we are."

"We'll deal with this once you get home."

I stood, needing to hurt something, but when I heard the water turn on, I reminded myself she was still here, not running.

"What has he been up to since we left?" I huffed out.

"He's been working closely with your father. To be honest, he's been great."

"That's something, then." I yawned and felt totally exhausted.

"I think you just need to lay it all out on the line for her, give her the benefit of the doubt. That little lady has shocked me from day one with how she deals with things, and after knowing all of that, and she still hasn't run…I think she's trying to tell you she's all right with it."

"Will she be, though? When I tell her the whole of it?"

"What choice do you have now? Give her a little credit, and you do owe her some honesty. I bet things will smooth out once you do."

"Yeah." I knew he was right, because never once had Francesco steered me wrong. "Why is it I can run our entire syndicate, take down another, kill someone with my bare hands and feel nothing, but one moment with Sienna, and I'm completely lost and can't navigate my next move?"

He laughed. "You're a natural born leader, Elio. It's in your blood to do what you do, but where there's strength there's always a weakness, and that little lady is yours. Remember, behind every strong man there's an equally strong woman."

"True." I had to smile, knowing he was right once again.

"I'll keep an eye on Mariano, and you go talk to her."

"Thanks." I hung up and rubbed my head, wondering how quickly we had gone from such intimacy to separate rooms in a blink of an eye.

Pouring myself another drink, just enough to coat the bottom of the glass, I slowly made my way into the bedroom. The bed hadn't been touched, and as I came farther into the room, I spotted her sitting on the edge of the marble stand-alone tub mixing milk wash under the rushing water. The robe she wore hung off one shoulder, exposing the flawless skin I had just enjoyed touching so much.

Moving to the corner of the room, I eased into a chair, stretched out my legs, and watched her from the darkness, needing to admire her again. The smell of the bathwater made me slip into a memory.

THIRTY

Sienna

I allowed my mind to slip into a daze as my hand swirled the milky water around, creating wispy clouds. Once the level was high enough, I dropped my robe and slipped into the warm water. I knew I desperately needed this, and I leaned back to rest my head on a rolled towel as a long breath expelled from deep within and I sank even lower in the water. I knew I had to get my head in order, but I fought the urge to think. The wooden table across the end of the tub held a fluffy face cloth, and as I reached for it, wanting to drape it over my tired eyes, something caught my attention.

Elio was in the corner of the room watching me in that sexy, mysterious way he had.

"I'm not answering any more questions." I sank into the water up to my chin.

"Remember the day we first met?" He spoke quietly. "You were so frightened and hungry."

I quickly pushed those bad memories back, as they threatened my relaxation, and wondered why he was bringing them up.

"I always wondered if Francesco hadn't forced me to go cool off at the pond that day if I ever would have met you." I heard him move in the chair. "What a shame that would have been, because the way you made me feel was so very special. You showed me what love is supposed to feel like."

I swallowed the lump in my throat, nervous what he might share next, and I wondered if we would be able to get through it.

"The only problem with loving someone like that is that when something really terrible happens you will do anything to protect that person from any harm that might come to them. I never wanted to leave you, Sienna." I heard the hitch in his voice, and I knew the truth was about to show itself. "It just all happened so fast, and I had to make a decision, and to this day I don't know if it was the right call or not."

I pressed the facecloth tight against my eyes to catch the tears that started to fall.

"That morning, I woke to Francesco rushing into my bedroom. He tossed a suitcase on my bed and started to pack my things. He told me to get dressed because we had to leave. There was a hit put out on my father, and they were on their way to the house. I was in shock as I jammed my things into a small box and was told the rest was replaceable. I flew downstairs and saw the madness that was unfolding, and all I could think about was how I was going to get to you in time. Francesco was the only one who would stop for two seconds to hear me out. He told me that I had to choose and quickly. Should I rush to get you and thrust you into a life of crime, pain, loss, and fear, and put your life in immediate danger along with ours? Or do I let you go to have a second chance at finding love and live a normal life, one you so desperately wanted."

His hand brushed down my arm as I silently sobbed.

"I'm a selfish man, Sienna. I couldn't get enough of your love. I was an addict, and you were a thirst that couldn't be quenched. But what kind of a man would I have been to rob you of your choice? You had been robbed of so many things already. It was the one unselfish thing I have ever done."

"Why?" I pulled the cloth away and stared up at him on the side of the tub. "Why didn't you just tell me who you were? Then I could have made that choice myself."

"I've asked myself that question since the day we first kissed, and I think it was because you loved me for me, the boy from the pond who waited every damn day to see your smile. Not the son of a mafia family."

"I always suspected something."

"I guess I underestimated you, or maybe I didn't want to believe that you saw it. I liked being in our bubble. We were so young and happy."

"Well." I sat up, and his eyes dropped down to my breasts for a second before he caught himself. "That's one thing you got wrong. When you decided to burst our bubble and leave everything behind, I didn't get the happy life you so wished I would."

He stood and tapped on his phone screen. "The other day, you said I left our photo behind because I didn't care about you, but that wasn't the case. I kept *this* one because it shows one of the happiest memories I have of us." He turned it around, and I saw a photo of me laughing at the camera. Elio was looking up at me as he kissed my fingers. "Do you really think I could ever leave without a trace of you? Our souls are entwined, Sienna." He dragged a finger down my jaw with a look that seemed a million miles away, no doubt reliving that horrific day. "I know we have more to discuss, but I just dropped a lot on you, so," he paused and looked at his phone, reading something that just came in, "I'll give you some space now."

As he left, I sank deeper into the tub and drifted below the waterline, tuning out the world while my mind sorted through the truth of what really happened that day.

I wasn't sure how long I lay there, but when the water turned cool, I peeled myself out of the tub and found the hotel room empty.

"Elio?" I held a hand to my stomach that begged for food, but everything in the place was either pre-wrapped healthy or just healthy. I picked up my phone and tapped on his name and waited for it to connect, but I was sent to voice mail.

"Damn." I tried a different number instead.

"I just fell asleep," Wyatt groaned.

"Elio disappeared. Is Vinni there with you?"

"Don't know." He yawned. "Why?"

I looked around the dark, quiet room and suddenly felt alone and raw from my emotions.

"You want me to come and keep you company?"

I smiled briefly, loving that he would do that for me.

"No," I lied, "I'm just going to head to bed."

"You know how to reach me if you change your mind."

"Thanks." I hung up and pulled my knees to my chest. When I flopped my head back, it hit something that crinkled. I picked up the glossy magazine I'd seen on the back table about the hotel. I turned to page four and scanned to the Rooftop bar ad and saw it was open twenty-four hours. After a moment of thought, I reached for my phone and decided to order room service since it was safer than going out or starving.

After I ordered a large pizza, a garden salad, and a cheesecake, I turned on the fireplace and flipped through the channels on the huge TV. I settled on a show called *Schitt's Creek*. Wyatt seemed to like it, and with the closed captioning I had an easier time making out the conversations.

After about five minutes, I lost track of the show and found myself looking outside at the stormy night. My mind drifted back to that awful day.

Pain burst through my chest as I picked up a picture frame from the floor and brushed my finger over the broken glass. I tucked the photo in my bag and bolted for the woods. I lost all sense of direction, but I didn't care. I just needed to run.

As the branches thinned out, I gained speed. Colors and sounds blurred together, and just when I thought my lungs would burst and my legs became Jell-O, I came to a screaming halt in the nick of time.

"Whoa!" I screamed and dug my heels into the dirt. I should've backed up, moved far away from the edge of the cliff, away from the jagged rocks below that foamed at the mouth like a wild beast. But I didn't. Instead, I flirted with death, let him hold me by the hand and let him decide. Just as I felt myself begin to tip forward, I caught a movement on the other ridge and froze. A baby roe deer was staring at me. He looked just as alone as I was, and dangerously close to the edge, too. In all the years of living here, I had never seen a deer, let alone one so close. It was almost like he was saying, "You jump, I jump." A suicide pact.

He was so young, and I was sure his parents were close by, thinking he was just playing in the tall grass.

"Fine," I huffed. Feeling like his death would be my fault, I pushed back and bent down, letting go an Earth-shattering scream that tore through me. I screamed until there was nothing left inside me. I panted and struggled to drag some oxygen back inside over my raw throat.

When I looked back over, I saw the deer hadn't been frightened off. He stood on the edge of the forest, and just before he disappeared, he glanced over his shoulder as if to make sure I was all right.

I needed a new plan, one that would get me out of there now.

A knock at the door had me on my feet and rushing across the hotel room. Lack of food and a wild, emotional night had me in its hold when I threw open the door.

"Please come in." I welcomed the bellman, but when I went to close the door behind him, someone's shoe blocked it from closing.

"Sit." Jacob Raine ordered the bellman to sit on the couch as he pointed a gun at me. I squelched a scream and held up my hands. "Don't even think of making a move." Jacob waited for two of his men to join us, blocking the doorway.

"I don't know who you really are, Anna." He gently touched the swollen cheek that Elio had hit earlier in the night. "But something tells me you're important to Elio."

"No." I shook my head. "I'm really not."

"See, here's the thing, I think you are, and you are going to get him to sign this damn contract."

"No," fell out of my mouth like a damned idiot.

"You should know I don't do well with that word." He slipped on a pair of gloves and came closer to me, and my bones rattled with fear. "So, let's try this again." He shoved the contract in my hand.

"I don't think I can get him to sign it." I knew I was testing my luck, but I was revved up from my memory, and once again I was flirting with death.

He nodded calmly then grabbed a handful of my hair and yanked me backward. I was tossed on the couch and pinned to the seat. His leg covered mine so I couldn't kick out. Again, that horrible nightclub smell lingered on his clothes, reminding me his men were probably not that far away.

"Just because your boyfriend sucker punched me doesn't mean I don't know how to inflict pain myself. You either get him to sign the contract or I will find another way to get it." His free hand moved inside my robe and massaged my breast.

My skin shivered as a wave of anger tore through me.

"Don't touch me." I spat in his face, and his eyes went wild. He reached back grabbed the whiskey glass and smashed it on the table. I yelped at the loud noise. My nerves were pretty much splattered all over the room at this point. He held the jagged edge to my arm and smiled like the crazy man he was.

"As sexy as your sass is, Anna, I don't like to be disrespected."

He pushed the glass into the skin of my arm, slicing through the top layer like a painful papercut. I gritted my teeth, afraid I would jump, and it would dig in deeper. Fear raced through me. What else would he do if I didn't agree?

"Listen to me." He pushed down and sliced deeper, and I cried out, seeing the bellman's face go pale. He looked like he might be sick. "Shhh." He kissed my temple, and I shook harder. "Will you do as I ask?"

"Yes," I whispered through my trembling lips.

He glanced down at the blood that oozed and slid the sharp edge across again, cutting even deeper as I struggled.

"Good girl." He inspected his handiwork, then I shrieked as he sliced again but harder. He tossed the glass aside and grabbed my face and kissed my cheek hard. I closed my eyes, holding back my stomach, and when I finally heard him leave, I waited, frozen in position.

"Miss?" The bellman's voice broke through my fear. He looked horrified. "Should I call the police?"

"No." I trembled through more tears. "No, just go."

I scrambled to grab my phone as he ran out, and I rushed toward the door to close it, tripping along the way.

"Ouch!" I held my burning, bloody arm as someone slammed into it, forcing it open again. "No!" I batted at a set of hands, but when I heard his voice I stopped.

"Jesus!" Vinni looked down at me, horrified. "What the hell happened?"

I threw myself into his arms, so thankful to see him.

"Help me," I cried.

"Elio!" he called, and a moment later I felt his strong arms wrap around me.

"Whose blood is that?" His voice was haunting.

"Hers," Vinni whispered.

They sat me in a chair and then closed and locked the door. Elio grabbed a towel and put pressure on my arm for a moment as he held me.

"Who did this?" he finally asked as his eyes drilled into me, but before I could reply, he removed the towel, and they both looked down at the deep cut.

"Is that a..." Vinni studied my arm, and for the first

time, I took a look at it. A crude, jagged J was cut into my flesh.

"He marked her!" Elio growled, and if I thought he was wound up before, I was sadly mistaken.

"He wanted you to sign the contract," I whispered, feeling the need to speak.

"Is that so?" he boomed as he stood. "Vinni, watch her." He went for the door, but I jumped to my feet, feeling like I might be sick if he left.

"Elio," I cried against his chest, "please don't leave me."

"This won't take long, I promise."

"No." I sobbed, desperately wanting him to see what I needed from him. "I need *you*, please."

I held his wild gaze with my terrified one, and after a moment, I knew he heard me. He buried his face into my neck and held me tight.

"Vinni." He lifted his head after a few beats. "Don't leave Wyatt alone tonight, but get Niccola…"

"You got it, boss." Vinni gave me a pat on the shoulder as he left us alone.

Elio helped me to bed. He gently tucked the covers high up around my chin then paused as though he wanted to say something. He didn't. I watched as he removed his suit jacket and bloodstained shirt then disappeared into the bathroom where I soon heard the shower running. I moved my attention to the electric fireplace and became mesmerized by the flames as they slowly flickered up over the artificial log. It gave me a chance to turn off my thoughts, if only for a few moments. I tuned in to the tenderness of the cut on my arm as I rolled over. Elio had wrapped it up after cleaning it when we were finally left alone. He also insisted I took a pain killer. I was glad I did; it hurt a lot now.

Thunder shook the windows, and I closed my eyes and swallowed hard. As much as I loved a good storm, it was a constant reminder of my time alone on the streets.

"Stop," I whispered, wanting to keep my mind from racing wildly through everything that had happened then and today, to force myself to focus on what was next.

"There's one more thing." His voice suddenly broke through my thoughts. I opened my eyes to see him and blinked hard to focus. He leaned against the mantel. A fresh pair of slacks rested low on his hips, and as he reached up with both hands to slick back his wet hair, he let go a long breath.

I pushed myself up to rest my back on the pillowed headboard, curious to know what he had to say. At the same time, I wondered if my head could take any more tonight.

I looked up at him with a question in my eyes. He seemed to gather his thoughts and sat. "I like to call it quiet wealth." He sat down on a chair by the bed, keeping his eyes on mine. "There's a reason our family got to where we are today, why we have so many eyes and ears keeping watch for us, why we have so many staff members, and why loyalty runs so deep..." He paused again, and I wondered where he was going with this, then he shook his head as if to get back on track. He stood and walked to the floor-length window and rested his arm on the glass. His reflection mirrored the storm outside.

"Fear, when used correctly, is one of the most powerful weapons." His voice was almost chilling. "When someone joins our syndicate, whether they are a staff member or a family friend, we arrange it so they become a witness to a crime. We also make sure that they know the killer saw their face." I swallowed hard, thinking immediately of the murder I had witnessed. "It sounds sick, I know, but it ensures that they keep quiet, and in return for their silence, we provide them with protection and money to feed their families. It's like an initiation to our world."

"And if they want out?" The words barely slipped past my lips.

"They don't." He kept his back to me.

"And if they speak up?"

"They are dealt with."

"I think," I cleared my throat trying to find my voice, "I think when we get back to Italy, I need to go home for a while, clear my head."

He turned to face me.

"Sienna," his expression was unreadable, "you just aren't getting it. Things are complicated now. After what you have seen, whether you like it or not, you are not going to be able to go back to the life you had. You need to give me time to figure this out, then you can leave if you wish."

"What?"

"It wasn't my hit," he finally admitted, and I suddenly

grew cold. "There's a lot going on, but whoever that was at the dockyard, it wasn't us. I don't know who did it."

"Which means you can't speak to him," I said more to myself, just needing to hear it.

Thunder rattled the glass, and lightning lit up the room. If he were anyone else, I would have run out of there so fast, but he wasn't. He was still my Elio, but with secrets rooted deep within him. A darker side of the man I fell in love with many moons ago.

"You're a target now, and when the word gets out that I have feelings for you," he stepped closer, and I felt a tear slip out, "the wolves will come out and play."

When he moved to come closer, I held up a hand, unsure of my own actions. I needed space.

"I just…" I held back, trying to process all he had said, "need a little time."

He nodded and checked the time on his phone.

"The plane leaves in five hours. You should try to get some sleep."

Chapter
THIRTY-ONE

I watched her fall under a trance caused by the shock of what happened. My coin flipped through my fingers as I tried to think of all the ways I could deal with Jacob and his men. We lived in a ruthless world cloaked in power and money. The fight to stay on top came with a price, and many sacrifices had to be made, but this one went too far. My phone lit up and showed only a number. It was the room number next to ours. Slipping on my suit jacket, I found Vinni at the door. His nod reassured me he wouldn't leave her side.

Plastic sheeting was a staple in our world. You never knew when a soul would be bought, or blood would be shed. The furniture had been pushed aside, and in the center of the room was one of Jacob's men tied to a chair, his face sweaty and pale. I recognized him as one of the bodyguards. I stepped on the plastic that covered the floor and made my way over to the chair facing him. I made a show as I slowly unbuttoned my jacket and eased myself onto the chair.

"Typically, I would have ordered my men to dispose of you like the trash you are." I plucked a piece of lint from the sleeve of my jacket. Each movement I made was deliberate, making him sweat what was coming. "But you have something I want."

"Which is?" he snarled at me.

"Information."

"I know nothing."

"On the contrary, you do." I changed my tone, hating that Sienna lay next door without me. "I know you knew the contract was dirty. I know that Jacob is working with someone, and you're going to tell me who."

"The hell I am, you asshole fool."

I winced and glanced at Niccola, who shook his head at the idiot in front of me. Words were powerful in our business. They were a representation of how we were perceived and how we expected to be treated in return. These men were dirty, foul-mouthed businessmen. Their lack of class was painfully obvious.

"Well," I held out my hand, and Niccola handed me a steak knife, "my men tell me you are a fan of playing football. It would be a shame to see you have to take the season off." His gaze shot down to the knife.

"I'm no snitch."

"I hear what you're saying, but…" In a quick jolt forward, I jammed the knife into the side of his knee and leaned back as he screamed and bucked against the ropes that held him in the chair. "This situation can very easily be avoided," I used my handkerchief to remove the blood from the blade, "with a simple answer. Who is Jacob working for?"

Sweat rolled down his forehead, and his face turned a dangerous shade of red.

"No doubt your heart is now pumping overtime, therefore sending massive amounts of blood to your wound." I pointed to one of my men who was holding a roll of gauze. "We always have options in life, so choose yours now."

"Screw you."

I shook my head, unimpressed with his decision, and reached toward the man on my right. He immediately stepped forward with a pair of shears in his hand. He grabbed hold of two of the bodyguard's fingers, ready to cut.

"No, no, no!" He bucked, and I held up a finger to pause my man momentarily.

"I'm listening."

He screamed. He knew I wasn't messing around. "I don't know everything," he tried to catch his breath through his pain, "but what I do know is that he had a meeting with someone three weeks ago and came back saying there was a change in plans. He needed to change the contract because we were working with another side."

"What does that mean?"

"I don't know!" His chest heaved, and his eyes rolled back in his head as he began to lose consciousness. My man slapped his face, bringing him back to us.

"Again," I repeated, "what does that mean?"

"Ah…" He blinked like he was trying to clear his thoughts.

I grew annoyed and tried a different angle. "Was it Stefano Coppola?"

"Who?" He seemed generally confused, and that instantly made me wonder what in the hell was brewing behind the scenes that I wasn't aware of.

"Enough of this." I stood and buttoned my jacket. "Carve an E in his chest, film it, and dump him where he can be found."

I headed back to my room, my mind in turmoil. I needed sleep.

To say I was on edge would be an understatement, and I knew Sienna had keyed in to my mood on the way down to the car in the morning. I must have touched the handle of my gun at least sixty times on the way from the hotel to JFK where my private plane awaited us. Normally, I'd stay in New York and finish off Jacob, but Papa felt strongly that we should return. It wasn't until we were in the air that I was able to take a full breath and relax a little.

Sienna had admitted to very little sleep at all last

night and was curled up on the couch in the back and had finally passed out. I noticed Wyatt seemed uneasy, and I took pity on him. Though I knew I should be working out the schedule of what needed to be done over the next few days with my cousins, I joined him instead, deciding he and I should have the talk now before the wheels hit the tarmac at home.

"Do you need anything?" I signaled for the flight attendant to bring my usual.

"I'll have whatever you're having. I could use something to take the edge of the last twenty-four hours." He gave a dry laugh.

"Two, please, Rita," I said softly, not wanting to wake Sienna where she slept only a few feet from us. I leaned back, stretched out, and tried to seem less intimating. It was important for me to know exactly how much her best friend knew about me. "I bet you have some questions for me."

"I do." He nodded. "Am I allowed to ask them?"

"Of course."

"Okay," he rubbed his lips while he thought, "I'm known to be blunt."

"So am I."

"You lived in Sicily and met Sienna when she was young." I nodded. "And your family is part of the mafia?"

"Head of our syndicate, yes." I took the drink from Rita.

"Wow." He set his drink on the table, using the napkin as a coaster. "And she never knew?"

"No."

"And now you live in Montepulciano, and you also are one of the Santoro brothers."

I shifted, uncomfortable with him knowing such an intimate detail about me. "That's correct."

"Jesus." He let out a nervous laugh. "You watch the movies, you know it happens but never hear anything concrete. I sure didn't see that coming."

"Has she told you anything else?"

"She tells me everything." He shrugged.

"I suspected so." I sipped my sidecar, thinking. "My turn. When did you and Sienna meet?"

"At a bar I was working at. She'd come in from time to time to eat, and I could tell she just needed someone to talk to, so I became that for her. A friend. Turned out she was living in a room she rented from an old lady, but the lady's granddaughter needed the room, and she had to be out by that weekend. She just had a few personal belongings, and I told her I had room and could use a roommate, at least until she could get her feet back on the ground."

"That was very nice of you."

"It's not what you think."

He misread my mind, but I was curious to see what he was going to say.

"I left everything to come to Italy. I wanted a change after my mom died. My dad and I were always on opposite sides of everything and argued a lot. I got a shitty job at a bar, but I had no one and had always been a little confused about myself." He hesitated. "Perhaps I still am, but Sienna sees past all that. She doesn't care.

She sees me for me."

"She's never been one to judge," I added to his compliment. "And for what it's worth," I took a deep breath and let him see inside me a little, "I left because I thought it was the right thing to do. I know now I was wrong, but now, more than ever, I'm concerned for her. Being with me and in my life puts a target on her back."

"You really care for her."

"No, Wyatt," I leaned forward, "I really love her. No matter how many times I tried to move on and live without her, I couldn't. I missed her every day, and now that she's back in my life, I'm prepared to do whatever it takes to make sure she's safe."

"I can sincerely see that." He glanced over at her. "So, what about the guy who did that to her arm?"

My blood ran cold, and I felt my temper rise. "He'll be dealt with."

"Good. Let me know if you need any help." I smiled and appreciated his offer to help protect her. He seemed very genuine, and I felt she was in good hands with him. "She mentioned something about not being able to go home."

"That's right, she didn't tell you about what happened at the dockyard?" He shook his head, waiting. "Well, she saw something she shouldn't have, and now her face has been seen by someone dangerous. I hate to say this, but you also walked in on something you shouldn't have been a party to, and your face has been seen by someone dangerous as well."

"What? When?" His eyes shifted from side to side

as he tried to remember. "Oh, my God, at the restaurant when I walked up to the table, is that the same guy who cut her?"

"Yes, so you will need to stay at my place where you will be protected until I figure this out."

"What about my things and my job?" His face showed his confusion at the sudden turn of events.

"I will have someone drive you to get your things. As for your job, I'm sure we can provide you with enough stories to keep your boss happy."

"Shit." He leaned back in his seat and let it all sink in.

I felt for him and the sudden change in his life. I wasn't sure how I would cope with all this if I was in his place.

"I never meant for any of this to happen. I'm still trying to understand it all myself. There seems to be something more going on than I know. I'll get to the bottom of it soon, and we can get your life back on track, but in the meantime…" I shrugged as if to say *it is what it is*.

"I appreciate your honesty on everything." He gave me a glance. "How is it I know nothing about the mafia? You never make it into the newspapers or any TV headlines."

"We never do any business in public. Ever."

We both settled into our seats and let the hum of the engine fill the silence. I mulled over our conversation, making a mental note to have someone watch over Wyatt when he was out on his own. Out of the corner of my eye, I saw him smirk, then when I looked over at him, he chuckled.

"What?"

"I don't know," he shrugged, "I guess it's weird being here, with a drink in hand, you know, chillin' with a villain'."

I laughed into my glass and went back to my emails.

After a bit, Vinni gave a soft whistle to get my attention and waved me over. I leaned over and gently kissed Sienna on the forehead, pulling the blanket up to her chin.

"For years," Wyatt stood next to me, "that girl cried for you every day, and if she wasn't in tears, she'd often slip into a memory and tell me about it. Anything to find a moment of happiness." His eyes grew glossy. "Never once did she ever say anything bad about you or your family. I feel that really says a lot about what you used to have. I don't know what your world is like now, but if it's anything like I'm imagining, please don't hurt her again, because I'm not sure I can put her back together."

"I'm not going to let anything hurt her," I promised, and I knew he believed me because he held out his hand and we shook on it. A man should keep his word, and that was exactly what I was going to do, no matter what the cost. With that, I joined my cousins.

Over the next two days, Vinni moved Wyatt's and Sienna's belongings to my parents' house, and they settled in. Mama was beside herself with excitement to have them there, while I paced my office trying to figure out where the hell Mariano had raced off to just before we arrived home.

Sienna seemed to be avoiding me while she digested everything that happened, which was hard to wrap my head around because I was used to having her again.

"Elio?" Francesco stood in the doorway of my office. "Everyone is about to leave for the church luncheon. They're leaving in fifteen. Did you still want to attend?"

I rested my elbows on the back of the chair and covered my face. I knew how important it was that the family was seen at these community events. We needed to show to our support, but I had so much on my mind.

"I know it's bad timing, but we haven't been out as a group in a very long time. It'll do us some good." When I didn't answer, he continued. "Sienna is going." He grinned and wiggled his brows at me when I looked up.

I rolled my eyes back at him and reached back for my phone. "Give me a few minutes to change, and I'll meet you out front."

I changed into my black Paul Stuart suit and slipped a gray and black silk handkerchief in my breast pocket. I wasn't feeling it, but I knew I needed to dress up when I was in front of the public. It was no secret to the town who we were and what we did, but we were respected because we never hurt those who didn't deserve it. Plus, we poured a lot of our oil revenue into the small businesses around the town, and in turn they grew deep roots to grow and expand.

Squinting at the sunlight as I opened the front door, I slipped on my Cartier sunglasses then stopped when I saw Francesco, Wyatt, and Sienna in the driveway, all studying me.

"Great," Wyatt tossed his hands up, "now I feel underdressed."

"Ready?" I smirked at her best friend, who turned out to be pretty funny at times.

"Is that a Paul Stuart?" Wyatt whispered enviously to Sienna, and she gave him a nod.

I opened the door for her, and she slipped inside, tucking her gorgeous black leather skirt down as she wiggled into the seat.

"Vinni, no stops. There and back."

"You got it." He settled into the driver's seat, and I nodded to Francesco, and he joined Vinni up front. I might not have been in the mood for an outing, but I knew appearances were everything, and I was going to act like all was well with our world. I knew I needed to find out what Stefano was up to, and I would soon figure it out. Even more than that, I needed Mariano to come the hell home. He had a lot of shit to answer for.

I joined the others in the back of the car and signaled to Vinni to get moving. Once we were out of the driveaway, we waited for bodyguards to catch up, and we drove three cars deep into town.

"How's the arm?" I peered down at Sienna's skin-colored bandage.

"Better." She ran her fingers gently down the length of it.

"Have you shared that you're not sleeping at night?" Wyatt asked.

"Wyatt, stop," she snapped.

I turned to move my arm to wrap around the back of the seat. "You're not sleeping?"

"I am."

"She's not." Wyatt shook his head. "You never lie to the mafia, Sienna."

I smirked at his comment, and she elbowed him. I would address the sleeping matter later. Right now, I just wanted them to enjoy themselves a little. It might be fun to show them what our small town could offer. I sat back. Maybe this would be just what we all needed.

"We got company, boss," Vinni called, and I saw the police were waving us over.

"Pull over," I ordered. I noted that our other cars had followed and pulled over as well. I knew my men would sit tight and wait for my instructions.

"Oh, shit, what did we do?" Wyatt sounded panicked as he pulled out his wallet and removed his ID. I rolled down my window as the officer approached Vinni's window.

As soon as he saw my face, he stood straighter and moved his hand off his weapon.

"Forgive me, Mr. Capri. We've had a few problems lately, and we are told to check any and all vehicles."

"Not a problem. You're just doing your job. You have a good day."

"You as well, sir."

I rolled the window up and signaled for Vinni to get

moving.

"Just like that?" Sienna shook her head as though she was blown away the police knew about my family.

"We donate a lot to the police department," I explained.

"It's like riding with John Gotti," Wyatt said. "You never actually hear about this kind of stuff happening, but you know it does." His nervous laugh turned into a cough.

"You watch too many American movies." Sienna laughed.

"You doubt *my* movie watching, but wasn't it you who used that good comeback with the guy holding the gun at Mariano's?"

She really did share everything with him.

"Yeah, and almost got my head blown off because of it."

"What about the time Renzo came to see you when you were living on the streets?"

That caught my attention. I glanced down at her and wondered why the hell that one was never mentioned before.

"She took a pipe to his knee," Wyatt bragged.

"What?" I looked hard at Sienna.

"It was self-defense, use whatever means necessary." She shrugged.

"What happened to Renzo after that?"

"Don't know." She shrugged again. "A man walked into the alley just after I hit him and spooked him enough to run. Last I saw, the guy was chasing him, and I bolted in the opposite direction. Never saw him again."

I wondered if that was one of Francesco's men. I leaned on the armrest, and something she said the other day at the graveyard hit me. She had used the word "weapon," not "gun." There was a lot to learn about this new Sienna.

"What?" Her eyes pried into mine.

"I'm just impressed. He deserved it."

"He did." She settled into her seat but still glared at Wyatt, but her friend seemed totally unfazed. I was pleased to see that she had someone in her life who challenged her and loved her enough to out her truths.

The church fundraiser was just as it was every year, band playing in the center of town, baked goods for sale, and homemade crafts donated by the same ladies who also made blankets for the local hospital.

"Elio Capri." The minister came over and greeted me and my entourage. "Thank you for coming. I was just speaking to your parents. It's wonderful to see you all looking so well."

"We wouldn't miss it." I scanned the faces, making sure we wouldn't stumble upon any unwelcome company. "I would like you to meet my friends, Sienna and Wyatt." I left out their last names on purpose.

While the minister chatted with Sienna and Wyatt, I stepped away and walked among the tables, making sure to speak to as many people as I could. Some of the women flirted with me, and I shot them a charming smile then moved quickly on to avoid conversation. Others were nervous and tried not to make eye contact.

"Lemonade?" A little girl tugged on my pant leg and held up a half-full cup of juice.

When she stepped forward, it sloshed on my shoe, and her mother popped out of nowhere spewing apologies.

"Sorry," the child said as her cheeks grew red and her eyes grew glossy at her mother's fussing.

I bent down and took the cup she still held and smiled. "I would love to buy one. How much?"

"Oh, no, please." Her mother frantically tried to get her friend's attention. "Let me get you a napkin for your shoe."

"I'm fine." I waved her off. "Nothing is free, now, is it?" I said to the child and pulled out twenty euros and handed it to her. I made a show to take a sip of the incredibly sour brew. "That," I tried to hide my face with my hand, "has a good bite to it."

"I made it myself."

"I bet you did, and that's impressive. Thank you for sharing it with me."

"You're welcome." She smiled and raced back over to her table.

Francesco smirked when I stood and turned around. "She got me last year, so it was only fair that you took one for the family."

"Thanks," I laughed, and we continued wishing everyone a good day.

"At least your good deed didn't go unnoticed." He gave a slight nod over to Sienna, who was watching us. I immediately twitched in her direction, drawn by her smile. Her expression changed suddenly, so I followed her line of sight.

"Well, look who finally decided to join the family," Francesco muttered.

"There's my girl!" Mariano scooped up Sienna and whirled her around. When he placed her back down, he grabbed her face, but she pulled away, and I saw red.

"Mariano," she hit his arm, "have a little respect for where we are."

Don't kill him. Don't kill him.

"Do you want to hurt him or shall I?" Papa appeared at my side.

"We could make it a family affair," Francesco huffed as he devoured something chocolate.

I reached behind me under my coat and discreetly handed Papa my gun. "I don't trust myself right now."

"Wise choice."

Making my way over to them, I felt my mouth go dry and my fists clench. Sienna caught wind of me first, and I could see the concern on her face.

"Mariano, a word."

He wrapped his arm around her shoulders and pulled her back against him. He leaned down and whispered loudly, "Be good. The boss is here."

"Mariano." I wasn't in the mood.

"All right," he sighed and kissed her on the cheek. I wanted to rub it away and replace it with one of my own.

I started walking, and he followed as he started to bring up something from last weekend, and it took all I had not to snap.

"Listen." I turned once we were deep into the church parking lot. "I want to know what is going on with you. You've been missing meetings, not showing up at the dockyard, and Niccola said you didn't even show up for a hit, one you definitely should have looked after yourself."

"Sorry." His defenses went up. "I've just been trying to figure out what's been going on with me, too."

"Meaning?"

"Look." He tucked his hands into his suit pockets and grinned at me. "I didn't mean to. I didn't see it coming, but I think I'm falling in love."

I swallowed down my desire to hurt him.

"Falling in love with whom?"

"Sienna." He covered his mouth, and his face lit up even more. It was the same expression I carried when I was twenty.

Shit.

"I never thought I would fall in love with someone. I mean nothing's happened, but damn, Elio, she makes me feel alive." His eyes danced wildly. "I tried understanding it, and that's why I went away after she got angry with me about something I did for her." I opened my mouth to rip him a new one but stopped myself. I wasn't sure why, but my gut told me to stay quiet…for now, at least. "I just drove and drove and slept in my car. I ended up calling Pauly."

"You called Pauly Milani?" The Milanis were a southern syndicate whose territory was in danger of being absorbed by the Coppola family. I knew Mariano was friends with Pauly, their son, but he had been warned many times not too share too much. Last I heard, Domenico Milani and his family were keeping a very low profile. Once again, Mariano was revealing his recklessness. "Tell me you didn't share anything."

"No," he waved me off as if he didn't really hear me, "I just needed time to work on me, and the only conclusion I came up with was…" He held my attention as I begged a higher power for him not to finish the sentence. "I'm in love, and I want her to be mine."

I blinked back at him, unable to speak, while my inner voice screamed at me to tell him she wasn't his and never would be. Just as I was about to protest, Stefano's face popped up in my head, reminding me that he was on to her.

"As great as that is, Mariano," I gritted through my teeth, "work comes first, and we apparently have a lot to discuss in that area."

"Like?" He seemed genuinely confused, which only further pissed me off.

"Like why did you take Sienna to the dockyard when you first brought her here? And how could you not have mentioned that she witnessed a murder?"

"I had it under control." He shrugged.

"How about the fact you introduced her to The Finder or Tieri Santoro?" I folded my arms in fear I'd throw a punch.

"She was going to leave. I needed something for her to stay. I needed more time to figure out what the hell I was feeling." He completely missed my murderous tone.

"Elio, love makes you do crazy things, and I know it was a little risky, but I was there with her the entire time. I wish you could have seen her excitement when I pitched the idea to her. It brought down some of her barriers, I can tell you. She isn't good at letting people in." He chuckled.

"Is that why she left for Mama's afterward?" I asked sardonically.

"It was a bump in the road, but we'll get past it." He gave me one of his cocky smiles, and I wondered if he was on something, because he was certainly delusional. "She didn't run when I saw her today, did she?"

Breathe.

"I'm sorry you're pissed at me. I see that vein in your forehead ticking to your heartbeat, but," he held up his arms and grinned wider, "I'm back, feeling a hundred percent, and I'm willing to do whatever it is you need from me."

I stopped myself from falling back to my normal habit of letting his shit go then giving him my typical debrief of what had been happening. Instead, I rolled my wrist and checked the time.

"I need papers from the dockyard."

"Actually," he pressed his lips together, and I knew this would be my last straw, "any chance I could have the night off? I want to take Sienna to dinner. I have a surprise for her."

At that very moment, I was glad my gun wasn't in my procession.

"*Cazzo*," I spat at him and turned away. He still

didn't recognize his duty to the family. "I'll do it my goddamn self!"

Storming past some of the locals, I attempted to curb my anger, but it was no use.

"You look like you could murder someone." Vinni tried to read my mind.

"Keys." I held out my hand to Vinni, and he suddenly looked very nervous.

"I'll drive, you just tell me where."

"Dockyard." I swung my murderous gaze toward my father, and he handed me my gun.

He stepped close and lowered his voice. "I'm not sure what's going on here, son, but don't let Mariano make you do something you will regret later."

"Watch her for me."

"I will."

I signaled for my cousins to follow me, and we headed over to the car.

"Elio," Sienna stepped in our path, "what's wrong?"

"Go find my father. He'll take you home."

"Elio," she snapped, and I had to remember she wasn't the one I was angry with.

I moved closer and whispered, "I'm sorry, but I have to go grab some papers from the dockyard. When it's time to go home, go with my parents."

"I will. But…" She grabbed my arm, and I looked over her head and saw Mariano watching us. I carefully removed her hand, not wanting Mariano to see she could get away with such behavior. "Whatever you're doing, just be careful, okay?"

I gave a tight nod and left.

Ten minutes into the drive, Vinni answered a call, and I caught his gaze in the rearview mirror.

"What?"

"We have to make a pit stop."

I cursed under my breath and wondered what the hell happened now. We turned down the old road that that led to my uncle's villa. The place sat near the edge of a cliff and was surrounded by an electric fence with multiple guards. We had our reasons to be paranoid, and my uncle spent good money on protecting the business. Seven years ago, the property was turned over for a place of business but still disguised as a summer home.

We parked in front of the giant maze my aunt had designed years ago. It was an amazing thing, and I had taken it over for my own personal use. Fifteen-foot-high hedges were placed on sliders that could be rotated to change up the pathways to vary the route. Red roses grew throughout the lush brush, masking any smell that might arise. It was incredible, but best of all, it was designed to be inescapable. I loved it, and it was the one place I enjoyed playing.

"Donatello found two of Stefano's soldiers sniffing around the dockyard this morning," Vinni said as he stepped out of the car. He then opened my door. "He figured you might like to conduct your business here this time."

"Excellent decision." I buttoned my jacket and headed toward the opening of the maze, but not before I felt my Nonna on the balcony looking down at us. Nonna was my father's mama and hadn't left the property in over ten years for reasons that were best left untold. She gave me a nod then drew a cross over her chest as if to bless the work I was about to do.

Making my way along the path to where it widened, I found them and nodded at Donatello that he had done well.

"Boss," he greeted me and smiled down at the two men who were blindfolded in front of him. Niccola came up and handed me the iPad that controlled the maze. With three little taps, I turned it to level C, *advanced*. Both men jumped when the sliders started to move the walls around us. Their heads moved about as they tried to understand what was happening. We were in the center of the puzzle, the one place that never changed. It was where the master motor sat like a spider with arms. It was a fascinating design and one I knew my clever aunt never thought we would ever use in this way.

I waved for the blindfolds to be removed. The young men blinked and froze when they spotted me. Fear washed over their faces as the shakes set in.

"Who wants to be my informant?" I jumped right in, not having the time for bullshit.

"We're loyal, sir." One of the guys puffed his chest. "We stand behind the Coppola name."

"You're soldiers who apparently mean very little to the Coppola family, because here you are on my territory, and," I made a motion of listening, "you've been missing for some time now, and it appears no one is coming for you."

"They will come for us." His voice was hopeful as he looked to his friend for support, but the friend looked to be in shock, so there was little help there.

I rolled my wrist to glance at my watch. We needed to get this rolling. Although I did enjoy these games, I had a tight schedule to keep.

"I'll tell you what," I motioned for Donatello to cut them loose, but they stayed on their knees, unsure what I was about to do, "whoever makes it out of the maze first can go home," I shrugged calmly, "and the other will be my informant. May the best man win."

"What?" Both men blinked up at me.

"Run."

Sienna

"I could really get used to this life." Wyatt rolled his head on the velvet pillow and grinned behind his sunglass.

"Mm," was all I offered because I could tell something was off. I wished I knew what the conversation was about with Elio and Mariano.

"Did you send the story to Georgio?"

"I did." I rolled onto my back, letting the sun bake my front. "He was very pleased."

"I'm sure." He laughed but then went quiet. I looked over and saw him fiddling with his straw in the slushed ice drink.

"What?"

"I heard something from work, and I'm not sure what it means."

"What did you hear?"

He shifted to his side and rested his head on his hand. "A woman was asking about you the other day."

"Oh?" I sipped my drink, thinking the pool seemed very inviting at this point. "Who told you that?"

"Our bird lover." He referenced our chatty secretary who we avoided like the plague. "It wasn't just that the woman was asking for you, but how adamant she was on finding you."

I stopped drinking my cocktail mid-sip and glanced over at him.

"Yeah." He pointed to my face and moved to swing his feet over the side of the lounge chair. "So, I did something."

"Wyatt?" I wasn't sure where this was going.

"Normally, I would never meddle, but it got me thinking. Maybe your plan did work? Maybe *she* finally found you."

"Oh, my God," escaped my lips as I flipped between scared and hopeful.

"She's meeting us tomorrow at eleven, by the field where the little road meets the main road." His hand covered mine, and I looked down at it. "I promised you years ago that I would help you track her down, but I can cancel—"

"No." I stopped him. "It's what I wanted, what I needed to happen."

Suddenly, loud voices could be heard, so we

scrambled to our feet and rushed inside, following them to the living room.

"Family meeting," Elio said to us as we approached. He looked ready to kill someone as he pointed to the couch, and I sat, pulling Wyatt down next to me.

He tapped a button, and a strange sound blanketed the room.

"Helps drown out our voices to the staff." Niccola filled in my unanswered question.

"What's going on, Elio?" Mama asked as she took a chair next to Francesco.

"One moment, Mama, I'm just waiting for Papa." He positively radiated anger, and I was filled with dread. Piero arrived a few moments later, then Vinni came in, looking rattled. The seven of us stared up at Elio. I couldn't resist the thought of how magnificent he looked as he stood there behind a grand leather chair with the family crest on the wall. The crow stood tall on the shield below the crown behind him. I thought of Piero's words—family, strength, loyalty, protection.

"My gut," he started and pulled my attention from my thoughts, "always told me to be careful. Yet, over the years, I overlooked many things, thinking I was paranoid. After all, our lifestyle lends itself to that. But this one has really taken its toll."

I glanced at Andrea. She was shaking her head, unsure of what he was saying.

"We have a traitor among us." He cleared his throat.

"What?" his father boomed, and I knew we were about to witness the darker side of the mafia.

"Someone is human trafficking through our ports and using our ships. It seems a young woman was found in one of the containers. Apparently, she is from Serbia, and there's more." He looked at his father. "She has numbers inked on her upper arm, numbers that correspond to the paper we recovered from Antonio, the one he was to deliver. Papa, our traitor is not just anyone," Elio's voice was eerie, "it is one of our very own." His gaze swung over to mine, and I felt like I was suddenly on trial. "I couldn't see it before. I was blinded with my own wounds from the past, but it all makes sense now." Holding a firm gaze on me, he spoke again. "Papa, what has always been your biggest weakness?"

"Your mother." He didn't miss a beat.

"Exactly," Elio paused, "and mine is Sienna."

I swallowed back the intensity from his words. Elio loved me hard, and I did him. I was just too scared to admit it out loud. Though some of the scars were healing, my trust was still weathered.

"But he doesn't know of your past." Vinni spoke up clearly, knowing more to the story than we did.

"But he *could*."

"Elio, who are you talking about?" His father grew impatient. "I'm a half a moment away from a stroke."

Elio held up his hand. "The girl said there were two men who arrived at our dock to transfer her into a waiting truck. One wore all white, Stefano, and the other kept making a snapping noise as he spoke."

"A snapping noise, as in—" Andrea's hand flew to her mouth as she connected the dots. "Mariano?"

Just like that, my blood turned to ice and my mouth went dry. My mind flashed with the memory of how many times he had put me in harm's way.

"Why?" came flying out of my mouth.

"I don't know yet." Elio sank into the chair as we all digested what he had shared. "He's been in our lives since I was twenty, and that's a long time to sink your claws into our family. He knows our ways, our secrets, and our weaknesses."

"His whole family does, son. So, what, exactly, do we know? How was the girl found?" Piero seemed to have fought his way out of the fog the rest of us were still in.

"She managed to hide under some debris in the back of the container, and while they searched for her, some of our men happened to come by, and they ran away. There is more to the story, but I have yet to get all the details." Elio pulled out his phone and read something. "The girl has been moved to the villa. We will have to decide how we want to handle the whole situation."

"And we don't know how much Mariano is involved?"

"No." Elio shook his head at his father.

"But he is involved."

"Seems that way, Papa."

"Sienna," Piero addressed me, "I'm sorry, sweet girl, that you were dragged into this mess, but I think it was for a reason. Whether Mariano knows who you really are to Elio or if it was a random coincidence that you two met, either way, I think we all need time to think about all this. Perhaps, as you have a relationship with him, it would be in all our best interests to keep things the way they are with him."

"No, no way." Elio waved a hand. "She will not be a player on our chess board."

"Wait, Elio." His father stopped him. "We would be watching her at all times. We just need to buy some more time."

"He claims he loves her," Elio huffed, and my jaw dropped open.

"He doesn't love me," I snapped and thought how insane that sounded. "He doesn't know me well enough to love me."

"I agree." Elio nodded. "But he told me today that he needed time to think and clear his head because he had come to the conclusion that he's in love with you."

"Do you believe him, Elio?" His father sounded skeptical.

"I'd like to say no, but I've never seen him act like that before. He's all over the damn place."

My head spun as the liquor I had by the pool hit my bloodstream and had me in a daze. Did Mariano actually help Stefano Coppola traffic girls to Italy? Was he really double-crossing Elio's family? Did he really know who I was to Elio? Did he really love me? Could you base love off the few small intimate moments we'd had?

"Sienna?" Piero sat down beside me. "I don't know exactly how you feel for Elio, and I will not pry, but I think it's best for now if everything remains as is. You and Elio need to keep whatever it is that you are a secret, behind closed doors, if you will. Just until we do more digging and buy us a little more time. I don't believe Mariano would hurt you. That being said, I would like you to remain living here in our house for now."

"Maybe she should leave," Wyatt interjected carefully. "And forgive me if I'm overstepping, it's just merely an idea, but we could disappear, and when the coast is clear we can return."

"I appreciate the thought, Wyatt," Andrea said kindly to him. "Sadly, anyone can be found with the right amount of money. The Coppola family have been after our territory and business for decades. If they even suspect that Sienna is important to our son, she would be in a grave or worse. Elio is next in line to take the family legacy." Her teary gaze moved to mine. "I don't want anything to happen to you, and I won't lose you again. The safest place for you to be is here with all of us."

"Of course, I'll stay if it will help." I was not going to argue with that. I was tired of running from my past, and if I could help the family, I would. As far as I was concerned, Andrea and Piero were my family.

"My dear Sienna." Francesco, who had been quiet the entire time, stepped away from the wall toward me. "Will you be able to act like yourself around Mariano? Because if he gets even a whiff of what is going on, the whole thing could go very badly." He bent down in front of me and covered my hands with his own. His warm eyes looked into mine, and I remembered the first time I met him at the family's old home and how welcoming he had been. "If you think you can, then that's wonderful, but you must be sure. Please speak your mind and let us know now, and we will think of a different direction."

"I can do this." I nodded at him, and he returned it with a hug then stood and joined Piero.

"Then it's settled," Piero said. "We'll hatch a plan." He clapped his hands and walked to the door and spoke to someone. "Now, where were we all before this meeting started?"

Donte stood at the door. "Dinner is ready outside. Please come and enjoy."

And just like that, we rewound time and fell into our respective roles.

Dinner was as wonderful as always, although I found my appetite a little less than great. Elio finished first and kept the conversation light. He didn't even blink when Mariano emerged from the side gate.

"Evening all. Please forgive me for interrupting your dinner. I'll just be a moment." He smiled over at Andrea, and she nodded. He gave a carefree wave as he took a spare seat at the table.

Elio's hand ever so slowly shifted over to my leg and rested it there for a moment. It took everything in me not to turn to him and bury my head in his chest.

"Nice to see you again, Wyatt."

"You as well." My best friend played it cool as could be.

"Sienna," he addressed me, and I froze.

"Breathe, *bella*," Elio whispered from behind his napkin, and my cold hand fell on top of his, just needing more of him.

"I would like to take you out tonight." Mariano smiled at me. He certainly acted the part of a young man in love. His eyes seemed to sparkle. Damn, Elio might be right. "I have some apologizing to do," he added and gave me a humbled look.

"I didn't realize you were coming by tonight, Mariano." Piero shrugged. "I have some friends coming by who want to meet Sienna."

Mariano's smile wavered into a frown as he thought about something. "Tomorrow night, then."

I hated how he told me rather than asked.

"Perhaps," I smiled, "although I do have to find another assignment before Georgio fires me." I tried to joke, but my throat was like sandpaper.

"Don't worry, I know you never have a hard time finding something to write about." He winked, and I nodded to be polite. "Let's do Friday, then. We can talk over dinner. Be ready by six."

Yes, sir.

Anna arrived a few minutes later, and I wanted to hug her. I was so pleased at the welcome distraction. Elio had mentioned before the house was a revolving door for people, so seeing her stroll in wasn't a total surprise. I just wished she had better manners.

An unexpected rainfall ended our dinner quickly, and once inside, everyone went their own way while I wandered into the solarium. Mariano was being entertained by Anna, and they both were into the rum, so the solarium was the perfect place to escape.

I loved the rain, so I curled up with a blanket and

a stiff drink and my book. The sound was soothing to my tired head, and the smell of plants around me was comforting.

Someone cleared their throat, and I turned to see Niccola leaning against the wall.

"I see you've found my hideout."

"Oh, I'm sorry."

"Don't be." He waved me off. "May I join you for a moment?"

"Of course." I didn't know Niccola as well as I did Vinni, so the fact he wanted to hang out felt nice. He was slightly taller than Vinni and had a few more muscled pounds on him. They were both very attractive men. Apparently, they were all blessed with good genes.

"Thank you," he said softly, "for not running and deciding to stay and help my family figure out all this mess. Although we are constantly at war with the other families, this one has really hit home. When Mariano and his family made a deal with Piero back in Sicily, it seemed like the best idea. Teaming up with a family that had ties with American and Libyan ports seemed like the perfect plan. The oil comes from Libya on ships to us, we sell it to the Americans, then the Americans send the ships back with the money. It's a smooth operation that we have controlled for years."

"Why not ship from Spain?" I was thinking of geography.

"Feds are on to Spain, plus we need to oversee everything ourselves." He cleared his throat as he shifted seats and sat next to me on the long couch. "I see the way my cousin looks at you." He studied my face for a beat. "I think it's time you knew the truth about something that Elio will most likely never admit to you on his own."

"I'm listening."

"Elio and I have always been close. Even though we lived far away, we were always there for one another. He was like an older brother to me. When he first arrived here after they had to leave Sicily, I barely recognized him. He was messed up and had lost a bunch of weight, and it took him days to finally tell me what had happened, that he had to leave you behind."

"He already shared with me why he had to leave." I didn't want another replay of the worst point in my life.

"But did you know he went back after you a short time later?"

"What are you talking about?" I had no idea.

"He didn't last long before he snapped, packed a bag, and went to leave. But when he got to his car, there was a note on his windshield. It was a picture of you in Sicily with the words, *you go after her and we'll kill her before you can ever reach her.*"

"What?" I set my drink down and changed my position to face him straight on. "I never knew that."

"We never figured out who it was that sent the note, but Elio vowed then that he would never bring you into his life because you were already a target."

"Wow." I pushed my hair back when I thought about how he gave me up so I would be happy and free.

"I've never met a man who loves someone the way he does you, Sienna."

I nodded, unsure what to say to that.

"Let's just get through this terrible situation with Mariano and see where the world takes the two of you next." He smiled warmly at me. "I'm looking forward to spending more time with you."

"Me too. Thanks, Niccola."

He tucked his hands in his pockets and started walking out of the small room. "Popsicles," he chuckled, "if you want to annoy Mariano, he hates the sound of someone sucking on a popsicle."

"Well, I'm glad it's summer." I grinned, thankful for the tip.

After a bit of mulling over Elio's secret, I headed toward the kitchen to see where everyone was. Donte zipped by and muttered the word *study*. I didn't know if he actually meant that for me, but I found myself heading in that direction.

Pushing the door open, I spotted Elio by the window, deep in thought. I admired his relaxed look of unbuttoned dress shirt and rolled up sleeves, and judging by the way his hands kept going to his head, it was clear how he got his messy hair. It was times like this I saw the boy who saved me. I'd spent so much of my life questioning and wondering why that I forgot to just live. With a deep breath, I stepped inside the room.

"Did you really try to come back for me?" I whispered, and his head dropped forward.

"Niccola," he hissed.

"Just answer me, Elio. Did you really change your mind and decide to come after me?"

"Yes."

My heart skipped a beat, and I let a little more of my armor flake away.

"Why didn't you tell me?"

"Because it didn't matter."

"It matters to me."

"I didn't go through with it." He shrugged and kept his back to me.

"Yes, but only because you got a warning not to, and that's not the point. The point was you *were* going to come for me."

"I should've."

"I wish you had, too, Elio, but it means so much to me that you really wanted to. I thought I was just an afterthought for you, but knowing you were going to risk it all and come find me, is…" I trailed off when he whirled around, and in three strides he was in was in front of me. Using his broad chest, he backed me up to the wall.

"I answered your question, now answer mine." His eyes pierced through me, and I felt like the air in the room had been sucked out. "Do you still love me? The way you used to?" I opened my mouth but slammed it shut. He shook his head, forbidding me to lie. "You know my secrets, now tell me yours."

"Yes," I whispered, and before I could think, his lips were on mine, devouring every last piece of me. I matched his intensity, not wanting to be anywhere but here. He leaned over and pushed the door closed, lifted me in the air, and carried me to the couch.

"No matter what," he huffed as he pulled my shirt off, tossing it to the floor, "I'm never leaving you again."

I pushed my hands on his chest to stop his kisses and stared up at the man who owned my heart since I was a child. "Promise me, Elio."

For the first time since he received it, he slid off his family ring and placed it on my ring finger. "I promise." He kissed my fingers.

I finally let go and gave in to him.

"One more thing," I stopped him and pressed my hand to his chest, feeling his heartbeat, "if we're going to do this, I think it's time I learned about family obligations."

"Really?" His face lit up, and I gave a nod.

It is time.

"First," he leaned me back, "let me show you just how much I still love you."

The next morning, after a hearty breakfast and a couple of pointed glances from Wyatt, who was no doubt wondering where my appetite came from, we waited for Vinni to find us.

"Ready?" He flipped his keys around his fingers.

"Let's go." Wyatt dragged me off the couch and outside to the car. "I know you're scared, and frankly, so am I, but you'll kick yourself in the butt later if you don't go."

"I know." I tried to shake my nerves off as we settled

in for the short car ride to the crossroads.

A few times, Vinni would answer some calls but spoke quietly so to not disturb us. I was becoming rather fond of him and Niccola. There was something strange about knowing that these men would kill with their bare hands without so much as a blink, but could still be so loving and kind. Wyatt always said he admired my ability to adapt to strange situations, and I had certainly proved that.

"Ready?" Wyatt touched my hand and brought me back to the present. I followed him out of the car, and we stood on the side of the road while the hot sun poured down on us.

As warm as it was, my hands were like ice, and my heart beat steadily against my breastbone. Was I really about to meet the woman who had given birth to me? Pain, heartbreak, and sheer excitement raced through me all at once. If I could, I would have wiggled right out of my skin. I was so amped up.

"Here we go." Wyatt let out a long breath as two cars came toward us.

They parked, and three men stepped out and stood to one side while the driver opened one of the back doors.

"This is it." He was just as nervous as I was.

A slim woman about my height, short hair to her shoulders, approached us. Her eyes were as deep blue as my own, and she was dressed like she was the one who just stepped out of *Fab Magazine* right down to her stunning heels. Her hand covered her mouth as she took another cautious step forward, mirroring my actions.

"Sienna?" she barely whispered, and I gave a small nod. "I'm Eleonora." She held herself with such confidence that I tried to match her stance.

"What did you give me when I was a child?" I blurted, not wanting to feel anything until I knew.

Her lips stretched into a smile, and her eyes softened. "A teddy bear pendant."

I burst into tears and pulled my necklace free from under my dress.

She reached out to touch me but stopped herself. "You still have it?"

I nodded and bit my lip as her gaze moved over my shoulder, and suddenly the mood swung in a different direction.

The sound of weapons being drawn and the glimmer of steel in the sunlight blinded me momentarily as Eleonora reached for me and quickly pulled me to her. Then she stepped in front of me with a gun in her hand.

"I know who you are!" she screamed at Elio, who seemed to arrive out of thin air. His gun was pointed at her as Vinni moved up next to him. "You wear the crow with the golden crown." She nodded at his ring that I had slipped back on his finger that morning.

My heart beat against her as I fought to see and to make sense of what was happening.

"How did you find her?" she screamed while the gun stayed steady in her hand. As I tensed and tried to step around Eleanora, she spoke sharply to one of her men, and I felt a hand reach around my waist, drawing me to him.

"Oscar," she commanded, "keep her safe."

"Of course," the man replied as his arm tightened around me.

"Let go of me," I hissed, but he didn't even seem to hear me. "Elio?" I whispered urgently, sending his attention over to me. His eyes moved down to the man's hold on me.

"I will kill you first, if you don't let her go." Elio's voice dripped with fury. "She's not going anywhere with you!"

Eleonora's men created a horseshoe around Vinni, Elio, and Wyatt. Wyatt's face was white with shock, and his eyes darted around in terror.

"I beg to differ," Oscar, the man holding me, said confidently.

Suddenly, Elenora took a hesitant step forward, and the gun wavered in her hand as I heard her whisper, "Francesco?"

La Fine

Acknowledgments

To Michela Martorella, for all your help with this book! You were invaluable to me.

To Vanessa Webb, for helping revamp a good chunk of this story.

To Christina DeTorio, for helping revamp a good chunk of this story and for opening the door to my dark side again and providing me with a wealth of knowledge that helped my mind untangle and run free.

To Steve and Jill Chamness, for all the white-collar crime information and for being a great sounding board for my ideas.

To Kim Kelchner and Veronica Nelson, who still beta read while enduring Covid. You ladies are rock stars.

To Elizabeth Clark, for beta reading and helping me find a fantastic show to help spin my wheels some more. I love that we are both sucked into that world together.

To Jamie Johnson, for beta reading and letting me pick your brain on the mafia.

To Rachel Womack, for sharing our love of Italy,

great food and wine.

To my mother, for once again being my person while I ride this author journey.

To my daughter Brooke, who relishes my love of "fun" endings.

To Tommy Tardie, for creating the perfect location for one of my key scenes. I can't wait to visit The Flatiron Room in New York someday.

Bring on book two!

About the Author

Author J.L. Drake was born and raised in Nova Scotia, Canada, later moving to Southern California where she lives with her husband and two children.

When she's not writing she loves to spend time with her family, traveling or just enjoying a night at home. One thing you might notice in her books is her love for the four seasons. Growing up on the east coast of Canada the change in the seasons is in her blood and is often mentioned in her writing.

Her books can be found in different languages around the world.

You can connect with J.L. Drake on Facebook, Instagram, Twitter, BookBub, and Goodreads!

You can also check out her website at www.authorjldrake.com.

Books by J.L. Drake

Broken
Shattered
Mended
Honor
Escape
Trigger
Demons
Unleashed
Freedom
Omertà
Courage
Darkness Lurks
Darkness Follows
Darkness Falls
Behind My Words
Christmas at the Cabin
All In
Quiet Wealth
Quiet Secrets
Quiet Power
Quiet Empire
Shadows
Whiskey
Alpha
Tango